# PROTECTIVE

LEGATUM
BOOK 1

## LULU M SYLVIAN

GRIFFYN INK

# ACKNOWLEDGMENTS

A construction worker with a proclivity for plaid shirts, who lived in a beat up old Airstream, moved into my brain, and wouldn't leave until I proved there was more to him than first impressions. I didn't even know there was more than one story for the plaid wearing guy until his cousin showed up, and said "me too." And before I knew it, I had a family that wanted their stories told.

Legatum, legacy. Thank you art history and mythology for giving my guys a rich complex background.

Thank you to Alana, Dana, and Lea for sciencing for me.

Thank you to my children who actually brainstormed and talked plot with me.

It took almost eight years before I realized this story in my head needed to be written. My husband knew years before I did, and was nothing but encouraging. So super thanks to him for the constant support.

# PROLOGUE

Morgan Palatine loosened the tie cinched around his neck. Weeks of wearing business suits made him feel as if he were being strangled by the thin strip of silk fabric. He felt confined. Confined by the tailored fabric he wore, confined by the human skin he walked around in.

He rolled his shoulders trying to release the tension that had been building for hours in the thick muscles along his neck and back. He could go months without shifting, but the past few weeks made it feel like years. He was not meant to spend his time in a leather chair at the head of a boardroom conference table. Morgan preferred to be hands-on, literally, when it came to work. He wanted steel-toed boots and rolled-up sleeves. What he really wanted right now was the freedom to be himself, this skin or fur.

A quick shift and a good hard run were his plans for as soon as he got home.

Home. His own bed.

That was it. That's what he needed to do. He needed to step up the diplomacy games and open his family home, Mission Run, to the Aventine family. Invite them to spend the weekend in the hills, give them the opportunity to shift and relax. Maybe then their alpha would chill, and realize that this pissing contest was not necessary. The old guard had moved on, Morgan was not interested in maintaining a family feud or continuing a centuries old grudge match.

There were few enough of their kind in the world, and they were well hidden, even from each other. It made more sense to be on friendly terms with the Aventines. Morgan was more than ready to shake hands and call it good, but the Aventine alpha, Blackston, and Morgan's sister Julia both seemed to think this accord needed to be full of legalese and have a consensus on the terms.

No, this was good. He would bring it up with Jinx in the morning. His household manager would know how to handle the situation. It wouldn't take much to fit the entire Aventine contingent in. Only a few of them had transferred to the Bay Area, and most of them were really only here for negotiating terms of this accord. Nancy Aventine, Blackston's wife would probably appreciate a nice weekend in wine country. She was the reason they were in California after all. Her illness brought her to the Stanford Medical Center.

Not that the Palatines were particularly territorial. It was mostly a formality, allowing the Aventine alpha and his mate to live in the region, and to prevent petty issues from snowballing.

Wolves liked to have space between themselves and the next family. Of course, the Aventines weren't just any other wolf family. There had been a special level of distrust and hate between them and the Palatines. The deep down anger of sibling rivalry gone too far for too long.

Yes, a weekend out of the city, a weekend where everyone could relax and drink good wine was just what the doctor ordered. Aventine's son, Roman, seemed like a decent enough guy, even if he was focused entirely too much on business, just like Julia. This would give everyone a chance to get to know one another in a relaxed more intimate setting.

Morgan barely registered the *click click click* of someone in heeled shoes walking quickly, as he continued his slow walk towards the parking garage. He should have hired a driver for the week. He should have gotten a hotel. He should have done too many damned things.

The stench of pot and body odor assaulted his senses. He would have ignored the kids if he hadn't picked up something one of the punks had just said. Lone woman. Street kids. Not a good combination.

Morgan straightened his posture as he tuned his senses into the situation at hand.

He turned around and headed back to where he thought he'd heard the click of heeled footsteps heading. He turned another corner.

"You little turd! Give me back my purse!" he heard a woman shout. Heavy running footsteps headed in the opposite direction.

Morgan took off after the purse snatchers and then he heard her scream.

He backtracked, catching a glimpse of motion disappearing into a walkway off the street.

He turned a corner and saw a woman with short black hair pressed against the brick wall, a large knife held in front of her face. The assailant had apparently taken advantage of her distraction when the potheads ran off with her bag. Looked like this guy wanted more from his victim than just her handbag.

Morgan didn't hesitate. In a single swift motion, he

pulled the attacker from the woman and tossed him down the walkway. The man crashed into a group of garbage cans.

The assailant began to get up. "What the fuck? I'll kill you for that."

The woman was on him, and in a few well-placed kicks and a knee to the nose, he was knocked out.

Morgan stepped back in appreciation of her skills. He opened his senses to see if there was more to her than met the eye. He had a hard time picking anything up from her. She wasn't one of his, and not human either, nor vampire. Only daywalkers messed with his senses this way.

Morgan watched as she brushed down her dress and smoothed her short hair into place.

"You really didn't need my help there, did you?" he asked.

"I would have figured it out eventually." Her accent hinted at origins in South America. "But your assistance was most fortuitous."

Morgan noticed long fingernails pointed like claws painted vibrant red as he engulfed her hand in his own. "Cyan del Fuego. And you are?" She raked him with a gaze that said I know *what* you are but not *who* you are

"Morgan Palatine, Ms. del Fuego. You really didn't need my protection," he said, recognizing her name. Cyan del Fuego, daughter of the local Del Fuego coven lord and head of Cyan Group, a potential client Morgan had been trying to contract with.

Cyan chuckled. "Against humans no. May I borrow your cell phone? Mine was in my purse that..." she nodded over her shoulder indicating the unconscious man behind them "...this idiot prevented me from retrieving."

Morgan held up his hand, asking for a moment. He turned and picked her bag up from the entrance to the walkway where he had dropped it. "I managed to snatch this back for you." He handed her the handbag.

"Why, thank you." She linked her arm through his. "Now, Morgan Palatine, walk me back to my car and tell me why your name is so familiar. And not just because you're the local alpha."

**1**

A cacophony of angry honking and yelling caught Honey's attention.

*Not another idiot who thinks traffic on Cannery Row would behave like normal city street traffic.*

She looked to see who would be so rude in this throng of tourism and froze. Fear and panic stopped her breathing as she recognized the angry man at the center of the commotion.

She couldn't think; she couldn't breathe. Her heart thudded in her throat. "Oh, God, not him," she said, barely a whisper. Her hand went to her neck, clasping her protective charm, her personal amulet.

Through the front windshield of a low-slung, silver sports car, she saw the once loved angles of Bryce Maplecourt's face, twisted into a familiar visage of rage. Only this time, it wasn't directed at her. This time those piercing blue eyes were blazing at another hapless victim of his undeserved vitriol.

Air flooded back into her lungs as she gasped and spun around, angling herself to face away from him.

"He didn't see me, he didn't see me, he didn't see me." She repeated over and over again under her breath as she rubbed the small charm between her fingers.

Honey focused on her breathing, trying to calm the surge of adrenaline. *He didn't see me, and he would never recognize me dressed this way.* Honey wore a comfortable old hoodie, one that had been broken in with years of abuse and washing, one that had mystery stains spattered on it and faded color. The Honey Bryce had known would never wear a hoodie, let alone one she purchased for a buck at a local thrift shop. *No*—she calmed herself—*Bryce didn't see me, and Bryce wouldn't recognize me if he did.*

Careful to keep herself turned away from the street, Honey carefully made her way through the crowd.

When she was half a block from work, she ran. The need to distance herself from Bryce increasing with each step.

She entered the crowded coffee shop and immediately headed to the back, through the office, and into the employee washroom/janitor closet. She slammed the door shut then crouched in the shower.

She had gotten away. He hadn't seen her. No matter how much she repeated this mantra, she could not shake the panicked thought that Bryce had followed her, that he somehow knew she was here.

Her breathing came in gasps. She gulped in air as she stared at the door.

Her eyes widened and her stomach lurched as she watched the door handle turn.

A comforting hand stroked along Honey's back as she emptied the contents of her stomach into the toilet.

"Shhh." Lana's voice soothed.

"You came running in here so fast that I came to check

on you. Are you doing okay? How much have you eaten today?" Lana's concern brought tears to Honey's eyes.

Honey finished retching and stood. She rinsed the sour taste of sick from her mouth before facing her boss. She gestured towards her throat as she explained, "This isn't food. This is panic." It was important to Honey that Lana knew she hadn't slipped back into old unhealthy habits. Honey swallowed hard, then returned to the sink to rinse her mouth again.

"I saw Bryce." Bryce who had fed on her insecurities like a vampire.

"Oh, shit," Lana murmured.

"I don't think he saw me. It's just..." Honey's voice quavered. "It's just I haven't seen him since... Ya' know?"

Tears rolled down her cheeks.

"You want to take the afternoon off? I can keep an eye out to see if he's around?"

Honey breathed deeply. "Yes. No. I don't know. I need to hang the show. I don't want to be around people, but I can't afford to take the time off."

Lana nodded. "How about you put on some headphones and hang the show. I'll get Joyce to stay later, and she can deal with people."

Honey nodded.

"Stay in here as long as you need to. I'm here for you. You know that, right?"

Honey nodded again.

Lana had been there ever since she first ran. Lana, who offered a job, guidance, and friendship.

Honey wouldn't turn tail and run away, she wouldn't do that. She needed to prove to Lana, and to herself, that Bryce and fear no longer controlled her. Her past did not dictate her future.

∼

Morgan stepped into the locally-owned coffee shop, The Corner, looking for an afternoon shot of caffeine and enough calories to carry him through to dinner. He opened his senses to the smell of hot coffee, expecting the aroma to fortify his energy and calm his nerves. What he didn't expect was to be assaulted by the distinct tangy scent of fear and panic.

The strong emotions came from a woman on a stepladder...a woman with the most perfect ass he had ever seen. Her panic had caught his attention; her shapely form held his stare and distracted him from what originally drew his eyes to her. He couldn't help himself but to stop and watch the ass. It was pert, would fit his palms perfectly. The rest of her shape was perfect as well. The long back immediately above tapered to a narrow waist and curved up to slender shoulders and long delicate arms. A messy bun of strawberry blond hair topped off this vision. Morgan had an overwhelming urge to fight for her, to wrap her in his arms, and shield her from the horrors that had scared her so badly.

He shut down the extra senses he had opened, clearing his head of his protective tendencies. Shaking off the overreaction to her fear, he continued to focus on the female who held his attention. She reached forward trying to level a large, unframed painting. Her reach lifted the back of her purple shirt, exposing a thin slice of skin and revealing a wide and extremely colorful tattoo. Morgan immediately found himself wanting to see the full extent of the body decoration. Did it merely accentuate the small of her back or did it swirl around and caress her hip bones as it wound its way to her lower abs? Did it twine down one of her legs and hug her thigh or did it reach up her back and wrap around her shoulders?

A sharp "like what you are looking at?" from another of the coffee shop's baristas brought him back to reality and his purpose for seeking caffeine.

"Uhm, yes I do," he said with a glance at the barista and a quick clearing of his throat.

His gaze shifted back to the woman on the stepladder. She turned her head and stared at Morgan. Her pale grey-green eyes slightly squinted as she looked at him but widened as he made eye contact with her. She had sharp, high cheekbones and a delicately pointed chin. She was beautiful and belonged in paintings, not hanging them. And she shimmered. A soft golden light surrounded her.

Morgan shook his head to clear his vision. Uncharacteristically self-conscious, Morgan ran his hand through his hair. Julia had convinced him to cut his shoulder-length hair for an important meeting. She had said it would make him appear more professional. Now it grew in an uneven shag, either needing a trim or time to allow it to grow out. He preferred the longer length; he was giving his hair time. He also hadn't shaved for a few days. Nothing like roguish stubble graced his chin; his beard was a scraggly mess. Unkempt, and in dusty work clothes, Morgan was painfully aware he was not making a good first impression, and it was suddenly very important to him that he do so. He would have to step up the charm and charisma.

The woman grabbed the level she had been using from the top of the canvas then jumped from the ladder and stood in front of Morgan. He noticed her exceptional height for a woman, even so he was still much taller. With the level grasped in one hand, she crossed her arms, tilted her head to one side then pointedly turned her attention to the other woman, and walked away.

Morgan knew he had been basically caught red-handed, staring at her backside, but in his defense, it was a very good ass.

Morgan watched as she walked past her coworker and disappeared into the back of the shop. He felt as if he had just been tag-teamed, passed off to the next player. He smirked. Fitting treatment for his blatant ogling.

"So you like art?" the other woman asked. Older, she had short, spiky black hair. Bold red-framed glasses emphasized her piercing blue eyes. Her eyebrows were raised and her expression said, *convince me.*

Without skipping a beat, he said, "I don't normally like Abstract Expressionism, but, there is something about how this artist uses the gradation of color as a form of movement that you can follow. You see there in the upper left corner, how the color seems to move and descend toward the middle of the canvas?" He gestured to the referred-to areas on the canvas with his hand. "There it expands and the darker colors sink to the lower portion of the canvas. The artist is clearly demonstrating despair. But see, there in the middle towards the right. There is a spark of yellow, and you can follow it rising to the upper right corner of the canvas where there is an explosion of light and movement showing joy and hope."

"You aren't a friend of Finney's. I know all his friends, so you aren't here for the art. Or are you? You interpreted that piece perfectly. I swear you even used Finney's exact words."

"Yeah, I actually came in for a cup of hot strong caffeine but got distracted..." His eyes followed the graceful fluid motion of the pale beauty as she walked past the counter carrying another oversized painting into the front of the shop, "...by the... ah... art show."

"Right, the art show. That's Honey's deal. She sets those up. Coffee, that's my gig. By the way, I'm Lana. So tell me about this cup of caffeine you are seeking. I believe you said hot?"

"Hot and strong and in the biggest cup you sell," Morgan said. He turned his head away from Lana at the counter as he continued to watch Honey attempt to hang another painting. Her arms appeared to be too delicate to wrangle the large canvas into position, yet Honey placed the painting level with skill and dexterity that said she clearly knew what she was doing.

"We would call that a large," Lana said patronizingly.

"Great. One large, hot caffeine and some sugared carbo-hydrates, I'll let you surprise me, just no chocolate." Morgan walked away from the counter and over to where Honey was hanging the next painting.

"Is this another of Finney's?" Morgan asked, nodding at the canvas.

Honey turned towards him, blinked her large green eyes, then left.

"Just noticing a consistency in color choices and painting techniques," Morgan said to the painting. He raised his hands, gesturing his defeat and returned to the counter.

The barista smirked. "She can't hear you." She tapped her ears. "Headphones. If you want to discuss color and technique, you really should come by tomorrow night. We're having an opening reception for the artist."

"Sounds like an interesting invitation. What time?" Morgan pulled out his wallet to pay for his coffee and the lemon bar she'd selected for him. He looked at the thin, delicately dusted with powdered sugar dessert. "I said surprise me, didn't I? I don't do lemon. Uhm, can you throw in a slice of that carrot cake to-go, as well? Thanks."

"My lemon bars are famous, I'll have you know." Lana opened the refrigerated case and extracted a healthy hunk of cake. She set it on the counter and swathed it in a sheet of plastic wrap. "The opening starts at seven, but things won't really get underway until about eight. She'll be here, and she won't have headphones on."

"Then I will see you tomorrow night at eight." With a nod of thanks, Morgan picked up his coffee and cake and headed back to work.

Morgan unwrapped the carrot cake as he walked out the front door. He glanced back as he turned to head up the street to the construction site. He caught a glimpse of the woman named Honey motioning towards him as if discussing his finer attributes with the other woman. He huffed a silent laugh. Morgan looked forward to tomorrow evening. The art might be tedious, but it would give him a chance to interact with the aloof Honey.

His phone rang. He pressed the Talk button.

"Palatine."

"Do you even know who your new client is?" Julia's voice demanded.

"Yes, why?"

"Do you know what your new client is, Morgan?"

"Very rich. Why?"

"Seriously. I just found out who our client is, and I have concerns regarding your safety on the site now."

"I've met with her several times. I know who and what she is. We have a mutual goal. She hasn't had issue with me, and I see no reason to have issue with her."

"Please tell me you aren't all rugged mountain man on the job. I would be embarrassed if the client saw you. No need feeding into their concepts of you being some feral wolf-man."

Morgan scoffed at her accurate description. He enjoyed taking a break from the rigors of daily shaving while onsite. "No need to worry, I'll clean up before she ever does an onsite inspection."

"I'm concerned you let this project go through, knowing who the client is."

"You're sounding prejudiced and paranoid, Julia."

"Just concerned. She can be dangerous."

"So can I." Morgan ended the call. He looked into his empty cup of coffee. When had he drunk it all?

## 2

Honey worked her way through the crowd, her tray full of dirty dishes held high so that she didn't accidentally crash into anyone. The turnout for Finney's opening indicated a success. Finney, a short, roundish, red-haired man, dressed in all black, animatedly spoke to someone sitting in one of the upholstered arm chairs the café provided. Honey couldn't tell who it was. She could see dark hair but no other identifying features. Finney threw his head back in a raucous giggle. The man speaking to Finney rose, also laughing. Honey noticed it was the tall man from the other day.

Previously, she had noticed his height, but she hadn't really appreciated how tall he stood until she saw him towering over Finney. She noticed he had cleaned up some. He wore another plaid work shirt, but at least this time it was tucked into clean pants and not the dirty cargos he had been wearing. His hair was incredibly unfashionable. He either needed to cut it all off or grow it out more, and it looked like he tried to shave with a rusty razor. His chin was still covered in stubble, and his sideburns were dangerously close to resembling muttonchops.

Finney caught her eye and waved to her. She nodded in acknowledgment. She worked her way back to the kitchen with the dirty dishes then returned to the front. Finney approached, dragging the tall man with him. "Honey, Honey, Honey. Where ever did you find Morgan? He's delightful. He actually knows something about art."

"She found me right about here." Morgan smiled.

"You actually came?" she asked incredulously. She seriously had not expected him to show up, figuring he had used up all his art knowledge trying to show off to Lana. She had heard everything he said through the headphones, even if she hadn't acknowledged it.

Morgan seemed to carefully study her face. "Your coworker did invite me, and it gives me a chance to properly meet you." His gaze lingered on her lips. He had warm hazel eyes that sparked with glints of glowing amber and were framed by ridiculously long and thick dark lashes. Something in his gaze left Honey breathless and unable to look away. She leaned on the counter; her knees didn't want to support her weight anymore.

Honey, taken aback by the intensity of his gaze, gave a nervous smile. "Well, yes, Lana did say you seemed rather insightful regarding Finney's work."

Lana had actually said a whole lot more than he had insight to Finney's art. Lana could sense people, read their intentions, and Honey learned that Lana's intuition was worth following. Lana had said there was something very trustworthy about this guy, that he would be worth Honey's time.

"We haven't officially met, have we, Honey?" Morgan's

voice, smooth and deep, felt almost like a caress. That made Honey a bit nervous. She didn't know if she wanted that kind of particular attention from him. Morgan was not her type. Honey preferred prettier men with more refined features. Morgan wasn't pretty. He had a strong, square jaw with a cleft dimple in his chin that she could just make out under the bad shave job. With a distinct, broad brow and wide cheekbones, he wasn't bad looking, just not pretty. Rugged, Honey thought. He was more rugged than refined. It also made her nervous because she felt like closing her eyes and leaning into the sound of his voice. After Bryce, she had no intention of falling for another guy anytime soon, regardless of how he made her feel.

"No, we haven't. I'm Honey Gould." She stuck out her hand and braced herself for commentary on her name. She felt certain Morgan would have some asinine thing to say. Most people did. She certainly didn't expect him capable of a witty pun. Inwardly, she flinched. She knew she was judging his intellect by his clothing and shave, and not for the first time. She had to stop that.

Morgan engulfed her hand in his large and warm one. Honey noticed the long tapered fingers were rough from use, but the skin on the back of his hand was smooth and his nails were clean and decently manicured. Those small personal grooming habits were the type of detail Honey always focused on.

"Morgan Palatine," he said.

"Morgan..." Finney grabbed the taller man by the elbow, "...I have some friends you have to meet."

As Finney steered Morgan back into the throng, Honey grinned. It was obvious Finney had a bit of a crush on him. As she watched the two men thread their way through the crowd, she realized Morgan hadn't said anything about her name. Honey couldn't remember the last time some guy who had been ogling her hadn't. They all seemed to think they were original, and that she would find it hysterical. She had heard all the lines, from being asked if she was sticky or easy to spread, to being called Golden Grahams after the cereal. She never found the name games to be witty, let alone to be hysterical. Morgan not commenting on her name was a notable relief.

Honey continued to clear away dishes, and fill orders as the night progressed. The majority of the crowd left by nine-thirty, a time considered fairly late around Cannery Row. Honey's gaze drifted over the front of the coffee shop. A few patrons stayed, gathered into cozy conversation groups. Finney still had Morgan cornered, and Morgan really didn't seem to mind. Her gaze settled on Lana and her wife Maggie, who seemed to be lost in each other's eyes. They looked at each other with such fathomless depths of love that it made Honey's heart ache. She completely understood why they loved each other. Lana was so witty and strong, a real business wiz, completely beautiful even though she didn't really focus on her own looks. She clearly adored Maggie. A local vet who spent most of her free time working with rescue animals, Maggie had a big heart and room enough for everyone she met. She naturally nurtured people and animals. She was amazingly beautiful inside and out.

Honey sighed. She wanted to love someone that way. To be content staring into each other's eyes for hours. She thought she had once, but he hadn't been kind or loving. Since then, she hadn't found anyone worth loving. Then again, she realized she hadn't been looking at who people really were. That's how she had ended up as an accessory for a vain, sadistic man. She had only paid attention to his exterior. He had turned out to not only *not* be loving, but to be someone to be afraid of, someone to run away from. She knew she had fallen into her old habit of looking at what people looked like, and how she perceived them to be. The last two men she dated had been exteriors only, well-groomed, pretty men who drove German phallic symbols. They dressed well, ate at the right restaurants, had the right job titles, and were complete assholes.

Lana had told her she needed to get over herself more than once. Honey needed to stop judging books by their covers. Read the first chapter, find out whether it was intriguing or not. After all, Honey realized, she wasn't that great of a book cover anymore herself. On the outside, she didn't look like a promising high-fashion model anymore and never worked as a museum curator, but inside she knew she was funny and had the capacity for love. No, she reminded herself, she wasn't a failed curator as some people might judge her; she just managed a different space than she had expected. In fact, everything in her life was much different than she had expected. She played with the charm at her neck. Much different.

Her gaze locked with Morgan's. She'd been aware that he had been watching her for some time. He smiled. It was a lovely smile, Honey thought, broad and full of gleaming white teeth. Now, this guy was not an exterior. Admittedly, he had a painful sense of fashion, but a girl could change that. His hair was positively a mess, but underneath the mess, he did have nice bone structure and friendly eyes. And, Honey noted, he was taller than her. When a girl stood one inch less than six feet, the height of one's date was a serious consideration. She knew she was being judgmental thinking about his looks, but what spoke to her, what made her think she maybe should give this guy a chance, wasn't just Lana telling her she should talk to him, but his actions.

He had spent the entire evening chatting with Finney and others. He didn't comment on her name. He had spent time in discussion with Lana and Maggie. He spoke knowledgeably about art. He did seem to understand it. Abstract expressionism was tough for a lot of people, yet he actually seemed to get it. A straight man who knew art—now that was intriguing.

Honey knew she needed to stop being so judgmental. Maybe she would practice on Morgan. See if she could do it. Get to know the person underneath the exterior. He seemed nice enough, and Lana had said he was a good person. *Hell,* he could be the best person to come her way in a long time and she would never find out because she wasn't impressed by his clothes or the fact that he did manual labor. *Hmm.* The next time he started to flirt, she would flirt right back. After all, little flirting never hurt. It gave the ego a boost.

Lana locked the café doors then headed back to the kitchen with the last tray of dishes. Maggie had pulled the register drawer and began counting the evening's receipts in the back office. Finney and his small group, including Morgan, were still ensconced in the overstuffed chairs in the middle of the café. Honey worked her way around the edges of the room cleaning towards the center, wiping down tables, and setting chairs on the table tops so she could mop. One of the chairs clattered to the floor.

"Crap," she bit out. She stood looking at the offending chair, wishing it would rise up and replace itself on the table. Her telekinesis mind powers worked in the form of Morgan. He picked up the chair and replaced it for her.

"Bad chair," he scolded.

"Thanks," she sighed.

"We should get out of your way. You're trying to close up, aren't you?" Finney stood up and motioned to the small group he always traveled with to begin gathering their things to head out. "Hey Morgan, we're going to head over to Pat's place for some wine. Care to join us?"

Finney's suggestion was chorused with a variety of *good idea* and *you are totally welcome.*

"Thanks, but maybe next time. I think I'll stay here and help with the heavy lifting." Morgan stood, holding a chair waiting for Honey to finish wiping down the table in front of them.

"You totally don't need to do that. It's my job to take care of it," she said.

"Think of it as a thank you. I haven't been in town that long. This was my first invitation out to something and I enjoyed myself." Morgan grinned at her. Something in his expression told her he enjoyed her company.

Finney air kissed her on both cheeks "Well, all right, Morgan. It was a pleasure, Honey. Delightful as always." She unlocked the doors and let him and his entourage out.

"He's quite the character," Morgan stated, watching Finney and his group walk up the sidewalk. "I think I got his whole life story."

"That's Finney. Sometimes I wonder when he finds time to paint. He loves people and he's a chatterbox." Honey returned to wiping down tables with disinfectant. Morgan followed behind and placed the chairs on each tabletop. She sighed. How to do this? Maybe Morgan wasn't her ideal of a good looking book cover, but she had to get an inside glimpse before she made any judgments. How to read Morgan's first chapter? What should she ask him? She thought about things he'd said, picking up on anything she could to ask about.

"So, you said you're new in town? Did you move here or just visiting?" Definitely, a good question to start a conversation.

"I'm only here for a few weeks—maybe six. Two months tops." Morgan explained. "I'm working on the new hotel about three blocks up on Wave."

"The one that's really a big hole in the ground right now?" Honey knew there had been a lot of community angst and anger over the hotel originally intended to be a high rise that no one wanted in this part of town. There had been lots of petitions and town hall meetings over it. In the end, the owners and architects modified the design to fit both local architectural styles and height specifications.

"That's the one," Morgan confirmed. "We're installing the foundation. Making sure everything is sound and as earthquake-proof as possible. A strong foundation means a strong building."

Honey paused. She could do this. A construction worker was a trained professional, not a mindless grunt worker. *I will not judge him by his cover. I will not judge him by his cover.* She repeated this mantra to herself several times. Though she had to admit, the more she talked to him, the more he seemed worth talking to.

"So tell me, Morgan, how does a construction worker know so much about Abstract Expressionism?"

Morgan laughed. "My family believes art is what makes us civilized. We always went to museums as kids. My parents taught us to appreciate art, even if we didn't find it appealing. I had to do projects on Abstract Expressionism since it's my least favorite. I really came to understand it."

"Your parents had you do projects? That almost sounds like you were homeschooled."

"Something like that. Small private school my parents helped to teach and run. Art is important. Too bad funding for it gets cut so frequently. When art is valued, the predominant culture is richer."

Honey had paused to watch him as he spoke, impressed with the views his parents had instilled in him regarding art and culture. If this is what Morgan had in his first few pages, maybe she should continue to read.

Lana rolled the mop out from the behind the counter. "Honey, mopping is all that's left to do. Why don't you go and head on out."

"You sure?" Honey asked as she reached behind her to untie her apron.

"Yeah. Maggie is almost done, so this is it for tonight. I'll see you tomorrow."

"Thanks, Lana." Honey disappeared into the back and returned with her bag and jacket.

"May I walk you to your car?" Morgan asked.

"Okay, sure." She unlocked the front door again, and they stepped out onto the sidewalk. Honey rooted in her bag for her keys and waited for Lana to lock the door behind her. She waved her keys at Lana and headed up the hill to the parking lot.

Morgan nodded at Honey's fist. "You always do that or is that for my benefit?" She had positioned two of her keys to stick out between her clenched fingers. They made a handy weapon. With enough force, the keys could puncture skin and scrape up an attacker, if needed, when used in self-defense.

"No, that's called force of habit. I used to have to take the train home at night when I lived in the Bay Area. Keys you don't have to explain away. Carrying a knife, you could get into trouble for that."

They didn't walk far when they reached her car, an old Japanese sedan. Honey liked its reliability, and as an older car, she didn't have to worry about computer parts failing her. Most importantly, she could actually take care of the basic maintenance herself.

"This is me." She unlocked and opened her door.

"Thank you for an interesting evening, Honey. I'll see you around." Morgan waited for her to slide into the driver's seat then closed her car door before backing away.

Honey started her car then watched him walk back down the hill in the direction they had come. She realized he had walked out of the way for her. Honey couldn't remember once when any other man had done something as considerate as that. He was definitely becoming more interesting.

## 3

Finney moved from painting to painting, examining the tags. He sighed dejectedly as he encountered another label without the telltale little dot indicating it had been sold. He slumped into one of the cushioned chairs. Finney wasn't up to his regular animated chatter. His opening party had been packed and full of bustling energy. The coffee shop did well in sales, but Finney had only sold one small painting. According to him, the opening had been a complete waste of time.

Seth rattled dishes as he made his way into the back and started the dishwasher. Honey cleaned the front counter, avoiding the midday maintenance on the coffee machine. Finney's dejected attitude was merely a reflection of the slow afternoon.

The bells over the door tinkled. Honey looked up from her task, prepared to rush around the counter and wash her hands before serving the new guest. She heard Finney gasp before she registered her own pleased reaction. *Morgan.*

"Morgan, you are a sight for sore eyes." Finney cooed. "Sit, sit, sit," he directed. "Hey, Honey, look. Morgan's here."

Morgan smiled broadly at her as he sat in the chair Finney directed.

"Hi, Morgan," she said, wiping her hands on the towel tucked into her apron. His presence was a welcome change in the monotony of the day.

"Honey. Finney." Morgan nodded to each in turn. He leaned back into his chair. "This is perfect, but," he began to rise. "I should order before I get too comfortable."

"Nonsense," Finney chided. "Honey will bring your order over, won't you, Honey?"

"Why not? It's not like I'm doing anything else," she harrumphed. "What can I get you?"

"You sure? Large, black, high octane, and something sweet," he paused.

"But not lemon." Honey finished for him, remembering he had left behind the lemon bar his first day in the shop. She remembered Lana eating it, claiming that after all, it was paid for and abandoned by the man because he "didn't do lemon."

"But not lemon," he confirmed.

"You want anything else while I'm at it, Finney?"

"Now that you mention it, I could use another tea and something sweet sounds great. Bring me whatever you bring him."

Honey shook her head as she walked behind the counter. Finney was obviously crushing on Morgan. Finney was a stickler for always having the right pastry with his tea. And if lemon bars were available, he always ate a lemon bar. Even if it was misdirected, at least Finney was branching out. Morgan wasn't Finney's type either. Finney tended to like younger men in lots of leather.

*Hmmm, misdirected.* She thought Morgan had been flirting with her, at least she realized she had wanted him to be flirting with her. Could she be sure? He could still be gay and flirt with her. He could be bi and flirt with her. Maybe he was just being nice.

She tried to eavesdrop on Finney and Morgan's conversation. Maybe she could pick up nuances that would tell her whether Morgan was responsive to Finney. Maybe Morgan secretly was a leather boy? But all Finney blathered on about was how much of his soul went into his paintings and how "the Philistines around here just don't appreciate good art."

Honey carried over a tray with Finney's hot water, a fresh tea bag, Morgan's large coffee, and two plates with gooey cinnamon rolls.

"Abstract Expressionism is hard to sell in a place full of tourists and all the galleries in Carmel, especially when most people are looking for something to commemorate their trip here," Honey tried to explain.

"I have to agree. Your work would probably sell better in a bigger city. LA, New York." Morgan added. He grinned at Honey as he took his plate from her and smelled the large frosted roll. "Smells great. Another of Lana's creations?"

Honey nodded.

"Well, I live and work here," Finney whined. "I don't like having to shill myself in those other places. Too crowded, too noisy."

"What you need, Finney is an agent," Morgan suggested. "They do all the legwork in the cities for you. You stay here and paint."

Honey watched as Finney played with his tea bag, thinking. She thought it a brilliant suggestion. Finney should as well, but Honey expected Finney to start making excuses as to why it wouldn't work.

The door bells tinkled again. A group of Asian tourists came chattering in the door. Honey moved to be of service behind the counter and left the two men to discuss Finney's abysmal career.

She smiled and returned the mini bows the tourists gave her as she delivered their drinks. She reflected on a time in her past when she would have been annoyed trying to order in a foreign country. She didn't speak any languages other than English, and she wasn't the most polite foreigner. In her previous life, she had never really appreciated the travel opportunities she had been given. It had all seemed like such a bore, an attitude she had clearly picked up from those around her.

She was in a better place mentally now. Sure the clothes weren't as exciting and the shoes were downright functional rather than decorative, but she was learning who she was inside. She was a different person than she had been.

Morgan's deep voice pulled her from her reverie. "Honey? Honey, hey."

She blinked at his close face. Damn, could that dimple in his chin actually be making him better looking? She had zoned out completely. Suddenly realizing she was staring at Morgan, she said, "Sorry. I got lost there for a moment. She shook her head to bring her awareness back to the here and now.

"I need to get back to work." He held something out to her. She glanced down at the credit card extended in front of her.

"Right, sorry." She took the card. While she hit keys on the register to total his bill, Morgan said, "Add Finney's tab to that. He's pretty down about not selling anything."

"Yeah, he really needs a sale and not just for the money.

If he doesn't sell something soon, he'll spiral into a depression. His work gets really bleak when he's depressed."

"It was just a cinnamon roll. I doubt it will fend off depression."

Honey added in Finney's tea and pastry. "It's still sweet of you. I think he likes you," she whispered conspiratorially.

"I think you're right," Morgan whispered back. "But we're clear where we stand. Buying a drink for a buddy who is feeling rejected isn't sending mixed signals, is it?"

"No, I think he'll appreciate the gesture. It's not like a secret come-on, especially since it's tea. Now if it were a martini and you'd showed up in studded leather chaps—" She snapped her thumb and third finger together then pointed her index finger at his chest. "—that would be mixed signals. You're safe, for now."

Morgan chuckled as he folded his receipt and put his credit card back in his wallet. He turned then pivoted back toward the counter. "Let Lana know her buns are the best."

A voice from behind Honey rang out, "I heard that!"

"You were supposed to!" He turned his attention back to Honey. "See ya'." He nodded and winked at her before leaving.

Morgan was different and surprising. He had only been around for a few days and already he fit in nicely with the regulars and everyone else at The Corner. He was being a good friend to Finney and trading teasing quips with Lana as if he's known her for years. If Honey let herself, she could really like him.

The tourists left. Finney sipped tea. Lana disappeared back into the office. Seth made too much noise banging dishes around, and Honey returned to cleaning parts of the counter. Everything returned to how it had been before the brief interlude with Morgan and the tourists.

The phone rang. Honey heard Lana answer then proceeded to ignore it.

"Finney." Lana's voice sounded stern, commanding. "You need to come over here. Give Honey your phone."

"What's going on?" Finney asked.

"Trust me on this. Give your phone to Honey." Cautiously, he handed the phone to Honey. She took it, a question in her eyes.

"Start recording this." Lana directed.

"What?" Honey was as confused as Finney.

Lana smirked. Honey recognized that expression, Lana was being mischievous. Something was up. "Trust me. This needs to be recorded."

Honey nodded and held up the phone to record. "Just keep it on Finney," she paused. "Tell me when you're ready."

"Okay, it's recording." Honey focused on Finney's confused expression.

Lana began speaking, "I just received a call from an anonymous buyer and a bank transfer is being made. I have a delivery address, but no name." Finney looked even more confused. Lana started walking towards the middle of the shop. "Camera on me for a sec."

Honey moved so that the phone recorded Lana. She held up a green dot on the tip of her finger. Finney squealed in delight. Honey refocused on him as Lana slowly walked past several small paintings. Honey continued recording Finney's anticipation. Lana carefully placed the dot next to the painting *Desespoir Agréable*. Finney's expression gave way to shock, then tears of joy as he realized the painting had sold.

"It sold? It sold!" Finney's voice rose in happy shock.

"Yep. The money transfer should be complete in the

next few days. The buyer expects it to ship when we pull the show down."

"Oh, my God! It sold!" Finney glowed, still absorbing the happy news.

Honey continued to record. She knew Finney would want the recording to share with all his friends.

"Where's it being shipped to? Who is the buyer?" He shot questions rapidly at Lana.

"Buyer—I honestly don't know. I spoke with a bank person. And the shipping address is in New York," Lana explained.

"New York?"

"New York."

"I need to call my mother." Finney patted all his pockets. "Where's my phone?" He returned to his chair and continued to look around. "Where the hell is my effing phone?"

Honey laughed as he looked directly at her and both realized she held his phone. She stopped the recording and handed Finney his phone. She knew that last part would be edited and put on the Internet. It was too funny not to share. And Finney was a member of the over-sharers club.

Finney took his phone, and in seconds, he happily chattered away with someone on the other end of the line.

"Seriously?" Honey asked Lana.

Lana nodded. "I've never done that before. Bank transfers and anonymous purchases. It felt all so very upmarket."

"Any idea who bought it?"

Lana shook her head.

"Well, I'm glad he has a fan with deep pockets. The commission on that piece does not suck."

"So now what?" Honey asked, not feeling like returning to cleaning after the excitement of Finney's big sale.

"Now we listen to Finney tell us repeatedly his version of the tale of intrigue over the big sale.

Honey laughed. Lana was right. Finney loved to share, and this was a particularly juicy story.

# 4

Honey sighed when she walked into the deli. The line for lunch was too long. She would never get her order filled in time to eat and get back to work within the time allotted for her lunch break. She could just skip eating. One meal wouldn't hurt her. One meal wouldn't trigger an avalanche back into old eating habits.

One meal. "Just give me one meal," her therapist used to say. "Eat one good meal for me today, and tomorrow we can start talking about eating two meals." *Recovery starts with one meal and so does a relapse.* Honey sighed. No skipping lunch today. It wouldn't be the healthiest option, but she could get pizza by the slice. She turned and began to push through the out-door when Morgan called her name.

"Honey, what do you want?" She turned and saw him already standing at the order counter waiting on a sandwich being made. He and the counter clerk were looking at her. She noticed how tall he really was. His head practically brushed the hanging salami display, and he looked to be twice as tall as the girl behind the counter.

"Uhm, I was going to get the Pesto Primavera." Honey

watched Morgan nod to the clerk before she moved off to scoop pasta salad into a clear to-go container.

"Grab me a bag of chips and an Orangina, and get yourself a drink. Meet me at the register," Morgan directed.

Honey was aware that everyone in line watched her. She had walked in the door, and by sheer dumb luck, had been propelled to the head of the line. This Morgan guy wasn't so bad after all. Now if he would just do something with his hair and stop it with those damn plaid shirts. She pulled a bottle of the orange soda he requested from the commercial glass-fronted cooler and a sparkling water for herself. Uncertain of Morgan's chip preference, she selected three different bags. She would eat one with lunch and save the one he didn't want for later.

She joined Morgan when he stepped forward in line.

"Hey, that was really nice. You didn't have to do that."

"No problem. You looked so despondent and about to leave."

"I appreciate it, I really do, but let me pay you back."

Morgan waved her suggestion aside. "No, I've got this. It's just a pasta salad, no strings attached."

"Are you sure?"

"Okay, how about one of your friendly smiles?"

"Really?" She crinkled her brow and stared at him in disbelief.

"Okay, how about a sarcastic retort?"

She couldn't help it. She smiled.

"Totally worth it," he crooned.

They headed out of the crowded deli and started walking back towards The Corner. Honey found a tall curb to sit on, and Morgan sat next to her.

"Orangina? You drink Orangina, but you wouldn't eat Lana's lemon bars?"

"No lemon, no chocolate. Lemon messes with my sense of taste and smell, and I'm allergic to chocolate. Oranges are fine. Besides, it's Orangina, it's not like drinking an orange soda at all. Makes your tongue feel like doing the Lambada." He licked his lips, swiping his tongue across his upper lip, and then wiggled his eyebrows up and down.

Honey giggled nervously at his blatant flirting. He was even better looking than she had let herself think on Friday night. His tongue had licked lips she hadn't realize she'd thought about licking herself.

"So, Morgan," she asked between bites. "You're just here for some job, right?" Honey was bound and determined to improve. She knew she had judgmental issues and that there were no grounds to make assumptions based on superficial reasons. So far he had proven to be a pretty nice guy. Lana would be proud of her progress.

"Yeah. I'm living out of an old Airstream I'm renovating. It's currently parked up in Moss Beach."

Honey nodded not sure what to say next.

"I could ask you the same, but your job is a little less transient than mine," Morgan observed.

"I moved down here from San Francisco a few years ago. A mutual friend introduced me to Lana. She had ideas for the café, and I was looking for something." She slowly shook her head at her own situation. Her hand reflexively wrapped around the charm at her neck. She remembered strange details about that day. Particularly the fog. The way the weather and her mood lightened considerably as she traveled south and away, as if the fog was releasing her from it's embrace.

"Did you find it?" Morgan's voice pulled her out of the mist in her head.

"What?" Honey, temporarily lost in her thoughts about

running away from San Francisco had lost track of the conversation.

"Did you find what you were looking for?"

"I'm not even sure what I was looking for at the time. I've found something different than intended, and for now, that's perfectly good. I feel safe here, and that's what counts, right?"

Honey stood up. Morgan watched as she brushed dirt off her backside. "I have to get back to work. Thanks for lunch. Next time you come in, your coffee and snack are on me." Honey stopped, realizing what she had just said. "Uhm, right," she stammered as her mind pictured images of Morgan licking whipped cream from her belly.

"Bye." Morgan laughed.

She wiggled her fingers in a nervous wave before spinning away from Morgan, hoping he didn't see her blush.

"Yeah," she sighed. "A construction worker who knows about the connection between Orangina and the Lambada." One being an orange soda from Brazil, the other a sexy dance from the soda's TV commercials. Getting into Morgan's first chapter so far had been worth it.

Honey stopped in her tracks as a chill traveled down her spine. For a split second, she thought she recognized a slender, dark-haired man. She blinked, focusing on the figure. He turned. She saw an unfamiliar smiling face with dark eyes. Honey shook herself and breathed a sigh of release. She needed to be clearheaded in order to deal with the workday ahead of her. She didn't need any man clouding her thoughts. Not Morgan and his lips and not that blue-eyed sadist who'd triggered a panic attack the last time she saw him.

∾

The fog bank rolled in earlier than normal. By four o'clock, all the unprepared tourists were making a rush on the shops that sold sweatshirts. It was the kind of day on which cups of comforting hot chocolate sold better than coffee.

"Rachelle," a familiar male voice mispronounced her middle name. Her head snapped up in recognition at the sound of rah-shell. Her nose twitched at the familiar smell of pungent aftershave. She felt the blood drain from her face. Her stomach lurched.

*Crap, crap, crap, crap.* "Why are you here?" Her tone held no friendly warmth of recognition.

"I came to buy a coffee. I was at a meeting with a client up the street, and they told me this was the best place to get a coffee. I had no idea you were here. Don't I get a hello?"

Honey glanced around, swallowing down the bile that burned the back of her throat. Seth was nowhere to be seen, and Lana wasn't due in for another hour. She was stuck having to deal with Bryce Maplecourt, her abusive ex-boyfriend, on her own, and she wasn't ready for it.

Bryce was tall and thin, with fine sharp features, ice-cold blue eyes, and short black hair slicked expertly to the side. Honey knew under his cashmere overcoat he would be wearing a designer suit. Bryce had always known how to put himself together. He dressed with as much care as most of the male models she had dated. It was what had drawn her to him originally.

Slowly and deliberately, Honey turned back toward the counter, positioning herself at the register.

"Hello. What can I get for you?" Her voice sounded robotic to her ears.

"Rachelle," Bryce's voice drew out her name, but there was no emotion to it. "I really had no idea you would be here. I thought you were further south, like in Santa Barbara all this time."

"My name is Honey, just like it always has been."

"I never liked that name. What were your parents thinking? Honey Gould. It's so, so trashy. At least they gave you a classic middle name."

"It doesn't matter what you think of my name. You don't even pronounce it correctly. If you are going to talk to me, use the name Honey. It's my name. I like it. Now, what can I get for you, Bryce?" She tried to look him directly in the eye but the piercing blueness of them held anger. She quickly averted her own.

"No catching up for old time's sake? You look," he paused eyeing her form, a sneer pulled at his upper lip, "settled. Older. You've put on some weight. You should ask about me now."

Honey stared at him blankly, her expression belied her inner turmoil.

"I am doing exceptionally well, Rachelle. Do you want to know more?"

The door opened behind him. A gaggle of cold tourists entered.

Honey felt her tension slip just a notch. She immediately felt safer with others around but not safe enough. She would never feel safe in the same room with Bryce. "Yes. I would like to know what you want? As you can see, I have other customers waiting. It's pretty straightforward here. Coffee, espresso, hot chocolate, tea, or something out of the cooler." Her brain kept repeating the mantra *just order and leave. Just order and leave.*

"I'll have a medium half-caf then."

Honey rang up his total, without even asking if it was for here or to-go or if he cared for anything else. She fixed the drink, repeating *just leave* in her head. She handed Bryce the paper cup full of coffee. "You can leave now." She kept her tone as unaffected as possible but she couldn't help but notice her hands were shaking.

Bryce also noticed and took his coffee. "Not very stable these days, hmm?" he muttered.

She carefully tried to not pay attention to the snide remark. If she was unstable, he certainly had done his best to contribute to that state. Once he moved away from the counter, she attempted to put all of her focus on the group of women waiting after him. It didn't work. She began to feel sick. Bryce took too long doctoring his drink. As much as Honey didn't want to pay attention to him, she couldn't help it. Every time she glanced in his direction, she caught him glaring at her through narrowed eyes.

The woman in front of her had to repeat her order. "I'm so sorry." Honey apologized, yet her eyes followed Bryce's back as he finally turned towards the door to leave.

It appeared as if he was about to turn and say something to her when Morgan walked in. With Morgan present, Honey felt herself relax. She instantly felt safer; she felt safe enough.

"I'm so sorry." She apologized again with a strained giggle. "That man was making me nervous."

She fixed four hot chocolates and plated two slices of cake, and delivered them to the women who surrounded the table furthest from the door.

"Honey." This time the voice saying her name felt soothing, warm, and deep. "Did I overhear you say that Maplecourt was bothering you?"

Honey nodded. "He's my ex-boyfriend. You know him?" Her breathing was shaky.

"He was at the site earlier. He's the client's accountant and a real asshole."

Honey nodded biting her lip. "He's an asshole all right. Remember when I told you I was looking for something when I moved down here?" Her eyes were wide, fear clearly lingering. "I was looking to get away from him." She took a ragged breath. "He didn't know exactly where I was until today." She started shaking again.

Morgan's body reacted to her instantly. Fear rolled off of Honey in waves. He longed to wrap her in his arms and protect her from Maplecourt and what he had exposed her to. Morgan reached behind the counter and eased her out, guiding her to a chair. He returned behind the counter and quickly poured her a cup of coffee. "Here." He handed her the cup, pulled up a chair next to her, and began tenderly stroking her arms, resisting the urge to wrap her in his protective embrace.

Honey held the warm cup and inhaled as if the pungent aroma strengthened her flagging fortitude. Closing her eyes, she began to talk.

"He wasn't just my boyfriend, he was my fiancé. I thought he loved me." She spoke softly and slowly. The words spilling from her on their own. "So pretty. Good family. Knew the right people. He seemed very supportive at first. Really proud when I graduated with my degree in gallery management. Said he would use his connections to get me into one of the museums." She took a sip of the coffee. She looked up at Morgan and snorted, more of a derisive sound than one of humor. "That never happened."

The bells over the door jingled.

"Honey are you all right?" Lana asked, rushing to where Honey sat.

"She's pretty shaken up," Morgan explained.

"What happened? She looks pale, even for her." Lana's voice sounded filled with concern.

"Bryce came in." Honey's voice sounded detached.

"Well, shit." Lana bit off the words. "Are you okay?"

"I'll be fine. I'm going to go in the back and hide for a bit I think. Maybe puke." She slowly got up and, as if in a daze, walked behind the counter and into the back.

Morgan glanced at Lana questioningly.

"They were engaged. He messed with her head pretty bad. He was abusive," Lana explained simply.

Morgan nodded in understanding.

"Look, I'm only telling you this 'cause I know you like her, and something tells me you wouldn't hurt her. She's had some serious issues in her past. She was working on herself, getting shit sorted out, and Bryce set her back. Messed with her head."

"Is he dangerous?"

"He's a bully, that's bad enough. He's a snake." Lana clearly was self-editing, she seemed to want to use a stronger word, but held herself in check with customers in the café.

"Look, I have to go back to the job site, but—" Morgan rubbed his forehead, thinking, "—uhm, don't let her walk to her car alone. Have her wait for me. If Maplecourt has decided to stick around for any reason, I'll deal with him."

"If you're really going to be Honey's friend, you have to know she comes with baggage."

"Don't we all?"

Morgan paused outside of the café to dial his phone.

"Dante, whatever you are doing, I've got something more important." Morgan paused to listen to the man on the other end of the line. He harrumphed. "No, you don't have to cause anyone to disappear under mysterious circumstances, at least not yet. Find anything and everything on an accountant for the Cyan Group, name of Bryce Maplecourt. Anything I can use as leverage."

Honey sat huddled in the corner, her purse sitting on the table in front of her. Next to it, a cup of coffee grew cold. She stared blankly in front of her. Morgan saw her looking despondent when he came back into The Corner.

He slid into the chair next to her, "Hi, Honey. You waiting for me?"

She nodded.

"I'm glad you waited. I don't want you walking to your car alone if Maplecourt is a threat to you."

She nodded again.

"I'm going to check in with Lana, okay?"

Honey kept nodding, not focusing on anything.

Morgan balled his hands into fists before spreading his fingers wide to ease out the tension he felt building. He frequently used this technique to keep his claws in check. Honey was terrified and withdrawing into shock. What had that asshole done to her? Morgan wanted to rip out his throat next time he saw the man. He couldn't, not while Maplecourt controlled the finances on the construction site. When this building was complete and the relationship with the client over and paid in full, Morgan thought about having a little chat with Maplecourt. Give him a demonstration on intimidation and abuse of power. Even if he never saw Honey again, Morgan would still pay Maplecourt a visit for scaring her like this. Morgan wondered if Maplecourt had set her on edge that first day he saw her. She had been terrified then too.

"How's she doing? Is she okay?" Morgan asked as he approached Lana at the counter.

Lana looked over to where Honey sat. Concern creased her brow. "He hasn't seen her for a few years. She thought she was done with him. I think it's hitting her hard. Last time she saw him, he didn't notice her, and she was still a mess. This time, she had to talk to him. She's strong, but sometimes there is only so much you can take." Lana looked over to where Honey sat. Concern creased her brow.

"I'll give Maggie a call. Maybe Honey needs to go to my place tonight. Bryce doesn't know where she lives. I seriously doubt he's out there stalking her, but I don't think she should be alone when she's like this."

"That's not a bad idea, at all," Morgan agreed.

Lana picked up her phone and held up a finger indicating that Morgan should wait for a minute. Her face softened into a broad smile, Maggie clearly picked up on the other end of the line. She nodded and made confirming noises. Morgan returned his focus to Honey, away from Lana's conversation. He didn't understand how anyone would want to hurt someone so frail and beautiful. Honey's eyes held fear, and her chin quivered as she appeared to fight back tears. Morgan wanted to hold and protect her delicate beauty. He wanted to eviscerate Maplecourt.

"Maggie agrees. If you could follow her to make sure she gets to my place, that would be great."

Morgan nodded in agreement.

"Hey, Honey," Lana's voice was soothing as she slid into a chair next to Honey. "Maggie wants you to stay with us tonight, okay? She said she would feel better knowing you were not alone. I'll go feed Calliope tonight so you don't have to worry about your cat."

Honey seemed to refocus on the world around her. She

turned to Lana. "Thanks, that's a real nice idea." She focused on Morgan, "I don't really want to go home right now, not anyone's. Would it be okay if we walked around for a while? I don't want to feel closed in."

A slow grin spread across Morgan's lips. "Sure, Honey, whatever you want."

"I'll let Maggie know it could be a while. But you *are* staying with us tonight." Lana's tone was firm. She would take no excuses or arguments.

"Thanks, Lana. Yes, I'll stay. I'm sorry I got a little weird there for a bit."

"It's okay Honey, it really is."

Morgan followed Honey out of the café.

"Where to?" he asked. His deep voice calmed Honey's nervous stomach.

"You mind just wandering up and down the tourist spots a bit? I want to distract my mind."

"Sure." Morgan placed his hand on the small of her back and led her past a group on the sidewalk.

The sidewalks were fairly empty, the fog having chased most people indoors.

"When I first moved here, it was always like this. Too quiet." Honey began. "No night life. The fog always rolls in around four in the afternoon, just like today, and then the sidewalks roll up soon after. Too quiet for me. Especially after having lived in nothing but cities for years."

They wandered past the aquarium. Normally crawling with tourists, after hours it was spookily quiet. They passed several shop fronts before Honey turned to Morgan, suggesting they enter one, a typical tourist shop for the region full of jewelry, tchotchkes made from shells, and T-shirts with sea otters and Monterey Cannery Row emblazoned across the front. The repeating themes of the shop were coastal and golf.

Honey led Morgan into another shop. Another repetition of similar touristy gift items. Morgan kept an eye on Honey, watching to see if any of these items sparked an interest in her. She seemed oddly detached as if she barely registered what her eyes were seeing. He realized that Maplecourt must have seriously hurt her, and not just physically.

Honey clearly processed information and feelings inside somewhere. That or she was shutting down. Morgan knew he could protect her from any physical harm, but from what Lana had said and based on Honey's reactions, Maplecourt's damage had been psychological. It sounded like he joyfully fed her demons and doubts. That was something Morgan could not confront and face down. There was nothing to take a bite out of to make everything better. He wasn't sure how to protect her from that kind of past abuse. He could be here for her now, and that was the best he could do. As long as she allowed him to stay around, he would make sure those demons would never be fed again.

Morgan positioned himself close behind her. "Honey." He gently placed a hand on her shoulder, breaking the silence of their wanderings.

She jumped at his touch. "Yeah?"

"You feel like talking about it? I'm a good listener." Morgan wasn't sure what to do, all he knew was that he wanted Honey to be happy, not sad and frightened.

She turned a wan smile towards him. "Not right now if that's okay, Morgan. Right now I think I just want to feel safe." She removed her hand from the charm at her neck to place her fingers on the back of his hand. "I feel safe with you."

Morgan gave her a brief nod then folded his fingers around her slim hand, engulfing it. She was safe with him, safer than she realized.

They wandered in and out of several shops in silence holding hands.

"I want to go look at the water," Honey announced. Quietly, they strolled back past all the shops and the aquarium and walked along the bike path until they were next to the water. The tide rolled out. No large waves crashed against the coastal rocks. The smooth lapping of water covered rocks then receded. California harbor seals perched on top of lonely rocks.

Honey continued walking, pulling Morgan with her as she headed further out on the rocks. She let go of his hand as she jumped from one rock to another and began climbing higher before sitting on a flat surface. Morgan followed her, sitting on the rock next to her.

"I forget sometimes that I can walk out the door of work and come sit here." A car passed behind them on the road, the sound muffled and distant. "The fog makes it feel like we're the only people for miles and miles. Isolated. Lonely." She spoke softly, voicing the thoughts in her head. "It can be depressing. But not when I come to the water. It all goes away. It's not desolate, it's beautiful. It's like the waves and air cleanse my spirit." She huffed through her nose. "Salt-water therapy, sea air, and ocean waves. This is almost as good as a therapist. I mean, a good therapist makes you think about your issues so that you can solve them on your own. The ocean clears my head so I can think straight and figure out what my problems are." She glanced at Morgan, seeing if he understood her meaning.

He nodded at her. She noticed a glint of amber light flickering in his dark eyes.

"You still want to listen? I can talk for a while."

"I don't have any plans, except to see you safely to Lana's for the night." Morgan grinned at her. "Until then, I'm all yours."

"Okay." Honey took a deep cleansing breath and stared out into the water. "I met Bryce my last year of school. I was interning at a gallery." Her hand zipped the charm from side to side along the chain at her neck.

She could picture the first time she and Bryce met. It was a slow, dreary, drizzly winter afternoon, and she was minding the gallery on her own, first-time solo. She was nervous but glad it was the kind of afternoon people didn't window shop. She had never really had to talk to anyone before, never had to try to sell anything. Her mentor said she would do fine and not to try to sell a piece. Instead, she should approach a prospective client like trying to set up friends on a date. Her job was matchmaker for art, not painting seller.

Bryce acted as if he had been lured into the gallery by a particular painting. He was the prettiest man outside of modeling she had ever seen. Fine features, almost delicate bone structure, sharp blue eyes, a dazzling smile, black-black hair and pale-pale skin, tailored designer suit. Honey had tried to set him up with every painting in the gallery that afternoon. In the end, he insisted she go out to dinner with him. And for some reason, she did not refuse. Now she realized he had been playing head games with her from the very beginning.

"It started off with small things. Like my name. He always used my middle name, Rachael, but he pronounced it rah-shell instead of ray-chel. At the time I loved it, it sounded soft, elegant, sexy. He was the only person who called me Rachelle; everyone else called me Honey. It felt special. It took me a while to realize what he was doing. He started to point out how low-class he thought the name Honey really was. Classic abuse. Undermined me, cut me off from my friends, convinced me I didn't need therapy anymore. he was messing with me, making me think I was crazy."

It had been over food. The fights hadn't always been about food, but so many of the bad ones had been. Bryce would get angry with her for not eating then get angry with her for eating and ruining her figure. She couldn't win.

"He slapped me." She shook her head, trying to arrange her thoughts. "Bryce cried after he hit me and promised it would never happen again. That I had made him so angry. That it was my fault he hit me. I needed to trust him." She breathed deeply, turning her gaze to Morgan, "The sad part is I believed him. I let him convince me it had been my fault. He would blame me for his actions. At first, I believed him, then something clicked and I realized it wasn't me."

"How was it my fault he hit me?" Her gaze shifted back to the water. "He told me to trust him. How could I trust him when I didn't feel safe around him? I called my old therapist in a panic. She got me into her office the next day, on a Sunday. I talked for hours. She helped me to see that he was displaying abusive patterns, and now that the hitting had begun, it would not stop. It would only get worse. She helped me make an escape plan."

Honey sat quietly for a few minutes. She poked at the rock beneath her before she began talking again.

"I never made it to the escape plan. A few days later, Bryce pushed me then hit me. Hard. More than once. I saw stars, and my nose started bleeding. I thought he had broken it. He did that apologizing thing while still blaming me the entire time he cleaned me up. I let him put me to bed, and he even called in sick to work for me. Said I had nothing to worry about, I just needed to rest while he went to work. I waited to make sure he wasn't coming back. I packed up everything I could carry and I left." She looked down at her hand. "I found this in the car that afternoon. He had ripped it off me at some point. I thought it was lost."

She looked at Morgan again. His features tightened, and his face held a fury he kept in check. His eyes glowed and his lips were pursed as he glared at the horizon.

"You okay with this?" she asked.

Morgan kept his tone even and controlled, but his voice was rough with anger. "I should be the one asking if you're okay. I am angry for you."

Honey patted him on the knee. "That's sweet, but it's in the past."

"It still hurts you to think about it, and he scared you today just by showing up."

"He scared me today because I wasn't expecting to see him. But I know I am stronger than this." Honey said with all of her conviction. "I am a survivor, and Bryce Maplecourt cannot hurt me anymore. He has no leverage for threats, and if he tries to touch me, I'll have his ass arrested for assault."

Morgan gave Honey a small smile, his anger lifting. "Clearly, you have thought this through."

"Lana is helping me a lot. Actually, I came here to hide out with a friend for a few days. I needed to think. Needed to figure out what next. I met Finney my first night down here. He introduced me to Lana. Lana offered me a job immediately. Said she needed me, so I stayed."

Honey stood up abruptly. She spread her arms wide as if embracing the world in front of her. She breathed deeply. "God that felt good," she sighed. "Thank you. I needed to air that out. Thank you for listening and not trying to fix this for me."

"You don't sound like you need help fixing anything. You sound like you've got this." Morgan said as he stood. He stepped close to Honey.

"I'm working on it, definitely working on it." Honey stepped toward Morgan. Her pulse began racing again, this time it didn't feel like fear. "I'm trying to be my own hero, but that doesn't always work." She lifted slightly up onto her toes and placed her lips against Morgan's.

She lowered back onto her heels. Morgan hadn't kissed her back. *I shouldn't have done that.* "Thank you for listening."

Honey headed back towards the bike trail. "I think Lana knew I needed her. She's really seen me through these past few years. She's been my unofficial life coach since I started working for her. I don't need a knight in shining armor to save me. I can save myself. I don't need to be afraid of Bryce. Just need to stay away from him. I don't need a partner to complete myself, but it's nice to have the companionship. That one gave me a whole new perspective on dating. I am a worthy complete person all by myself. Me and my fat ass can do anything I set my mind to."

Morgan narrowed his eyes at her and then shrugged. "Good philosophy, I like that. Be your own hero."

They walked in silence back to Honey's car. Inside Honey's head was anything but quiet. *Why did I kiss him?* She decided if he was going to ignore it, she would too.

"I promised Lana I would follow you to her house. That I would see you safely home. Get in. Lock the doors. I need to get my bike. I'll be right back."

Honey followed Morgan's advice and locked her doors. She blared the CD she had in the player. Queen. Freddy

Mercury crooned, and everything felt better, even though Morgan hadn't kissed her back. Soon the loud, low rumble of a motorcycle caught her attention as Morgan pulled up next to her.

Honey lowered her car window. "Follow me."

Morgan gave her a thumbs up as she pulled out of her parking space. Morgan followed closely but not too closely as Honey navigated her way uphill into the residential area of New Monterey.

She parked her car and got out in front of a small house. "This is it," she announced. Honey waved as she walked into the house.

Big Dog greeted her with drool and a happy wagging tail. She dug her hand deep into the scruff of fur at his neck, and knew she would be alright.

# 5

-------

The café buzzed with motion when Morgan walked in for his afternoon coffee and daily visit with Honey. Ever since the afternoon Bryce Maplecourt had paid Honey a surprise visit, Morgan had made it his mission to check on Honey as often as possible. He knew exactly what days Maplecourt would be in town since it was his job site the man visited on behalf of their mutual client. Maplecourt wasn't due for another visit for two weeks. This gave Morgan plenty of time to warn Honey.

Honey perched on a ladder just as she had the first day he met her. This time, however, she was removing Finney's paintings from the walls. As soon as she stepped off the ladder, Joyce, another woman who worked at The Corner, climbed up the ladder. She draped vibrant swags of colorful fabric that looked like Indian saris.

Finney's paintings were stacked against one wall and the entire coffee shop was beginning to resemble something that belonged in 1001 Arabian Nights.

"Hi, Honey," Morgan greeted her once she had tucked the most recent painting carefully into the stack.

She smiled at him. She seemed to actually glow with joy. "What are you doing in here?"

Morgan gestured with his hand, indicating the change of décor. "Looks like you're setting up for a party."

"We are." Honey explained. "Last month we had Finney's art opening. This month Joyce's belly dance class is having a hafla." Her voice chipper, she radiated happiness.

"A what-la?"

"Hafla. It's what she calls a dance party. Her students get an opportunity to dance in public, and sometimes she even gets in a small band. It's a lot of fun."

"Belly dancers? That does sound like fun. You dance?" he asked with a smirk.

"Not like they do," she attempted to demonstrate her skills with a rather awkward chest gyration. She giggled. "Nope, not at all."

"So when is this haff-lah?"

"Saturday. You're coming, right?" Honey glanced up at him through lowered lashes.

*That was a flirt.* He followed her over to the counter. Without confirming his order, she began preparing a large cup of black coffee and a random pastry but not the lemon bar.

"Of course, I'm coming. That was an invitation, wasn't it?"

Honey blushed slightly and nodded.

"So, Honey," Morgan leaned forward on the counter separating them. His voice lowered. Morgan prepared to take this flirting to the next level. She had started something he planned to enjoy for as long as he could. "Tell me something." He licked his lips. "Why are you so happy this afternoon?"

Honey superstitiously glanced around. She leaned in

closer to Morgan. Momentarily distracted by her scent, so close, he could kiss her. But not yet.

"Don't tell anyone," she whispered, "but I am not a fan of Finney's paintings. They make this place gloomy and everything feels stagnant and superficial. It's like they have some weird negative energy vibe." She leaned back. "Joyce's parties always make me happy." Her voice returned to its normal pitch and volume. "Besides it's hard to not be happy with all these wonderful colors. When Lana gets back, she'll start making some special pastries, so the place will smell of honey and cardamom by tomorrow morning. And Joyce always plays good music."

Honey had been right. The entire mood of the café did feel different without Finney's splashes of gloom on the walls. It was a nice upbeat change.

A tour bus hissed as its air brakes brought it to a stop. Tourists piled out of the bus and straight into the shop. Joyce quickly maneuvered the ladder out of the middle of the room and into the back before she joined Honey at the counter.

Morgan watched Honey as she worked. She was busy with her customers, so he didn't have to hide his blatant staring.

Why hadn't he kissed her back the other day? That was stupid of him, especially when he wanted nothing more than to grab her and kiss her smiling face. No, kissing her back when she had been talking about Maplecourt would have been wrong. Too much like taking advantage of her. But this party sounded promising and she'd definitely flirted with him today. He liked that. He liked that a lot.

~

Friday evening music assailed Morgan when he opened the door to The Corner. Discordant to his ears, the music was clearly Eastern in origins. A rhythmic clank of finger cymbals accompanied the recorded music. He threaded his way through the crowd. He had never seen the café so crowded. His first task—locate a place to stand that wasn't in the doorway, then try to find Honey.

He looked up and saw the dancer. The café seemed so crowded because everyone gathered along the edges, clearing a space for her to perform. Decked in sparkling red and gold, her costume picked up light and threw it back at the eye in a thousand winks of sequins and beading as she swayed her hips in time to the music. As soon as he saw her, the music settled into a melody he could follow. The clank became another of the instruments. This was a full sensory experience. Morgan noticed the place smelled like patchouli, honey, and cardamom.

The dancer swirled in a mist of fabric and hair, as the music came to crescendo. She ended in a pose, her hand reaching for the sky, her face, smiling at the ceiling.

The audience broke out in ululations and applause. She ducked a quick bow then scurried off towards Lana's office.

Joyce, clad in a caftan, makeup that would do a drag queen proud, and an enormous mound of hair walked into the center of the dance space. Her hand covered her mouth as she continued with a high-pitched ululation. "Kazeema!" She indicated with a gesture the dancer who just left them. "So next we have Raks Habibi. They are a few of my students who put together their own little dance troupe. They have been working hard on this little choreography for you. Everybody be nice and make a lot of noise. This is their first time performing together! Welcome, Raks Habibi."

Joyce backed out of the space as music began playing.

This time the music had a more western rock'n'roll feel to it. Heavy metal guitar ground out a rhythm accompanied by the pop and thump of Middle Eastern drums.

Three dancers in full black skirts, bright crop tops, and floral hip scarves entered into the dance space. Their arms were lifted at shoulder height with their wrists undulating like snakes. Morgan found it to be an interesting dichotomy of heavy metal music with smooth motions.

Their movement changed with the music. A smooth crooning voice began singing in a foreign language, while the dancers' hips lifted and popped and were tossed around as if they weren't attached to the rest of the body. He could see why Honey enjoyed these parties. His ear took a minute to adjust to the music, but that was only because it was new. He actually enjoyed the combination of dancing, costuming, and music. It was a show, and he enjoyed a good show. The music changed again, and the dancers began moving in a slow sinuous way. They were still in time with the music and they were well synchronized. Morgan became confused when several members of the audience started hissing.

"Hey." Honey surprised him as she suddenly appeared next to him. He smiled, she glowed. Distracted by the dancers, Morgan hadn't had a chance to look for Honey. Now she was next to him, he wanted to reach up and play with the wispy curl in front of her ear to see if it had spring.

He leaned over to speak into her ear. "Why are they hissing? Am I missing something? They seem to be doing a pretty good job."

"It's a belly dance thing," Honey explained. "They are doing really good, and it's slow and snaky, so the audience is hissing in appreciation. Those are mostly other dancers making all the noise. They're the ones who do that la-la-la-la-la thing instead of clapping."

Morgan nodded in understanding.

"You want anything?" she asked.

"Yeah, sure, but it's kind of packed in here. Hard to eat."

"Drink then?"

"The usual," he answered. The dancing mesmerized Morgan. He found that he wanted to keep watching.

Honey moved away to get Morgan's order. The troupe left the stage, and Joyce returned announcing another first-time performer. This one was clearly nervous, but the audience supported her by clapping to the music and hissing when she did slow turns and arm waves.

Honey returned to stand next to Morgan. She elbowed him slightly to get his attention before handing him his coffee.

"This is fascinating," he said, leaning over to speak into her ear again.

"Scantly-clad women gyrating—isn't it every man's fantasy?" Honey asked with dripping sarcasm.

"Not that at all. I mean, most of the crowd here are women. And I hadn't even thought of any of these dancers that way—yet. Thanks for the hint." He glanced sideways at her, smirking. "No, the whole performance and showmanship of it all. The decorations, the music, the costumes. I mean, that's Joyce right?" He indicated the woman standing against the pastry counter who had emceed earlier. "I didn't recognize her at first under all that hair and makeup."

"It is a show and a lot of fun. And Lana even bakes a special batch of baklava for the event. Some of the dancers are the most normal people under all that glitter and makeup."

Morgan nodded. "It gives them a chance to be exotic, not normal, don't you think?"

Honey turned to look at Morgan. "That was incredibly observant of the human psyche."

"Naw." Morgan shook his head. "Just me coming up with random BS."

Honey stayed next to Morgan, and they watched the dancer finish by rapidly vibrating her hips, before slamming them to the side in time to the last recorded drum beat. Joyce announced the end of the show and that everyone was welcome to stay for the rest of the party, but it was time to put the tables back into place.

That was Honey's cue to start moving tables. Half the audience filtered out the front door. The other half helped with the furnishings arrangement, before claiming tables and chairs for themselves. Morgan managed to procure a small table against the side wall with a single chair.

Middle Eastern music continued to play, only not so loud. A few of the dancers emerged from Lana's office draped in caftans, carrying large duffle bags and swords. Morgan wondered what he had missed. Honey stopped by his table as the crowd shifted and settled into the after-show dynamic.

"You want something to eat now that you have a table? Surprise you, no lemon bars?"

Morgan laughed at his predictability as far as his ordering at the café. "How about a piece of baklava?"

"I thought you'd say that." Honey slid a plate she had been holding behind her back onto the table in front of him. "The last one. I actually saved it for you."

"Why, Honey, I'm touched."

"I saw you look like you were gonna drool when I mentioned that Lana made baklava. So I made sure you got a piece." She posed wiggling her fingers around her face

"Stellar customer service." She paused, holding the pose with a silly grin on her face.

Morgan laughed. "Yes, it is." He shook his head at her silliness, grinning. She left to return to her job. He liked that she had started to loosen up around him, being silly. That, he thought, was a very good sign.

Honey had made a fool out herself in front of Morgan. He had laughed, but still, she felt stupid.

*Well, crap! He's not going to like me. He's going to think I'm a weirdo.*

Now that the show had ended, the work began. More orders were coming in, more drinks to make, more dishes to pick up and dump in the kitchen for later. Lana would normally be at the party for the entire time, but something had happened to one of their dogs, and she wasn't coming in until it was practically time to shut down. Joyce would help out a bit but tonight her job was party hostess, not café worker-bee. Honey could handle the café on her own during busy times, but she wasn't free to socialize, which meant no blatant flirting with Morgan tonight.

She noticed a few tables had been moved again to clear the way for a tiny dance area. Nothing like the earlier performance space, but enough room for a few people to move. Dancers were already up having a good time. It wasn't until the cheering got louder and on the rowdy side that Honey really looked up from her work.

Morgan danced in the middle of the floor, surrounded by other dancers cheering him on. He had a handkerchief swirling from one hand, held way above his head, as he stomped around following the foot patterns of the dancer holding his other hand. No wonder the hooting and hollering had increased. When his eyes found hers, her breath caught in her chest. He really was incredibly handsome when he smiled like that. He had shaved off the beard, but a shadow of stubble graced his chin. Stubble that made her want to scrape her teeth over that damned dimple in his chin. Stubble that looked entirely too good on him.

## 6

"What is going on? Why is today so insane?" Seth quietly whined to Honey, so that the tourists wouldn't hear him. "Have I mentioned I hate Mondays?"

Customers waiting their turn in line packed The Corner. Honey and Seth worked behind the counter moving with as much speed as the espresso machine would allow. They filled orders with precision and charm to stave off the wrath of a herd of hungry, cranky tourists in need of their afternoon decaf and cinnamon rolls. Slowly, the crowd filtered out and onto the waiting buses. When the last of the crowd left, Honey and Seth both wilted, draping their bodies onto the counter.

Morgan stood over them. "You look like you're ready for a break."

Honey smiled up at the deep warm voice. She rolled her head to the side, too tired to lift up. "Hi, Morgan." Her voice sounded so tired that her words slurred together. "I am so ready for a break."

"You can't go yet." Seth snapped up as if his batteries had

instantly recharged. "I haven't had my fifteen yet, and you're gonna be gone for thirty. So, no, you're not ready for a break. I have to take mine first."

Honey rolled her head to the other side so she could glare at Seth. He had a bad habit of doing this to her. No, he hadn't had his break yet, but honestly, he could wait. She had been there for over four hours and he hadn't. She needed to get out of the café. More importantly, Morgan was here. She sighed, pushing herself back into an upright position. Laying on the counter was probably not on the health inspector's list of acceptable activities for the surface anyway. She rolled her eyes in Seth's direction. "Do you mind waiting a bit longer, so Wonder Boy can take his fifteen?"

"Sure." Morgan took a seat in one of the heavily cushioned chairs.

She turned to Seth. "Run." She said the word in a menacing tone as if the permission for him to leave on break was a threat.

With the tourists gone, it was quiet in the café. Honey picked up a wipe cloth, meandered to be near Morgan, and began flicking the rag mindlessly across the top of a table.

Honey rubbed the back of her neck. "It's been nuts today. Like it's some holiday or a long weekend. It's not, is it?"

Morgan shook his head.

"Monday's aren't usually this busy. Lots of big groups came through today, like that one that just left. But lots of them. Bus after bus after bus. It's the kind of day Lana loves. Lots of customers, lots of coffee, lots of extra things getting sold."

"Did you see?" Honey asked, gesturing.

Morgan's gaze followed her pointing finger to a display of coffee mugs and refillable drinking cups. "That's new." Morgan acknowledged.

"Yep. Lana put it up yesterday. We also now have post-cards and other little things. It's going to be a pain in the ass because all that stuff is taxable. So we now have to make sure sales tax is calculated on the taxable items and not the food items. It's a mess. It's why that last group took so freaking long. In fact, every group has taken freaking long today. Just like Seth is." Honey looked around to see if she could see Seth approaching through one of the windows. "How long has that little stinker been gone?"

Honey turned, tripped over Morgan's feet, staggered trying to regain her balance then fell heavily into his lap. She blinked a few times, staring into Morgan's hazel eyes. They seemed to flash with gold. She blinked some more trying to get her orientation back.

"Oh God, I'm so sorry." She started to shift out of his lap.

Morgan put his arms around her. "Stay."

Honey stopped moving and looked at him. His lips were a lean away from a kiss. *Kiss him. Just lean in and kiss him.*

Morgan snickered, "I won't tell anyone you took a pre-break break. I'm the only one in here right now anyway." Morgan reached up, and with one of his large hands, covered the middle of her shoulders. She let out a low groan as he began massaging the muscles along the top of her back and neck.

"Oh, that feels good." She moaned and leaned back into his touch. Honey closed her eyes, and let the tension melt away under Morgan's warm hand. She didn't notice time as Morgan rubbed with his fingers and dug into her back with his thumb.

Morgan lifted her arm and pushed up her sleeve exposing a tattoo of delicate pink blossoms encircling her thin arm slightly above her elbow. He traced their path for a moment. His fingers tickled, Honey's nerves danced in response, wanting him to trace more than just her ink work.

"They are from Botticelli's *Birth of Venus*. They are the flowers floating in the air around the Zephyrs, as they blow life into Venus. They don't symbolize anything. I just liked them." She watched Morgan's face as he looked at her tattoo. How had she not considered him handsome before? He had a few character lines from smiling and laughing around his eyes, and working in the sun helped to emphasize his swarthy completion.

"They're very well done. What's the piece on your back?" Morgan's attention was still on her skin. Her toes curled from watching his mouth move this close up.

"When did you see my back? It's always covered."

"I caught a glimpse when you were moving paintings around."

"It's a big close up of a lotus blossom, sort of Georgia O'Keeffe meets Buddhism. I got it to symbolize that I had grown past my modeling and materialistic needs. Of course, I realize now I hadn't really. I was with Bryce. He was very much a materialistic choice."

"And Zephyr's flowers what do they signify?" Morgan shifted his attention and looked Honey in the eyes. She dropped her gaze away from his intense look.

"I like flowers. I got them for kicks and giggles. The big piece on my back I never finished because I left San Francisco before I could get it done. Actually, Bryce hated it. He wanted me to have it lasered off. I had the Zephyr flowers when we met. He never said boo about them. But when I started the back piece, he pitched a fit. He controlled the money, so he made sure I never really had enough to get it finished." Honey scoffed. "I should have left him then. My body, my art, my rules."

Morgan nodded. "Are you going to get it finished?"

"Definitely. Funny thing is, now that I really am past my materialistic self, I don't have the money to finish it. It's at least five more hours of work." She shrugged. "Do you have any tattoos?"

*I could trace them with my tongue if you do.* Honey bit her lips together as if that would ensure her thoughts wouldn't fall out of her mouth.

"Count tattoos in with lemons and chocolate for me. My cousin tried one once. We have similar allergies. After his failed attempt, I never bothered. But I like them. Your flowers are pretty. They suit you." Tattoos were not going to be a deal breaker with Morgan. That made Honey very happy.

Honey wanted to reach up and brush his hair with her fingers. There was so much more to this man than a good smile and plaid shirts. Why couldn't she see that before? She reached for her pendant, a safe alternative.

"You keep playing with this." Morgan's fingers grazed her collarbone as he captured her pendant. Her breath caught. His fingers made her skin tingle. She could feel the heat radiating from him.

"It was a gift," Honey whispered. The pendant had *forza* engraved on one side. "Strength." Morgan translated the Italian.

"You speak Italian?"

"Some. Not enough to say I speak it. Do you know what the pattern is?"

"Just a pattern." Honey found it hard to focus. Morgan filled her senses, and she wanted more.

He dropped the pendant. "Just a pattern? And I thought you were into art."

"Fine," she huffed. "It's the pattern from the Piazza del Campidoglio. Most people wouldn't know what that means, so I tell them it's a pretty pattern. I gather you recognized it?"

"Yeah, I'm familiar with the Capitoline Hill and Michelangelo's work. I was wondering if you were."

"Honestly, I am because of this." She held the small gold disk up. "The last designer I worked for sent it to me. Sophia di Lorenti, an Italian designer. I missed out working on this collection, which was inspired by Roman architecture. Anyway, it's become my talisman, a reminder to keep strong."

The bell of the door jingled and Seth clattered back into the café. Honey jumped nervously from Morgan's lap. She grabbed Morgan's hand and was out the door before Seth could say anything.

Honey walked towards the pizza-by-the-slice place. She felt like she never had enough time for break, even so, she dragged her feet. She should be seeking a meal with more protein to keep her going until closing. For some reason, anything with meat on it would simply take too long. The deli would be closing, if it wasn't already closed, so no pasta salad. As she navigated her way between tourists, she chided herself. She could have gone up the hill to the grocery store or succumbed and gone to the fast food place. But pizza had sounded so good.

She walked past an open air bar when she thought she heard her name.

She paused and looked around confused.

"Honey, in here." A deep voice called to her from inside the bar.

She turned and saw Morgan inside waving to her. She walked up to the fencing separating the sidewalk from the restaurant. "Oh, hi, Morgan. I didn't see you there at first." Morgan sat a few tables in from the open patio at a tall round bar table with a beer.

"Where you headed?" he asked.

"I'm on break. I was headed over to get some food." She pointed over her shoulder indicating the direction of the pizza place.

"Come join me." He waved her in.

"I don't have time. I just need to grab something."

"I have a big order of wings coming. You can share." He grinned at her. "You do eat chicken?"

"Yes, I eat chicken," she chuckled. "Sure." She shrugged and turned to head back into the bar.

She arrived at his table as the waitress delivered a platter of chicken wings. Honey sat to join Morgan and asked for a glass of water.

"You sure I'm not taking food away from you? What is this—a double party plate?"

"I was hungry, and I like chicken wings," Morgan explained with a grin. "Look, if I think you're eating too much—" Honey froze at the words. Bryce had always been overly critical when he thought she was eating too much. "—and I'm still hungry, I can always order more." Honey sighed in relief. No commentary on her eating.

"Well, thank you." Honey reminded herself Morgan was

not Bryce. Other than being male and having dark hair, they were nothing alike. Nothing. "More protein and good company," Honey finished.

She bit into a meaty wing piece and hummed in appreciation of the taste. "I always forget they have really good wings here," she said between bites.

"Do you eat here often?"

She shook her head. "Not enough time. They don't take phone-in to-go orders. That's the only way I would be able to have enough time on one of my breaks. It's a tourist place. They want to get you in and drinking. Not so much feeding the locals."

Morgan nodded in agreement. They ate in silence for a few minutes. Honey furtively looked at Morgan through her lashes. No eye contact. He was always focused on something else when she glanced at him. Looking around to see what Morgan might be looking at, Honey became distracted by a broadcast report on one of the bar's many televisions.

"What's up?"

Honey shook her head. "Stupid news over stupid things."

Morgan looked at her quizzically.

"We live in the future, right? I mean we are well into the new century and these things—" she waved her hand at the TV, a chicken bone in her grasp "—shouldn't still be an issue. Race riots, human rights, marriage issues. Shouldn't all of this have been worked out by now?" She noticed the bone in her hand and set it on the side of the plate where they were placing the remains of their wing feast.

"How so?" Morgan prompted.

"People are not only how they appear or who they love. And no one else should prevent someone from access to human rights based on skin color or who they want to marry. They've passed laws—time to move on." She shrugged.

"What if they are simply trying to protect people?" Morgan gave her an odd little smile, just at the corner of his lips. *What was that all about?*

"From what?" she snapped. She did not like the idea that she was eating with someone who did not support human rights, crush be damned.

"Mutants. Aliens." Morgan announced.

Honey relaxed. Morgan was making conversation not arguing politics with her. "You mean like in the movies? Like the guy who can freeze the air, or transport from place to place, or the guy with the knives that pop out of his knuckles?"

Morgan made a fist and a *kakshew* noise as he mimicked the motions of the character with the long blades bursting from his fists.

"That's hot." Honey pointed at his fist. "Okay, yes, including mutants and blue aliens."

Morgan cocked an eyebrow at her.

"What? I watched a lot of anime as a kid. Blue aliens are totally hot." Honey defended herself.

"Okay, so if you wanted to marry a blue alien or mutants with dangerous knuckles, you should be allowed to?" Honey nodded at his understanding. "What if excessive body hair was your mutant power?"

Honey laughed. "You mean like a yeti or something?"

Morgan nodded.

"Well, yes, they should be allowed to marry whomever they want. It won't be me. I don't have a furry fetish."

Caught off guard, Morgan laughed up his drink. He grabbed a napkin over his face to stop the beer from spraying all over the wings and Honey. She snorted with laughter. Morgan laughed with her.

"Well, that's good to know," he said once he regained his composure. "No excessive hair for Honey, not even if it's blue?"

She shook her head as she continued to laugh.

"Okay, what about supernaturals?" he asked.

"Supernaturals? Ghosts? It would be really hard to marry a ghost." Honey's brows furrowed as she tried to figure out where Morgan was going with this line of questioning.

"Like vampires and werewolves," he corrected.

"Totally hot." Honey put her hands up.

"So you're telling me that you would knowingly marry a vampire or a werewolf?" Morgan sat back watching her.

Honey was animated, her arms gesticulating as she explained her thoughts on the matter. "It all depends really. I mean are we talking the original legends or any variation of modern versions? Dracula was freaking sexy in his pursuit of youth, but the whole ripping-the-throat-out thingy, not so good. Now if he could magically seal the wound and having your neck sucked on was really as orgasmic as they want you to believe in the books, sure, why not?"

"Do you think they're out there? Vampires, werewolves?"

"Mutants? I don't even think as humans we really know what it is we don't know. Too many weird situations that can't be explained. Too many species we haven't even discovered. Who's to say mutants aren't real. If vampires can hide really well, how do we know they don't exist?"

Morgan nodded as she talked. "How many vampire movies have you seen?"

"All of them."

"What about werewolves?" he asked.

"Probably. I've always thought of myself as a vampire girl really. I think their aesthetic appeals to me. Ethereal, yet powerful. I've always been drawn to things that are more tragic and beautiful. I can see why Goth culture is so alluring. But the idea of werewolves is pretty darn cool. I guess it would depend. I mean you can prepare for the full moon and what that entails. Just make sure you're always in a place with a safe room. Shapeshifters, werepanthers, tigers, yeah. That's scary and sexy all at once. The lack of control into a dangerous beast that's truly frightening, but then they are always supposed to be hyper-über sexy beings." She paused and leaned forward on the table. She pointed at Morgan. "What was the point I was making?"

"Consensual adults should be the ones deciding who they are going to marry and not policy makers," Morgan said smoothly.

"Right," Honey chuckled, "I got lost with the vampires."

"Don't forget the furries." Morgan chuckled.

Honey rolled her eyes and shook her head. She picked up her phone to check the time.

"Sorry I have to eat and run." She stood up. "Thank you for the wings. Do I owe you anything?"

Morgan also stood. "I've enjoyed your company immensely. That's payment enough."

"Good night, Morgan. I'll see you later." She turned to leave. She didn't want to go. Honey stopped and turned around. She could do this.

"Honey," Morgan started before she got a chance to speak. "Would you have dinner with me sometime?" He waved at their impromptu meal. "One where we can really sit and talk. Not one where you have to run back to work."

"Like a dinner date?" Honey asked.

Morgan nodded. "Yes, a dinner date."

"I'd like that." *I'd like that a lot, and maybe you could kiss me back.* She smiled then nervously bit her lips together. He had beat her to the punch.

---

## 7

Honey followed the lights of the motorcycle in front of her. So far this date was weird. Odd. Morgan had arrived at The Corner just before she was scheduled to get off work. It had started sprinkling, and he didn't have an extra helmet, so he suggested she follow him in her car.

"Great start. I'm alone in the car, and I'm following him into the unknown." Honey said out loud to her empty car.

"I should have told Lana where I was going or something. It looks like he's taking me out into the wilds to off me." Honey overdramatized her narrative as she followed the bike's tail lights around corners. Verbalizing her worst fears made it all sound ridiculous. The light sprinkling turned into a drizzle as the sun set. The night grew darker and wetter.

Honey stopped the car in front of a long vintage trailer. The aluminum siding gleamed like brushed silver in her headlights. She could tell the trailer was an Airstream by the shape. It appeared to be new.

Morgan dismounted his bike and approached Honey's driver-side door. "I wanted to show off my little project.

Come on in." He opened the door to the trailer and gestured for her to step inside.

Morgan switched on the lights. Recessed lamps running the entire length of the ceiling lit up the interior space. "I've been revamping this for a few months," Morgan said. "It's not done yet, but I needed someplace to live while on location for this job. I'll finish it after I'm done here in Monterey."

She and Morgan stood in the kitchen. Honey didn't know what to expect, but this was not like the interior of any camper trailer she had ever been in. The interior encompassed one wide open space. The kitchen was the only area where the renovation appeared to be complete. The pale blond wood cabinets and gas range were obviously new and recently installed. Clear blue tiles had been partially installed as a backsplash, and the counter tops were a silvery gray. To Honey's right, a folding table and a chair occupied the space under a bank of windows. The kitchen configuration made a small L-shape that separated the kitchen area from the next open space.

"You aren't restoring this, are you?" she asked as she looked around.

"No, I think the original spaces are broken up awkwardly. I was going to gut it anyway, so it helped that it was in bad shape when I found it."

Honey noticed Morgan wasn't standing fully upright. He dominated the space, filling it completely.

"You barely fit in here."

He patted the ceiling, "I don't stand up much inside. Usually, I'm sitting down or asleep."

"You have no bathroom door." Honey pointed to a shower curtain hanging across the end wall.

"Yeah," Morgan chuckled. "I didn't get to the back wall

yet. I got lucky that this one originally had a rear bath, so I didn't have to completely rework the plumbing. I had to restore it, but that's easier than having to move and re-plumb things." Morgan stepped past Honey to indicate with his hands the bath area that featured a large jacuzzi tub. "I'm going to put in a bank of cabinets here. The same wood as in the kitchen." He motioned to the area next to the toilet and across half the width of the trailer. "Then I'll finish right here with a folding wall that will tuck in." Morgan swung the large screen television out and away from the wall. "I'll be able to watch movies from the tub."

The tub aspect surprised Honey. "You like baths?"

"Sore muscles from work like a good soak. Yes, I like baths." Morgan huffed. "I still have to add a shower. Right now the only plumbing that works back here is the toilet."

Honey nodded in appreciation of this new information about Morgan. Baths. She added it to her mental list: art, no lemons, no chocolate, Orangina, and now baths and remodeling vintage RVs.

"This isn't the final furniture. I'll have a fold-out bed here." Morgan indicated the current worn couch. "I plan to get a pale tan leather sofa and bolt it into place." He turned and gestured enthusiastically to a space next to the kitchen counter. "There will also be a chair. Right now everything is removable so I can finish the construction when I get home. I don't have my tools with me so I can't work on it down here. The kitchen is done, which is why I could bring the trailer out. The tiling on the backsplash needs to be finished, but otherwise, everything works. A table and bench seats will be installed there." He pointed past the kitchen to the area under the bank of windows. "When it's finished, it will be a luxury studio apartment on wheels. I can live in here more economically when I have to be on job sites for a prolonged period of time, like my current project."

"How did you get it here? I didn't see a truck outside."

"The company hauled it down here for me. The driver took the truck back with him when he left. I'll ride my bike back and pick up the truck when it's time to haul this thing out of here," Morgan explained.

"So you don't live in here all the time?" Honey twirled her finger indicating the trailer. *Oh gods, what am I doing?* He was a construction worker who lived in a trailer. He was nice. He was actually really handsome. And she had assured herself she was past the materialism. Honey breathed deeply, mentally girding her loins as she realized she was falling for a guy who was the antithesis of Bryce. He was genuine; he had a warm smile; he wore plaid. Bryce had an ice cold grin and never wore plaid unless it was underwear. Bryce had also had a very large, very luxurious penthouse apartment in San Francisco. Bryce was also someone to run away from. So far Morgan had been someone to run to.

Lana had been right. Honey had to get past a person's cover, maybe even get past their first chapter. She was well past Morgan's first chapter, and she had started to freak out. They had similar ideals; he liked her tattoos even though he didn't have any. But he lived in a trailer and wore plaid. She started to pull into herself. Maybe she couldn't do this. She couldn't see herself living in a trailer with a man who wore plaid. The construction work she could handle. She just wasn't sure about the rest of his foibles. She scoffed at herself. They had barely had a real date yet, and she was already thinking about living with him.

"No, this is temporary location living. I have a regular apartment at home."

Honey sighed in relief. Somehow she had got it into her

mind that Morgan lived in the trailer permanently, even though he had said otherwise. More than once.

～

Morgan sensed a shift in Honey as he showed her the trailer. Maybe this had been a mistake. Maybe she wasn't impressed with his renovation abilities. She became quiet, and her posture slumped. Time to charm her properly. He hadn't planned this date very well; he hadn't thought about dinner. He opened the refrigerator to see if he had enough to make her a dinner. That should impress her. He wanted to show her he was capable of building, cooking, providing.

"How does steak and green beans sound?" he asked as he stood up from looking in the refrigerator.

"You're going to cook?" Honey asked a little nervously.

"Is that okay with you?"

"Yeah, sure." Honey hesitated. "Uhm, I have to use the bathroom, and..." She paused pointing at the shower curtain.

Morgan nodded in understanding. "I'll step outside. You can let me know when you're finished. The sink back there isn't hooked up yet, so use the kitchen sink to wash your hands." Morgan saw Honey nodding as he stepped outside.

Rain drizzled on him as he waited next to the door while Honey did her business. *Okay, asshole, this may not have been the smartest move to make. You're trying to impress the girl, not scare her off. Face it, you have gone creepy. Cooking for her in a rundown trailer—bad move.*

The trailer door opened behind him. "All set, thanks," Honey said as he stepped in. "Hey, I saw you had some pictures posted up back there. Are those the ideas for how the interior is going to look when it's done?"

"Thats exactly what those are for. Help to remind me there is a reason to finish this project."

"This should be really nice when it's done." Honey nodded, a smile finally crossing her lips, the first smile since he brought her here, and more notably, she was glowing again. A soft golden aura surrounded Honey. Morgan couldn't blame the lighting this time.

"Why don't you have a seat, and I'll start grilling these steaks." His throat went dry as he tried to focus on making dinner. Honey continued to glow. Suddenly, it became very important to make a good impression on her.

"I should offer to help, but the kitchen area is barely big enough for you," Honey said from her perch on the couch.

Morgan chuckled. "Yeah it is tight, but I can't help it. I've always wanted an Airstream."

He placed the steaks on a plate and sprinkled them with salt and pepper. While they sat warming up, Morgan chopped an onion and mixed it in with the green beans and added some garlic. Between tasks, Morgan kept glancing at Honey to see if she still glowed. A smile played across his lips.

The click-click-click sound of the gas range not lighting started to annoy Morgan. This range had always been easy to light. Being new, it had not given him any problems. *Until now, when I'm trying it impress Honey. And she's glowing.*

It dawned on Morgan that he had been thinking he needed to protect her, that she needed him, when in reality he needed her. He looked at her, the light surrounding Honey seemed to jump across the small space and pierce him. Light exploded behind his eyes as realization of her importance to him spread throughout his being. He stopped fiddling with the range and stared at the wall in front of him. It really felt like a hit upside the head. He glanced back over at Honey sitting on the ratty couch. She radiated soft light. She was his. He smiled to himself.

She was surrounded by what could only be the mate aura—something Morgan had only thought of as a family myth. No wonder he hadn't recognized it earlier. He was a clueless clot. The mate aura, as he understood it, was a visible glow surrounding the best possible mate for one of his kind. The fates were telling him she was the one he needed. Now he needed to convince her that she needed him. It certainly didn't look like that was going to happen tonight.

*Click-click-click.* The range would not light.

"Sounds like it's not getting any gas." Honey chimed in. "At least, that's what my stove does at home when the gas gets messed up."

"Fuck," Morgan grumbled. He checked the settings for the propane on the read-out above the stove. It didn't light up at all. That meant the hook up had somehow disconnected and no pressure was being read or—Morgan groaned—it meant there was no pressure at all. When had he last replaced the tank? He couldn't even remember.

"Great. I'm out of propane. No cooking tonight."

Honey sighed.

"Sorry, my big impressive plan fizzled out." Morgan thought fast on his feet. He hadn't any plan to begin with. He needed to compensate for this flop. "There's a nice-looking family restaurant just up the road. How about we go there instead?"

"Sure." Honey said as she stood up, slinging her purse onto her shoulder.

Morgan slid the steaks and vegetables back into the refrigerator. "You don't mind driving, do you?"

~

"This doesn't look too promising, Morgan. Have you been here before?" Honey squinted through the rain speckled windshield at the building with no lights.

Morgan shook his head. "Hold on." He got out of the car and poked around the front of the restaurant. It appeared to have been closed for a while.

He got back in the car. "I guess I never noticed it's been closed all this time. I just saw restaurant, ya' know."

Honey nodded, pursing her lips. "Any place else?"

"Let's just drive around and see if we can find something." Morgan ran his fingers through his hair. He seemed nervous —or maybe he was getting frustrated with her.

After driving around for over half an hour, Honey pulled into the parking lot of a fast food chain.

"Food," she announced. "It's fast food, but it will have to do."

Honey found a table and wiped it down with a handful of napkins. The interior of this franchise location had clearly seen better days.

Morgan slid the tray with her food onto the table in front of her. She shoved a handful of french fries into her mouth and began unwrapping her sandwich.

"Sorry about dinner."

"Whatever," she mumbled, peeking under the bun of her sandwich. She tossed the tray away from her in frustration. "It's fried. I said grilled. Grilled chicken. It's not that hard."

Morgan slid the tray toward him. "I'll have them fix that." He picked up the offending article and approached the counter. Returning a few minutes later, he placed a fresh-grilled sandwich in front of her.

Honey frowned at the new version, then proceeded to eat the chicken breast and tomato, leaving the bread.

They ate in strained silence.

"I'm going to need more fries," she announced as she emptied the container in front of her.

"More fries?" he asked.

She thought he had given her that look, that *I'm judging you and the food you eat* look. She didn't react well to that look. She was hangry—hungry and angry—and this date was not going well.

She nodded sharply.

"Are you sure you want fries? Anything else while I'm up?"

"What? You don't think my fat ass needs more fries?" Honey replied tersely.

"I don't think your ass is fat, and I meant did you want a sundae or something. I thought I might get one." Morgan's tone was even, controlled. This date was crashing and burning around her.

"Sundae, extra fudge, no nuts," Honey muttered, abashed.

She blinked up at him as he delivered another order of fries and a fudge sundae.

"Thank you," she muttered.

Uncertainty about the feelings that had accosted her in Morgan's trailer, then the hunger and anger over the food situation had made everything worse. She noticed Morgan hadn't finished his sundae when they got up to leave.

"Thank you for coming up to see the Airstream. I'm sorry dinner didn't work out."

Honey didn't say anything. She held onto the steering wheel and focused in front of the car looking out the windshield. She didn't think she could look at Morgan right now. She was embarrassed at her behavior.

Morgan paused before getting out of the car.

The door closed and Honey backed out, turning her car onto the road. She sank emotionally as she drove home. *No good night kiss, not even a hug. What a royal cock-up.* Windshield wipers swishing rain from her view. Too bad they couldn't swipe away the dread that had settled on her.

## 8

Morgan stood in the rain watching Honey's car drive away. Rain soaked his clothes. He didn't particularly care.

"Well, that sucked," he said out loud. At least he hadn't insulted her parents or kicked her dog. Hopefully, Honey would be willing to try him again, but next time he would actually have a plan and not attempt to wing it. Dinner reservations, maybe tickets to a show. He heard that Monterey had a little melodrama theater. Those were supposed to be good fun. Next date would be quality. He decided he would contact Jinx to have some clothes sent down so he didn't dress like he was still on the job.

His phone rang. He checked caller ID. What did his sister Julia want?

"Palatine."

"I don't care what you have going on, Morgan. You need to get your butt up to San Francisco tomorrow. We have a meeting with Roman Aventine first thing in the morning." Julia's voice sounded demanding as always.

Morgan groaned. "I'm not cutting my hair again, Julia."

His hair was still growing out from the time she insisted he have a power cut for the alliance meetings with the Aventine family.

Roman Aventine was Morgan's business rival and despite their alliance, Morgan wasn't certain Aventine wasn't after his territory. Aventine had recently positioned himself to take over a healthy market share of the construction industry Morgan's Seven Hills company successfully held. Based on Julia's tone and insistence, this upcoming meeting had nothing to do with a little friendly market competition and nothing to do with the alliance they recently formed.

"You had better shave. I know how you get out on the job. You go all wild-man native-hairy."

"Fine, I'll shave."

"Do you trust Remi to pick something suitable to wear from your closet?"

He chuckled. "Jinx or Remi can pick something suitable. Now can you tell me what this is about?"

"Nope, it's Roman Aventine's baby. Besides I don't have all the details. He does. I agreed to the meeting and to make sure you were there. My gut tells me it's big, Morgan. Important."

No, Morgan thought, Honey is important, and he needed to make sure she knew that despite his piss-poor behavior tonight. Anything with Aventine could wait.

"Fine. Fine. What time do I need to be there?" Morgan asked, exasperated.

"Nine in the morning, Roman said prepare for it to be a long day."

"No kidding. I guess I'll head up tonight. That way I can spend my time more wisely in the morning. I've got a long drive ahead of me. Could you please make sure I have a room waiting for me at the Fairmont?"

"I'm not your secretary, Morgan."

Morgan's voice was grim, annoyance clearly evident in his tone. "No, you're not. You're the one giving me less than twelve hours' notice for a meeting I don't have clothes for and am over two hours away from. It's raining and I'm on a bike. I'm walking into this blind on your recommendation, Julia. You can arrange for me to have a bed tonight. You have a secretary. Call her."

"I'll text you your confirmation. I'll meet you at the hotel with your clothes at eight tomorrow. See you in the morning." She huffed then rang off the line.

Morgan blew air out his nose. He didn't want to spend the day in meetings at Aventine Industries. He enjoyed his break from office politics, working directly on the site of the new hotel. This meeting meant he wouldn't be back until late tomorrow. He wouldn't get to stop by and see Honey's lovely smile while he got a coffee. He wouldn't get a chance to ask her out again. She would think he didn't like her if he didn't follow up tomorrow after tonight's fiasco. He didn't want her to think that at all.

He dialed her number. Of course she let it ring. He wouldn't pick up after tonight either. "I want to apologize for the poor quality of tonight's date. If you would let me make it up to you I would like to take you out to a restaurant of your choosing. I'm headed to San Francisco tomorrow, so I can't ask you this in person. And I sound like a dork," he huffed in frustration. "I really botched tonight, and I'm botching this apology. I would really like to take you out again if you'll let me." Morgan ended the call and stared at his phone. Hopefully she would listen to his voicemail, and not send it straight to the trash.

∾

A sharp knock rapped on the door. Morgan stepped out of the bath room, shaving cream slathered over half of his face, and a thick fluffy white towel wrapped low around his hips. His visitor had to be his sister since his morning meal service tray sat on the table.

"Good morning, Morgan," Julia said sharply as she brushed past him into the room. A suit bag hung from one finger and a pair of shoes dangled in the other hand. She wore a black pant suit and had swept back her dark brown hair into a low ponytail. Several thick gold chains draped around her neck and hung in front below the pointed collar of her red blouse.

He closed the door behind her. "You know you could have had a valet bring those up."

"Nice to see you too, brother." She laid the suit bag across the bottom of his rumpled bed. Morgan returned to the bathroom. "I see your hair is growing back. Please tell me you are shaving that mange off your face." she said with an I-told-you-so tone to her voice.

Morgan growled a low rumble of disagreement in his chest. "It's too early for you to be this bossy, Julia." He leaned out from the bathroom to glare at her, "You still going to make me wait until we are in Aventine's office to tell me what this is about?"

"Hmm-mmm. And I'm not bossy. It's called leadership skills and effective decision making. You don't want to appear all scruffy when you meet Aventine since he will be wearing some custom tailored suit and not that off the rack special." Julia picked up a piece of untouched toast and slathered jam across the top. "Honestly, Roman didn't tell me much. Only that this is mutually beneficial and histori-cally important."

"Roman? You're on first name basis now?" He picked up

the suit bag, removed slacks and a shirt and returned to the bathroom.

"Shut up, Morgan. You're in a foul mood."

Morgan emerged from the bathroom in dress slacks and a crisp, pale blue shirt. He reached back into the suit bag to retrieve a pair of socks and a red tie. He sat, put the socks and shoes on, then began knotting the tie. "Yes, I am. I had to ride up here late, in the rain, on my Harley, and I still don't know why. You're telling me what to do. I'm pretty sure I recently met the mother of my children, and I'm fairly certain I completely blew it like some thirteen-year-old dweeb who doesn't know how to talk to girls." He shrugged into the suit jacket. "Are you done eating my breakfast?"

"It was only the toast. You never eat your toast, Morgan. Did you just call yourself a dweeb?"

"A thirteen-year-old dweeb. There is a difference. This had better be worth my time. I really should be in Monterey trying to figure out how to make it up to Honey."

Morgan followed Julia out of his room and down to the lobby.

"Her name is Honey?" Julia paused. "You're serious? Mother of your children? The whole mate thing?"

They were met by Julia's driver outside the door.

"Yes," Morgan grumbled getting into the car. "The whole mate thing. You think you're merely flirting, then BAM, you realize this is the one. Felt like a frying pan to the back of the skull. It really threw me off last night. I was less than impressive."

"I don't want to hear about your sex life, brother."

"You're not, and there isn't going to be one if I blow this." Morgan watched the city slide by through the car window.

"Your mate? I always thought that was a bunch of hokum our parents fed us. You know, wait for your true love.

You don't need to date around, you'll know, you'll profoundly know."

"Julia, they were so right. I wish I could tell Mom how right she was. She'd really like Honey. You and Caro will. JoJo will adore her." He was sure his sisters would be as impressed with Honey as he was.

"Well, you can make things up with her after the meeting then bring her up for JoJo's wedding."

Morgan shook his head, recalling the evening before. "If she's still speaking to me."

"That bad?" Julia tilted her head to the side.

"Worse."

Roman Aventine stood behind his desk when Morgan and Julia entered his office He wore a gray pin-striped suit that skimmed his slender frame. As tall as Morgan, Aventine was of a much thinner build so he appeared to not be as large. He wore his pale blond hair short, clipped close on the sides. His blue eyes were enhanced by the royal blue tie he wore.

He stepped out and offered Morgan his large hand. "Palatine." Morgan shook it. Roman nodded to Julia "Julia." Roman's gaze noticeably lingered on her face, and his tongue lingered on her name.

"That's Ms. Palatine, Mr. Aventine," she smirked as he took her hand and stepped in a little closer than professionally necessary.

"Roman, please," he corrected her.

"Look at this," Roman slid a stack of papers across his desk to Morgan.

Morgan flipped through the stack, shaking his head.

"I'm looking at what? This looks like genetic code. G-A, C-A, T-A."

"Exactly. It's a DNA report from a genealogy lab."

"So?"

"On the second page, the fifth group of gene data." Roman picked up a second set of test papers, flipping to the area of data indicated. "See here." He pointed between the two groups. "The report you hold belongs to one of my cousins. This report—" he tapped the second document, "—was included at random to be a control, basically. Do you see here? This gene pair on my cousin's report isn't recorded on the control report."

Roman walked across his office to close the door. He returned to his desk and tapped out commands on a keypad. A soft swishing sound could be heard as sound proofing baffles slid into place, the windows dimmed. "My cousin is full wolf. The control is full human. When this was first brought to my attention, she had already run tests on random family members, those who turn and those who don't."

Roman added more reports to the pile on his desk and pointed to different pages.

"Look, I don't have all the scientific terms, but this is how it was explained to me." He tapped a specific sequence. "This is a full genetic marker, indicating whether the subject is one of us—wolf. When a person has a full gene set, the person turns. When a person doesn't have a full marker, they don't turn. Now this one is interesting," he opened another report and indicated the area where the gene showed on previous reports. There was no mutant gene pair present. "This is my second cousin or something. Neither of his parents was capable of turning. He can't either. I'm betting that none of his children will have the gene since he doesn't. We're still waiting on their results. But get this, his brother has the gene, but the indicator is only for one of them, not for a full pair. He can't turn but will be able to pass the gene along to his offspring who might be able to if they inherit a full pair."

"Do you know what this means?" Julia asked breathlessly.

"We can be traced." Morgan's voice was calm.

"It means we need to start buying into genetics labs and getting people into position in them. How did you come by this, Roman?"

"One of the family works for a lab, ran her own DNA test. Came to me as soon as she figured out what was going on. Right now we are in a position to leverage this to our advantage. Our gene signature is going to start showing up as an anomaly as more and more people start using DNA for their genealogy hunts."

"We need to be part of the lab that all anomalies are sent to. How do we do that?" Morgan said.

"Leave that up to me," Julia jumped in. "We need to buy out a genetics company, become someone who is already leading in this area." She bit her lip calculating. "Aventine, I know you aren't in a position to take on something like that on your own."

Roman raised his eyebrows at her. Julia was on top of business knowledge for her company and her competition.

"I'm going to confess neither are we," she said. "Guys, you're both going to have to agree to a joint venture or it's not going to happen. I doubt we will be able to do this amicably, so we have to provide a united front and stage a hostile takeover of a genetics company." She began typing frantically on her tablet, her fingers flying to keep up with her brain. "Need to either stage a coup with the board of directors and supersede them or get them on board fast. Roman, your people are going to need to get moving on this as well if they already haven't started."

"We've started. Aventine Industries is in process of buying out the lab facility in Emeryville where our scientist is. I actually want to head over there this morning, and she can explain the situation better and maybe show us how we can tap into their network of other labs. We already have the one geneticist in our ranks. What both families need to do is find out who else is a geneticist and get them into some of these jobs ASAP. And we need to start making sure all data showing anomalies with that gene signature comes to us."

"My understanding is with the simple genealogy tests, they don't have enough information to find out what this mutation does. We are currently ahead of the game in that we have identified it as ours. As long as we trace that gene, and every instance of it that comes through, we can still control the knowledge about our kind."

Morgan glanced up from the report he stared at, "We no longer need to go on hearsay regarding other families. As long as people are voluntarily sending in for these tests, we can find who we have lost track of."

"Great. You two go visit that lab and start strategizing on how we become a clearinghouse for that piece of information. I have to go back to my office and get started on whats needed. I have to do some research, find who we can partner with, buyout or take over. Roman, who in your camp is going to be my contact regarding this venture?"

Roman smirked. "Sorry, Julia looks like you are going to be stuck with me since I'm the one who takes care of mergers and acquisitions. We're going to be spending a lot of time together."

Julia rolled her eyes. "Fine, I'm scheduling us for something early next week. I'll see you two later." She picked up her purse and headed out the door.

Roman paused admiring the view as she left. He pressed a button on his desk phone. "Have the car pulled around. Let Jeeves know we are headed to SeaQuence Labs."

"Your driver's name is Jeeves?"

"Hell, I don't know their names. I call them all Jeeves." Roman collected the reports from his desk and stuffed them back into a folder.

# 9

The car was large, but not large enough as far as Morgan was concerned. Two tall men, both dominant in an enclosed space, was never a good idea, especially since Morgan wasn't sure about Aventine's commitment to playing nice.

A few months previously, Julia had come to Morgan with a plan to strengthen the family. Her concept was that if the Palatines could play nice with the Aventines then they could stop wasting a lot of needless energy on grudge matches, even if those grudges went back thousands of years. Turns out she had been approached by Roman's mother. Whoever originated the idea, it was a good one.

Morgan began losing sleep and business when the Aventine family moved into the neighborhood and set up shop. The Palatines had held onto the northern California foundations market for years, decades even. Their diversified interests in construction, wine, and renewable energy had made them a very wealthy family. Julia's business acumen made sure they stayed one.

The Aventines, a very similar family, had been located

and focused in New England for over a century. Their move to a San Francisco base of operations could be clearly interpreted as a hostile maneuver, especially since they were actively cutting into Morgan's Seven Hills construction business.

The move was driven by the alpha's wife, who currently received medical treatments at Stanford Cancer Institute. Blackston Aventine was not ready to release control over the family or the business; however, he had been willing to negotiate a peace with the Palatines, since his focus was now on his wife and her health. He didn't want the hassle of petty rival arguments between the two families which could be disastrous, both financially and physically.

Roman Aventine was not his family's alpha. His father was. Even if his father decreed a peace with the Palatines, it didn't mean Roman would necessarily follow suit. But he had been active in the accord meetings, and he was the one to set up this morning's meeting. He had been the one to share the information regarding the DNA find.

Aventine had introduced the venture, that clearly indicated he was willing to play nice. If Morgan faced facts, he was uncomfortable because he sat in a car headed towards the East Bay and not back to Honey in Monterey.

He combed his fingers through his hair. He was a grown-ass man, and he had messed up his date with Honey as if he had never been on one before. He shook his head. Honey was so beautiful he couldn't think straight. Morgan sighed. Loudly.

"You seem distracted a bit, Palatine. Not getting car sick, are you?" Aventine's voice cut with sarcasm. Morgan had no plans on sharing his personal defeat with this man. He quickly brought the conversation back to business and concerns with the newly discovered genetic evidence. "No, just lots to think about. This DNA evidence—it means we have to be even more careful."

"It's why I brought you in first. I thought if we can get some kind of containment on the information, then when we start to let other families know, we actually have solid information plus actionable solutions. Right now, if I start alerting other groups to the ability to identify wolf shifters by DNA, we're going to have a lot of panic. Unnecessary panic," the blond man explained with cool demeanor.

"Have you begun analyzing the international implications?"

"That's exactly why I wanted to bring your sister in on this. Her business mind is ten steps ahead of the competition. I'm brilliant, but she's better."

Morgan slid his gaze sidelong to glance at Roman Aventine. Not in so many words, but Roman had revealed a weakness for Julia. It could be purely appreciation of her professional skills, but Morgan didn't think so. Not after what he witnessed back in Aventine's office. He shook his head, jogging his thoughts back into position.

"So our businesses partner up, make a game plan for the information. Then what? Sell it to the highest bidder? Keep some families in the dark?"

"Not at all. This gets shared freely with all parties concerned. Otherwise, we end up on the front page of every newspaper in the country—and not just the National Inquisitor. Know what I mean?"

Morgan nodded. This was good. Aventine showed concern for the greater good of their kind and not the greater good of his wallet.

The car maneuvered into an office park and stopped in front of a long low building of white stucco and blue glass. The sign out front indicated they had arrived at SeaQuence.

Roman took long confident strides as he approached the reception desk. The young woman behind the tall desk stammered over his name, clearly impressed by his clean-cut good looks, and continuously glanced at him through her lowered lashes.

A woman in a white lab coat approached them. "Roman Aventine, nice to see you again." They shook then Aventine introduced her to Morgan.

"Doctor Stacey Barnes, this is Morgan Palatine."

She paused slightly in recognition. Morgan's position in his family was well known among the Aventine family.

"Mr. Palatine, a pleasure." Dr. Barnes turned and headed back through the double doors she had previously emerged from. "If you gentlemen will follow me."

The two men followed her through several corridors of white walls. She led them into a large open area filled with laboratory benches. They passed a bank of equipment along one wall. Lights flashed and containers spun. On the far side of the room, she opened a glass door and held out her hand indicating they should enter.

"Please sit." She motioned towards two chairs facing a desk. The men each took a seat.

"Stacey, could you please review the information with Mr. Palatine that you shared with me the other day?" Aventine asked.

She nodded then began pulling out stacks of paper similar to those Aventine had shown Morgan and Julia in his office.

"We're learning more and more about human DNA every year. Keep in mind twenty years ago we didn't have half the DNA information we had ten years ago. So all this is new. To everyone. I'm sorry if I'm repeating anything you already know. At SeaQuence, we run genetic sequencing and identification. We are one of the labs that courts use in paternity testing cases, and we do DNA identification for crime labs. We also run some of the tests that those genealogy places now offer, the ones that help you identify your ethnic heritage." She carefully looked from one man to the next. "That's how I found the marker for wolf."

"Okay." She spread several sheets of paper on her desk. Alphanumeric codes covered the page. Some of the codes were outlined in green, others yellow, others blue. One set of codes had a bright orange starburst clearly drawn around them with a highlighter. "I ran my DNA through the system. Might as well get a heads-up on any inclinations towards heart disease and the like. But this showed up unexpectedly." She tapped the starburst of orange. "This page shows my ethnic breakdown. This is what it looks like before it's evaluated and translated for the average Joe to understand. This group shows Nordic ancestry," she circled a cluster of codes with her finger. "This group is the Mediterranean-Aegean ancestry. Nothing unexpected." She circled the cluster of codes around the highlighted mark again. "At first I thought this was junk code—DNA with markers but no actual genes or DNA that codes for a gene or genes with no know function. All DNA has some, so it's nothing actually unusual. I was reviewing some other reports, and I noticed their junk DNA looked different. The sequences in this region were unique to me. I wanted to find out if it was me individually or me as wolf." She nodded looking back up at the men. "Make sense?"

Morgan leaned in, focused on her information. Mostly a repeat of what Aventine had said, but hearing it a second time, the information started to take a more comprehensible shape.

"That's when you tested other family members," Aventine added.

"Exactly. This pattern showed up on the known wolves I tested. I then started testing non-shifter family members. That's when I really narrowed it down to the exact coding region."

She shuffled papers. "I can now identify the specific allele—" She looked at Morgan and assessed his puzzled look. "—that's a variation of a gene that shows up in the same place on the same chromosome. Like we know what location on the chromosome has eye color, so I can identify which is the set that determines if a person is wolf, ethnically. With this information, we can start to identify what other genes and chromosomal regions determine if offspring will have the ability to change or not." She looked from Aventine to Palatine. "You realize, gentlemen, this might make us somewhat of a sub mutation of the genus Homo?" Dr. Barnes sat back, sighing.

"Or the next step in evolution?"

Morgan cut Roman a side-eye glance. "Superiority complex?"

Roman laughed.

"Of course, there is some margin of error, but with the little testing I've done, the gene is showing up consistently and predictably. Currently, I have only identified it showing up here as an ethnicity trait. There are most likely additional gene sets. Just as we have genes that identify us ethnically, there are related genes that will show up in some of the medical panels. Genes sometimes travel in packs that way, its called linkage disequilibrium. The other genetic players haven't been found yet, but trust me, they are in there. There will be other correlations between wolf alleles and other medical issues. I'd put money on there being a tie into our longevity and ability to fight disease and heal quickly. Even non-changers possess and exhibit those traits."

"Interesting," Morgan muttered.

"Scientifically, this is beyond interesting. It opens up so many questions. If we are a subgroup of Homo, how far did our kind interact with Homo sapiens to become integrated with them? Are we from a previously unknown species that somehow interbred with Homo sapiens, became absorbed into the species, and disappeared as a standalone group the way Neanderthals did? How far back before we run into dormant markers in the general population? How can we breed with an unknown, assumed regular Homo sapiens and come up with one of us?" Dr. Barnes pulled off her glasses and placed them on her desk. "You're familiar with the mate aura?" She gave the term air quotes with her fingers.

"But that's only among our kind," Aventine said.

"No, it's not." Morgan corrected, thinking about how Honey had looked bathed in golden light.

"Right." She pointed at Morgan. "While I think we're the only ones who see it, humans can glow. It's how we can all have that one human grandmother and can still shift. I'd say —educated guess here—this means that either wolf is a dominant gene set, or somewhere in that person's genome, they have wolf. I haven't yet tested a human mate to really be able to drill down into their DNA."

Morgan listened intently. Would Honey be willing to be tested? He couldn't ask her just yet. It wasn't a matter of if Honey would have him back, but how soon. She was his. His mate. He would do whatever it took for her to accept him.

"Clearly, you have years of research ahead of you. But how do we take this information and corral it?" Morgan asked. "We can't buy out every lab that does this work?"

Roman shook his head, "No, but we do need to establish a presence in this business community and access the data."

"If we alert other labs to the gene signature, their radar goes off and red flags start flying. That would basically be alerting the community that something is up with this code. That would result in noses we don't want sniffing around in our business and investigating people we don't want investigated," Dr. Barnes added.

Morgan leaned forward, placing his elbows on the table, hands fisted together. "Could we infiltrate their databases with some kind of filtering program? Have all matches sent to us?" He rested his lips on his fingers. "We need a piggyback program. Something that runs behind the database software. Something that we can use to get into all the systems, that alerts us without their knowing about it."

"That's one solution." Barnes agreed. "But programming and infiltrating other databases is going to take time. Fortunately, this is not a widely expressed allele and no one is studying its function yet.

"I've already checked our database. We run hundreds of thousands of DNA tests, and the only cases of the gene are found in the tests I've run." Dr. Barnes collected the papers spread across her desk. "I have an idea that should work in the short-term, while you figure out the big picture and how to harvest this information from other databases. I am a clinical researcher. I can put a call out to other labs in the US and Canada for this information. Right now its junk code as far as anyone is concerned. I tell them I'm looking for a few different sets of junk code. Give them several options, so nothing is pointing to our identifier specifically. Tell them I'm researching if it is, in fact, junk code or a placeholder for related medical issues." She nodded to herself. "Tell them it's viral related. Really send them in the wrong direction."

"This way I can start collecting the information, and we can see how far spread this really is. In the meantime, tell everyone you know to not go in for genetic testing.

"The only problem I can see with that," Roman drawled, "is if you get a match. We won't have patient information associated to it."

"No, but we'll be able to see how many more are out there being tested. Are the labs regional? Will we be able to pick up that type of data?" Morgan asked.

Dr. Barnes shook her head. "Labs are all over the place and not regional. I might be able to get location information from the other labs, but you're right, nothing identifying who the DNA belongs to. Not unless they happen to be a perp in the national and federal database of criminals who has been tested for DNA."

"It's a start," Roman noted. "How soon can you take action and get this moving?"

"You mean start contacting other labs regarding bogus research? A few days. I need to come up with a brilliant and feasible hypothesis to present along with my request. I can get that started right away." She motioned with her hands. "It's going to have to be good to sound convincing." She turned to Roman, "I'm going to need funding. Rumor says you're trying to purchase SeaQuence. I think once that's done, you can officially green light my research project. In the meantime I can get everything set up and ready to go."

"Do that. We'll keep brainstorming on how to access the information on a more permanent basis." Roman stood, indicating the meeting had come to an end.

Morgan also stood. "Julia has probably already started the process of locating a genetics group to buy out. If I know her, she'll be putting together prospectuses for our directors that will be ready by the end of week." He swept his hand in a motion to indicate the business office. "So this the facility Aventine Industries is working on acquiring?"

Roman nodded. "Yes, Aventine Industries is already moving forward with a purchase option for SeaQuence Labs."

Reaching forward to shake Dr. Barnes hand, Morgan said, "Thank you, Dr. Barnes. This has been most enlightening. We all have a lot of work ahead of us. Let me know if you want to run some tests on Palatine DNA to confirm any of your findings and ensure this is not an Aventine specific anomaly."

"Thank you for offering. Would you mind giving me a sample right now?" she asked.

"You need blood?"

"I can take blood, hair, urine, spit. A buccal swab is the easiest and the cleanest," she explained. "I'll be right back." She stepped out of her office.

Roman clapped him on the back. "I'm going to leave you here. Let you do your swab test. I will have a car called for you to take you back to your hotel in San Francisco. I have more meetings on this side of the bay this afternoon, so no need for you to wait on me, right?" He stuck out his hand for Morgan to shake.

"Right." Morgan shook the offered hand. "Aventine, you're not what I expected, based on your father's reputation."

"Thank God. That old wolf is a bit too antiquated for my tastes. But he's the boss."

Morgan chuckled. He knew that sentiment, but now he was the boss. "I'm sure Julia will be in contact soon regarding the specifics."

"I look forward to it."

Morgan stood waiting for Dr. Barnes to return after Aventine left.

She directed him to open his mouth while she ran a cotton swab over the inside of his cheek. He obliged her then filled out a short form identifying the swab as his.

Dr. Barnes thanked him, then guided him back out to the lobby.

The receptionist confirmed a car had been called and would arrive shortly. Her sneer indicated she was not as impressed with Morgan as she had been with Roman Aventine.

Morgan waited less than five minutes before the receptionist approached him letting him know that his car had arrived. Morgan slid into the back of the black Lincoln Town Car and told the driver which hotel to take him to in San Francisco. He settled back in his seat and began texting Julia notes from his second meeting with Aventine and the doctor. Morgan's large thumbs made typing awkward on the phone's small keyboard display. Most of what he sent Julia was ideas and the related obstacles that might prevent a course of action from being viable.

Identification was always something they had to be careful with. Family members who couldn't change still had to be welcomed into the fold, else they might feel ostracized and feel the need for retaliation of some kind.

Now to have confirmation they could be traced on a genetic level brought with it a whole new set of concerns for all his kind. *His kind.* They had lived, hiding in plain sight for centuries. They weren't even certain they were the only type of shifter out there. Rumors of others surfaced from time to time certainly, but never confirmation. And they were not exactly the werewolf of legend, but certainly wolf-shifters. They had a level of control and could decide when to change. They did not rely on the magic of the moon for their shifting abilities. That did not mean there were not werewolves out there that the moon controlled, but if they existed they remained well hidden. Just as the Palatine family had. Just as the Aventines had.

Morgan made a quick note to contact Dr. Barnes and have her on the look-out for other potential shifter races. *Race.* Was Wolf now a race? Was that even the correct term? Wasn't race considered purely a social construct? Wolf as ethnicity, a sub-species, a scientific classification? Morgan had always thought of himself as Californian, which super-seded his Italian and Portuguese heritage. Of course, he had always figured the arguments and one-upmanship was wolf, pack order, and not the typical, hot-blooded, Mediterranean heritage. Most likely the hot headed temperament came from both.

Always heavy, traffic was noticeably slower for this time of day approaching the bridge. The interior of the car grew dark. He looked up. They were boxed in between two semis, not moving in the traffic jam. Normally, this wouldn't have fazed Morgan, but this time, something felt off. He leaned forward to speak to the driver. A sharp *ppst* sound popped in Morgan's ears, and the driver slumped over the steering wheel. The windshield shattered and a canister dropped onto the front passenger seat.

Morgan grabbed for the door handle and shoved against his door. *Crap!* The door would not open. A low hiss sounded, followed by billowing white clouds of pungent, chemical-smelling smoke that filled the interior of the car. Morgan covered his mouth and nose with his sleeve and threw himself against the door again.

In seconds, all went black.

## 10

M organ felt like he had been kicked in the head. His mouth tasted bitter, like chemicals. His face pressed against something smooth, like paper. The rumbling and movement suggested he rode in the back of a truck. He blinked, attempting to bring focus to his eyes. Nothing.

He closed them again and tried to shift his position. His hands were tied behind his back. He tried to rotate his wrists, straining with his fingers to feel what bound his wrists together. Whatever the binding was, it was just out of reach. He pulled his wrists apart, expecting to break through his restraints. In his weakened condition, all that motion did was hurt.

He tried to open his eyes again. Dark. Some filtering light. He blinked and let his eyes adjust to the lack of light. A flat expanse blocked part of his vision. He leaned, face first against a cardboard box. Morgan used his shoulder to right himself to a more comfortable sitting position. Comfortable was subjective. Now that he could see, he realized he sat on the sheet metal flooring of a panel truck.

Morgan assessed his situation, reviewing everything he knew. Which wasn't much. His driver had been shot. He had been drugged. His head throbbed. He was now in the back of a cargo truck, not too big from the dimensions, so not a semi, and they were moving. From the constant and continuous rocking, Morgan surmised they were on a freeway, headed away from the Bay Area and its constant traffic jams. The aftereffects of the drug left him groggy and weak. There was little for him to do except sit and wait.

The truck pulled off the freeway and stopped once briefly before getting back on the road. The rocking motion and lack of sensory input lulled Morgan to sleep. He awoke as the back door to the cargo area rolled up with a clatter. Morgan squinted at the back-lit figure that stepped up into the cargo hold. Night. A fluorescent lit marquee advertising cigarettes and beer. They were stopped at a gas station.

Morgan turned his focus to the man in front of him. He tried to open his senses to identify who had kidnapped him. *Nothing.* He quickly assessed his captor's physical appearance. The man wasn't overly tall and had a military-style buzz cut. Morgan considered neither piece of information to be useful.

"Who are you?" Morgan asked gruffly, his words mere mumbles of sound.

His answer was a blow to the head and a sharp needle prick in the side of his neck. The man shoved Morgan away, so he landed with his face against the flooring of the truck. The lights outside of the truck blurred out of focus seconds before Morgan blacked out again.

～

Morgan groaned. His head felt like he had been hit repeatedly. The constant frantic throbbing in his temples wasn't helping any. A sharp slap stung the side of his face. A second slap was followed by a kick to the ribs.

"Wake up," a voice growled.

Morgan slowly moved his pounding head. Consciousness flooded him. Thumping that didn't originate inside his head assaulted him. The rapid thud of helicopter blades created the backbeat to the pain in his skull.

Keeping his eyes closed, Morgan assessed his predicament. He was no longer in the back of a truck—that much was certain. He sat upright in an upholstered swivel chair. Pounding, aching head—check. Bitter chemical taste combined with morning-after mouth, demon breath, and fuzzy teeth—check. Wrists bound behind back—check. Weak as shit—check. He opened his senses to gather more information, this time with a little more success. A human pilot sat behind him—that meant he was rear facing. A wolf-shifter in front of him. A not-quite-human who didn't smell right—sick or drugs, Morgan couldn't hone in on the smell. It was being masked by the unmistakable cloying stench of French designer aftershave on another human.

His lids still clenched, Morgan let his eyes open enough to let light flood his brain. He closed his eyes again and breathed. Slowly, he opened his eyes again, letting his vision focus on the man directly across from him. *Wolf.* A Japanese man with short black hair and black eyes stared back at him. Next to the wolf, in a separate captain's style chair, sat an extremely pale man with a military haircut. Morgan recognized his shape as the one who'd stuck a needle into his neck earlier.

"Good, he's awake." A familiar snide voice pierced

Morgan's brain. That explained the cologne, Morgan thought. He turned to face the man next to him, his entire chair rotated.

Morgan huffed. "What the fuck are you doing here, Maplecourt?"

"I should ask you the same thing."

"I'm the one with his hands tied behind his back. So I get that you think I have some information you want or need. Let's start by asking me something I might actually know?"

"Why do they think you have any power? You're a construction worker." The confusion in Maplecourt's tone told Morgan the man was out of his league, and he didn't know who, or rather what, he was keeping company with.

"Again, try asking me something I might actually know, Maplecourt. Last time I was awake, I was in traffic headed for the Bay Bridge. Now—" Morgan swiveled his chair away from Maplecourt, looking out of the helicopter window as they passed over a ski lift and treeless side of a ski slope. "—we appear to be flying over the Sierras. Maybe your new friends here could help you out?" Morgan nodded to the wolf. "What do you say, fellows? Want to fill Maplecourt in on what's going on so that I can get out of here?"

They stared back at him enigmatically.

"Nothing?"

The Japanese man pulled a cell phone from his pocket and placed it up to his right ear. He nodded as he listened. He placed the phone back into his pocket.

"Morgan Palatine," the wolf-shifter began, "our Lordship has a proposition for you."

"Lord? God told you over the phone to offer me a job? No thanks, I have one."

"Shut up!" Maplecourt hissed." You don't know who

these people are. They are very powerful. If you don't accept their offer, they'll kill you."

Morgan caught a whiff of adrenaline and fear under Maplecourt's assaulting aftershave. He was nervous, excited, and clearly in over his head.

"I get the feeling—" Morgan addressed Bryce directly, "—that you don't really know who these people are either. Do your friend's at Cyan Group know you're here?" He needed to keep the man unbalanced before he figured out it was his job to kill Morgan.

"Cyan Group is a bunch of daisy scouts." Maplecourt scoffed. "They act all tough like they're Russian mafia or something. They don't know shit. They don't have real power." He gestured towards the men sitting across the luxury passenger cabin. "Their Lordship has real power, controls real money. This—" His gesture included the helicopter. "—is not even a show of the magnitude of his wealth."

"What have you gotten yourself into?" Morgan asked. Cyan Group was definitely an *or something* and more frightening than the Russian mafia. This helicopter was for show. It wasn't a personal vehicle. Morgan had picked up on the little nuances from the interior that gave it away as a chartered ride, little stickers of communication that someone who rode in this cabin frequently would know and remember, and have removed.

"I've gotten into the real game, real wealth, real influence. And Cyan Group won't be able to touch me, not with what I have on them. If they make one move I don't like, I'll go public with my information, and they'll be out of business and in jail. They won't even get to enjoy watching it go viral."

Morgan shook his head. Real stupid and real dead.

Maplecourt was proving himself to be an idiot. A dangerous idiot. He turned back to the Japanese man.

"What does your boss want from me?"

"Bring down the alpha of the Aventine pack."

"Nature is already doing that. His wife is dying of cancer. He no longer pays attention to his family or his business."

"Take out the second, the son."

"Why? To what end?"

"Destroy the Aventines."

"And if I refuse this offer?" Morgan's eyes cut away from the Japanese man, quickly glancing at Maplecourt. "He's supposed to shoot me?" Clearly, this was a set-up. Maplecourt needed to prove his loyalty to the new master so they'd let him into their little club. Have him kill someone in front of witnesses, and they would have Maplecourt by the balls for the rest of his life. At this rate, it was going to be a very short life.

Maplecourt chuckled. "Do you even know who they are talking about? Aventine Industries is a bigger conglomerate than that paltry little get-up you work for. Taking them down will cause a disruption in the market. Not ripples, but a tsunami. A tidal wave I plan to surf to financial glory." Maplecourt turned to face the men opposite. "I told you when he was unconscious, he's a nobody, a construction site manager. I don't know why he's in a suit. Must have been meeting with the boss, and you grabbed the wrong guy. He's not who you think he is."

Maplecourt was an even bigger idiot than Morgan thought moments ago. How many meetings had they had and he still thought Morgan was the site manager. He let his gaze rest on the pale man. This one hadn't said anything.

"He's a real moron, isn't he?" Morgan asked, inclining his head towards Maplecourt. The other man grimaced, flashing his teeth. Naturally sharpened canines. A daywalker. That explained why Morgan couldn't figure out the man's scent. They never smelled right, and if he was drugged, that would explain why Morgan couldn't identify his smell earlier.

Daywalkers were the biological offspring of mated vampires. Vampires were not exactly the undead of legend, but close. They had fangs and a physical need to consume blood. They possessed extreme strength, had proclivity towards psychic abilities, and developed extreme burns when exposed to sunlight. Unlike their progenitors, daywalkers' fangs were neither as large or retractable. The need for blood also differed in daywalkers. They did not need to consume it for sustenance; however, they required infusions of clean blood on a regular basis. With comparable strength but without the need to avoid daylight, daywalkers tended to be the assistants and henchmen in the vampire world. While vampires tended to have a higher occurrence of telepaths in their ranks, the mental development of daywalkers leaned towards the unbalanced. Daywalkers were beneficial to vampires because they didn't have to avoid the sun which had fatal consequences for vampires.

Morgan stared at the daywalker. What would make a daywalker and a wolf work together? Typically, the two groups couldn't stand each other. The rivalry that made the centuries-long feud between the Palatine family and the Aventines look like the petty corporate squabble between Coke and Pepsi. And why did they want him?

Morgan addressed the wolf. "Okay, I'll bite. Why me? What purpose will killing Aventine serve?"

"It will serve our Lordship's purpose. That is all that

concerns you. If you do not comply, our friend here will shoot you."

Morgan pursed his lips and looked out the window. The helicopter dipped, following the tree line down to fly low over a body of water. *Lake Tahoe?* He let his gaze wander around the cabin. Idiot boy Maplecourt, no physical threat, sat to his left. He probably couldn't even aim a gun properly, let alone hit him even in this confined space.

"Don't shoot me in here. You'll never get the deposit back." Morgan muttered. The daywalker sat furthest away and was buckled in. The only real threat was the wolf across from him. Morgan focused on the door and the little sticker that indicated which way the lever pivoted to unlock and slide the door open.

"I think—" Morgan leaned forward towards the wolf. The Japanese man sat back, relaxing into his cushioned seat, assured he had won. "—that will be a no." Moving quickly he rolled back, kicked the lever then kicked a second time to open the door.

The helicopter wobbled as wind buffeted the cabin. Maplecourt let out an undignified squeal, and a shot rang past Morgan's head as he jumped.

Another shot, and a sharp sting bit into Morgan's arm. Adrenaline-fueled rage brought Morgan's strength roaring back. He snapped his restraints in time to pull his arms in tight as he hit the water feet first.

Rising to the surface, Morgan searched for the helicopter. He saw it circling low ahead of him. They hadn't seen him. Morgan gulped down air then sank below the surface of the water, striking out in the opposite direction.

He felt the fabric of his trousers tear when his knee crashed into a rock as he climbed to shore. His muscles felt shaky after the long swim. He still had the sedative in his system. It made him feel weak. Morgan looked around. The helicopter was nowhere in sight, but he could hear it.

His first inclination was to call for some backup, get Shane out here. Find out what the hell was going on. He pulled his cell phone from his jacket breast pocket. *Damn.* Plan A ruined by water-soaked technology. He began working on plan B: getting the hell out of there. Morgan removed his clothes and shoes, then tied them into an easy to carry bundle. He was going to need them later.

He reached out in a stretch. The muscles in his long legs and arms clenched and bunched as he willed the shift. He blinked, and his vision changed. The world shifted from flat and full color to infinite depths and details in black, white, and shades of gray. His bones shifted. He reached forward and landed on large paws. He shook as if he shook water from his dry, mottled brown fur. The sluggishness from the drugs left his muscles. The pain from the shot in his arm was now a dull, ignorable ache, as his natural accelerated healing began repairing the flesh and muscle.

A shot rang out. The *psfft* of a bullet sped past him. Morgan froze. Another shot. This one closer, hitting a tree less than a yard away. Morgan lowered his body and ran. Another bullet exploded into a tree as he ran past. They were in pursuit.

He hadn't smelled them or heard them approaching. That could only mean they hadn't brought the human Maplecourt along. Good. Then he still had no idea what Morgan was.

He ditched the bundle of clothes he carried and ran faster, circling around behind his hunters. Once downwind of them, his nose confirmed his pursuer was the daywalker from the helicopter. Morgan couldn't smell the wolf. Maybe he had stayed behind. The daywalker stood with his back to Morgan looking in the other direction for him.

Morgan attacked.

He clamped his teeth onto the wrist holding the gun. The daywalker shrieked as the large brown wolf bit through sinew and muscle. The pistol forgotten, Morgan dropped the wrist then lunged for the man's neck. He fought back, but not with the ferocity Morgan expected. This one was weak, all bluff and bluster. There was no fighting power in his arms. Morgan fought with teeth and claws. The man fought with knees and punches. In the end, teeth won against soft belly flesh.

The daywalker was down, possibly dead. Morgan circled back to where he dropped his clothes, picked up the bundle with blood soaked jaws, and ran back to the body.

In an instant, Morgan changed back to his human form. Momentarily, he thought about trying to hide the body, but he didn't have time for that. He had to get out of there before the wolf showed up. He searched the man's pockets for a cell phone. Nothing. What kind of person didn't carry a cell phone these days? No cell phone, but there was the gun. He didn't need that in wolf form, but he might need it as a human. He rearranged his bundle to now include the gun.

Back in wolf form, Morgan headed deeper into the forest. He had to find out what was going on. Daywalkers and wolves, and who was this Lordship guy? He also had to get back to Honey, keep her away from Maplecourt. That ass had just proven himself to be more dangerous than merely being a sadistic, abusive ex-boyfriend. They were grooming Maplecourt to be a fucking minion and he was clueless. By the time the vampires were feeding from him, he would welcome it. And worse, Maplecourt was stupid and dangerous enough they might turn him he was good-looking enough they would want him—that is, if they could control him. If they couldn't, then that was his tough luck.

Morgan needed to speak with Cyan del Fuego from Cyan Group. See what she knew about this "Lordship" person. Morgan had an idea, but he needed confirmation. This mess came with a whole list of questions without answers. More fucking work for him, and all he wanted to do was get back to Honey and make sure she was safe.

## 11

"Lana's on a rampage," Seth announced. He and Honey leaned on the counter looking out of the large picture window front of the coffee shop. They watched the short black spikes bob as Lana stomped along the sidewalk into the shop. Lana only ever bobbed when she was spitting mad.

"Whatever it was, I didn't do it," Seth said as he slunk away from the counter.

"Have you seen this?" Lana slammed the newspaper down on the counter. It was folded to a random interior page of the paper. The headline Lana pointed to stated *Potential Rape Spree on the Peninsula.*

"How is a rape spree potential, I ask you?"

Honey knew best not to interrupt Lana.

"It says there is a serial attacker. His style is much like a rape. He attacks from behind, cuts clothing, hits, threatens. Basically everything except for penetration. Then he steals the victim's stuff and takes off. Now, get this. Apparently, he's a complete moron He wears the same yellow jogging jacket."

Lana looked at Honey quizzically. "What the hell is a jogging jacket?"

Lana leaned over the counter, "Seth, get your butt out here!"

Seth looked completely guilty entering the serving area "I di—"

"Shut up and listen. Look, this guy has attacked at the Wharf and few places in Carmel. He's targeting tourist spots and hitting the employees who have to work late. He probably has already, or is about to, target down here. I don't want Honey or Joyce closing alone anymore. Got me?"

Both Honey and Seth nodded in agreement. One thing about Lana, she didn't get mad without also getting a plan. Honey, go get the schedule from the office, please."

Returning from the office, Honey slid the clipboard with the weekly schedule in front of Lana. "I want this schedule changed until this guy gets caught. Seth, how many closing nights can you give me?"

Honey's attention drifted as Seth and Lana set up the details of his new closing schedule to thoughts of Morgan. He would meet her as she closed and would walk her to her car. Her vision blurred as she just experienced pain, pure empty pain.

"Honey, got that?"

"Eight friggin' days— Huh? Sorry, I guess not."

"Honey, I need you to open tomorrow, Thursday, and Friday and do standard day shifts on your regular scheduled days. Seth will close on the weekends and Wednesdays and Thursdays."

Seth's look suggested a deer caught in a car's headlights. "But I'm no good at closing, remember. I keep fucking up the register."

"Shit. That's right." Lana glared at the floor thinking.

"Okay, Seth, you still close but just pull the tape and lock it and the cash drawer in the safe. Honey, you come in early the next day and close Seth out before you open the drawer. I'd rather risk a little mess-up with the drawer than risk Honey or Joyce. I will close on Mondays and Tuesdays."

"You can't close alone, Lana. Do ya—" Honey began.

"I won't be alone, I'll bring Big Dog to work."

"He can't come in here, you know that," Seth said, using his Mr. Know-it-all voice.

"No, he can't, but he can hang out on the back-loading dock. No one will mess with me when I'm with him." Big Dog's size was intimidating, especially to those who didn't know he was really a snuggly, fluffy, oversized puppy. Lana picked up the revised schedule, "Okay, Seth, you can pull this off tonight, right?" She waited for his nod. "I'll go call Joyce and let her know what's going on even though it doesn't really affect her schedule." Lana scooped the clipboard off the counter as she breezed past behind the counter and off towards the office.

Seth quickly resumed his slouching posture next to Honey.

"You'd think that with the boss here we would be inclined to look busy or something."

"Well, all of the *or somethings* have been done." Honey ticked off all the maintenance chores on her fingers. "Everything is cleaned, dusted, inventoried and restocked. There is very little for her to have us do. If there is no one coming in, and since the work is done, then we wait. Besides, I'm not cleaning the coffee maker midday. I officially protest doing that job."

"You certainly took care all of the to-dos."

"Nothing better to do. Keeps my mind occupied."

"Still mooning after that construction worker?" Seth quirked an eyebrow at her.

Honey cut him off. "I'm not mooning. I stopped mooning two days ago. He was only worth six days of mooning. Now I'm just, I'm just..." Honey pursed her lips and stared at Seth. Her eyes bore a hole into the center of his nose. "Gaaaa!" She stormed out of the front of the shop, trying to fight off tears.

Honey still mooned. She was more than mooning. She missed Morgan. She felt hurt and left behind. She played the voicemail he left, again. But he never answered whenever she called back. She didn't know if she was abandoned, or if something happened to him, or had their date really been that bad and he changed his mind after the message. She felt conflicted. Should she be worried or mad? Or both?

Twelve days ago he smiled that smile at her, and she could have sworn he was about to kiss her. Twelve days ago he had said he had a good time and that they should go out on a real date. Nine days ago their date had been a royal disaster, and she wanted to ask him for a do-over. She attempted to return his call the next day, and the next day after that. Honey had been waiting for eight days to ask him to go out with her again and not to hate her. Waiting for him to saunter into The Corner and ask when her next break was. Waiting to hear the deep tones of his voice. Waiting to hear him say her name again.

Honey dropped the pendant and used her fists to rub the tears from her cheeks. She stopped. Tourists bustled around her as her abrupt halt interrupted the flow of pedestrian traffic. She spun around on her heel and stalked back to the café.

Honey returned to the counter. Seth handed her a

whipped fruity tea concoction he had been developing. "Here, it's pink and fruity. Whatcha think?"

Honey sat and took a long hard sip through the straw. She closed her eyes as her tongue enjoyed the sparkling frozen berry flavors mixed with green tea and honey. Then she clenched her eyes and pinched the bridge of her nose. "Brain freeze!"

When she recovered from the cranial chill effects of the blended ice drink, she blinked at Seth. "Thanks. Sorry I..." She twisted and pointed at the door. "Ya' know, he never once made a comment about my name."

"Seriously? Not one crack about the color of golden honey?"

Honey sniffled. "Not one. I thought that was a sign or something."

"It certainly seems like it would have been. I was sorta hoping he wasn't a jerk to you, but I guess he was."

"Yeah, I guess he was." Honey said sadly.

## 12

————

Morgan had been wrong. Disastrously wrong. South and east only revealed more forest, not civilization. That assumed he still traveled in that compass direction. And followers of the Lord person hadn't given up pursuing him. The daywalker had not been their last attempt at eliminating him. Morgan sensed the other wolf followed him. Whiffs of the other wolf's scent when the wind changed alerted him to his constant danger. Morgan realized his adversary was a skilled tracker. His strategy of circling to position himself downwind of the other wolf worked only for a short while. They spent days like this, circling each other, in a constant rotation to be downwind of the other.

Morgan rested against his paws, letting his eyes drift shut if only for a moment. He instinctively ducked when bark exploded when a bullet impacted the tree above him. There was no way he could be seen, he was certain. The fallen branches provided excellent coverage. He waited. When another bullet shattered branches on a nearby tree, he knew the shooter couldn't see him but was targeting by scent.

Morgan dropped his bundle of clothes on the ground and slipped from his hiding spot and ran. The sound of shots grew faint as he put distance between himself and the shooter. Counting on his pursuer tracking by smell and not visually, Morgan crossed a stream. He ran back and forth several times, pooling his scent into a dead-end for his tracker. Once his smell was concentrated in the small area, Morgan trotted in the middle the stream, following the flow of water uphill. When the creek thinned to a trickle Morgan rolled in the mud of the stream bed to further hide his scent.

The next time Morgan heard shots, they were ahead of him. Good. Keep the other wolf thinking he was behind Morgan when the opposite was true. Morgan approached the other wolf, who was currently in human form. Morgan crouched low, crawling forward on his belly. He didn't want the other man to realize he was there or give him a chance to change. Wolf versus man was always easier, faster. As humans, shifters were strong but never as strong as in their wolf form. They also had all the weaknesses and frailties of the human body.

Morgan didn't want a prolonged fight. He wanted a strategic strike, an opportunity to get this battle over with quickly, and return to the task of finding civilization.

Morgan watched as the man stalked passed him. In a single movement, Morgan was on him. He sunk his over-sized canines into the back of his stalker's neck. Bones crushed under the power of his jaws. The man dropped to the ground, twitched briefly, and went still.

Morgan stood over the body of the wolf-shifter, blood dripping from his muzzle. Something seemed wrong about this fight. It was almost as if the Japanese man hadn't tried to protect himself. Either he was submissive to the point of not knowing how to fight or he wanted to die. But why?

Staying in wolf form became a necessity for survival. He tracked back to where he had left his clothes. Eventually he would need them again when—and if—he found civilization.

Nights were cold in the Sierra Nevada Mountains. Morgan found shallow caves to hide in, to rest. It was easier to watch one entrance for danger than it was to sleep out in the open. Fortunately, Morgan had a thick fur coat to protect him. Without the ability to shift, Morgan in human form and dressed only in his suit would have been in grave danger of succumbing to exposure while lost in the mountains. Clearly, his concept of south and east were either not correct, or as he had started to suspect, he had not jumped into Lake Tahoe.

With no knowledge of his point of origin, Morgan could only hope he would cross a road or find a town soon. Morgan decided to head west towards the setting sun and downhill.

His nose twitched as he scented body spray. He followed the strong scent and then picked up the smell of a campfire. Morgan couldn't safely approach a campsite in his current form. He shifted and dressed in the clothes he had continued to carry.

His suit was rumpled, blood stained, and torn. Morgan knew he did not look like a camper accidentally separated from his group. He looked like some moron who had decided to take a walk in the woods in a business suit. He ran his fingers through his hair, concocting an excuse story as he approached the campers.

"Hey, guys," he said as he entered their campsite.

Two young men stared at him bewildered.

"Do either of you have a cell phone I could borrow?" He held up his defunct phone. "Mine's dead."

"There's no service out here," one of them replied. "You lost?"

"I am so very lost it isn't even funny," Morgan drawled, without a hint of sarcasm.

After introductions, Morgan explained that he had been driving around and got turned around. He had no cell signal and a rapidly diminishing battery. Then his car died. After a day of waiting in his vehicle for someone to drive by, he decided to start walking. He had been walking along the road, and clearly, his mind had wandered, because he found himself in the middle of the woods, falling into a shallow ravine.

Morgan continued with his story, telling the campers that when he tried to find the road again he couldn't. He began hiking west and downhill. He let the young men think he had been out in the woods for two days and not the almost two weeks it really had been.

"We're heading back in in the morning. We'll give you a ride," The taller of the two men offered.

"I would appreciate that."

They rustled up a serviceable car blanket for Morgan to sleep under. It felt scratchy, but it was better than nothing since Morgan couldn't transform for the night. At dawn, he helped them break down camp. He rode in the backseat of their jeep into a small town which consisted of a diner and a gas station. They had cell phone service.

Morgan held the borrowed phone, staring at the number pad in front of him. He hadn't needed to remember a phone number since he started carrying a cell. It had been years.

He entered the only number he could remember.

"Mission Run, how may I assist you?" a cool even-toned female voiced answered.

"Remi, I need Remi." Morgan's own voice sounded hoarse even to himself.

"Who may I..."

"It's Morgan. Get me Remi," he growled.

"Morgan! Where have you been? It's Jinx. Everyone here has been frantic." The voice on the other end of the line was muffled as Jinx began talking rapidly to someone at the other location. "Are you safe? Are you hurt?"

"I'm safe at the moment. I'm not hurt."

"Morgan!" a second, deeper voice roared through the phone. "Where the hell have you been?"

"Missing, Remi, I've been missing."

Morgan sat at one end of the large dining room table, still in the same rumpled suit he had been carrying around since his escape from the helicopter. The formal dining room served double duty as a meeting room whenever business had to be discussed at the house. Remi, an older bearded man, in an electric wheelchair positioned himself next to Morgan. Shane, a large body builder type and Joe, a tall rangy man, were also seated around the table.

"Dante's out on a job. He won't be joining us." Remi explained.

"What job?" Morgan asked. He figured everyone had been called in as soon as he had been located.

"He's acting bodyguard for JoJo and her friends while they wreak havoc on Las Vegas for her bachelorette outing," Remi explained.

"In other words, he's hitting on all her friends then plans to abandon them and find some party girls." Shane scoffed.

"For any normal trip, I'd agree with you, but this is JoJo. He won't leave her side. He will hit on all her friends, that's a given." Remi explained. Morgan needed Dante in on this. He would just have to catch him up later.

Morgan breathed out his nose. He was tired from his ordeal and his earlier phone call to Julia. He needed her to get in touch with Aventine, let him know what had happened, and see if he knew anything. Morgan also wanted extra security around her, in case whomever it was who had targeted him would try the same with her. She had argued she would be fine. He countered-argued they were already killing people, starting with his driver that fateful afternoon just over two weeks ago.

Morgan glanced between Remi, Shane, and Joe. "We've got daywalkers and wolves working for an unknown party. And Bryce Maplecourt, a human, has gotten himself into the middle of it."

Shane blanched, noticeably flinching when he heard the term daywalker. "Are you sure, daywalkers? And who the hell is Bryce Maplecourt?"

"Yes, I'm sure. I killed the daywalker. There was another man. Wolf. Japanese. Didn't say much, and I would bet even money he was a Smith. Japanese. I don't even know if that's a connection we can follow up on." Smiths were wolves who had renounced all family connections, loners. Typically, Smiths had delusions of grandeur. Non-dominants who fancied themselves to be leaders. He glanced pointedly at Shane. "Kept referring to their boss as 'Lord' and 'Lordship.'"

"'Lordship?' That sounds entirely too familiar for comfort." Shane said.

Morgan nodded. "That's what I thought." Morgan

nodded. "We need to make sure our clients at Cyan Group are our friends."

"Wait," Shane stopped Morgan. "You're working for Cyan Group. What does this have to do with them?"

"Cyan del Fuego is a daywalker. And Maplecourt works for her. I know him from the construction site. Fortunately, I'm certain I got out of there with him still not knowing what or who I really am. He thinks they picked up the wrong guy. He's an asshole—a stupid, dangerous, egotistical asshole. I already have Dante doing some digging on him. I need to know what information he's gotten so far. Why did he have to go with JoJo?" Morgan answered himself. "Because, Vegas."

"No," Joe cut in. "Because you were missing, and Dante didn't trust any of us to protect her."

Morgan sighed. "Okay. Look, Shane, I know you've tried to distance yourself from daywalkers as much as possible, I need you asking some old friends what they know." Morgan watched as Shane clenched his jaw.

A vein pulsed in his forehead, as Shane visibly fought to control his emotions. "I'll let Julia talk to the suckers at Cyan Group." He shook his head. "I'll make some calls."

"Good."

"I'll get started on the Smith, see if any families we have contact with have a lost one out there. Anything else you can tell me about him other than his being Japanese?" Remi asked.

Morgan shook his head. "It's all I got."

Remi nodded. "That gives me something to work with." Remi turned his chair and began wheeling out of the room.

Morgan clapped Shane on the back. "You got this, man?"

"Yeah, I got this. Don't like it, but I got it." Shane confirmed. "Good to see you back, my brother. This place has been in chaos without you. Poor JoJo. Thought everyone was going to demand she cancel the wedding. She actually wanted to cancel it. Everyone was doing the opposite, assuring her to go on with it, and you'd be home soon."

"I'm not here most of the time. How could chaos ensue because I go missing?"

"That's just it, man. Our alpha went missing. No ransom request. No notifications. No cell phone to track. No one in Monterey knew where you were. Nothing."

They stared at each other for a long minute.

Shane shook his head, "Daywalkers. I fucking hate daywalkers."

A slender, middle-aged woman, hair pulled back into a ponytail entered, passing Shane on his way out of the dining room.

"Morgan, I have a bath full of epsom salts started for you. I also pulled out a selection of essential oils. They are on your counter. One drop of each on your tongue, then hold against the roof of your mouth," she began.

"Jinx, I'm fine. Merely tired."

Jinx followed Morgan out of the dining room and up a wide grand staircase.

"I'm sure you do feel fine, but you've been out in the woods eating who knows what..." She paused, holding up her hands. "No, I don't want to know. The oils just bolster your already exceptional immune system. Just as the bath feels good and is more psychological than physical for you, this is psychological for me." She stopped. Morgan turned to face her. "Morgan, you've been gone. Everyone has been worried. Your family put up a good front, but they were almost frantic. And the staff—well, we're really glad you're safe."

Morgan stepped down to be on the same level as Jinx

and pulled her into a brief hug. "You take good care of me, Jinx, and you always have. You're part of the family too."

"Stop or you're going to cause emotions I'm uncomfortable with." Jinx declared.

Morgan chuckled. They continued up the stairs and into Morgan's apartments. He had a three-room suite within the larger family home. Jinx pulled out clean towels, and laid out a dressing gown.

She paused on her way out the door, glancing up and down his tall disheveled form. "I loved that suit. I don't think even the dry cleaners can save it. Want me to try anyway?"

Morgan shook his head. "No, I think it's dead." He examined the holes in the pants' knees. "I don't even think its salvageable for donating. You can have it burned once I get out of it."

"One does not burn Armani. Put it in the hamper. I'll take care of it later."

Jinx closed the door behind her as she left.

Morgan was alone again, but home. He disrobed as he walked towards the bath, leaving articles of clothing in his wake. He hissed in appreciation as he sank into the deep tub of hot water. Jinx was right. He wasn't muscle-weary; he was mentally weary. Physiologically he didn't need to soak in a hot tub. His muscles were fine, changing as often as he had the past weeks healed any wounds or minor contusions. Sure he had been shot, but the bullet had gone straight through, and within a change, it had begun healing at an accelerated pace. Within three changes, it had scabbed over, and now it was nothing more than a pink pucker. A few more changes and he wouldn't even have a scar. Morgan wasn't muscle-weary, he was mentally weary.

Who was this 'Lord?' Why were wolves working with daywalkers? What were they doing with Maplecourt? What did Maplecourt think he was doing with them? Did this in any way have anything to do with Aventine's DNA discoveries? Morgan leaned his head back against the edge of the tub and closed his eyes.

It felt like he had closed his eyes for only a few minutes, but Shane standing over him and the chill of the water indicated it had been much longer.

"Ever heard of knocking?" He grumbled as he sat up in the water.

"Yep, but it doesn't do much good when you're asleep. I've got intel."

Morgan nodded, indicating his sitting room. "I'll be out in two." He exited the tub and tied the sash of a terry dressing gown around his damp waist and stepped into the comfortably furnished room where Shane waited.

"Remi has contacted Dante. Apparently, JoJo is anxiously awaiting a call from you." Shane started.

Morgan nodded in understanding. JoJo was his much-younger adopted sister. Her single mother had worked for the Palatine family, and the family had taken them in and treated them as their own. When her mother had been killed in a freak boating accident, Morgan's parents legally adopted JoJo. No need to change the young girl's life any more than it had already been. Several years younger than Morgan and his sisters, they helped to raise her. Morgan treated her as a much-adored baby sister, and she treated him as a much-loved older brother. Morgan took that attachment seriously, and he watched out for her, her safety, her wellbeing, and her excessive spending habits. That meant having to call her while she partied in Las Vegas, gearing up for her forthcoming wedding.

"I'll give her a call after you tell me what you've got."

"Okay. Julia called back. Our friends at Cyan Group are

definitely friends. Cyan herself is most interested in learning more about what we know about that Maplecourt guy." Shane leaned back into the leather couch. "Apparently, she told Julia to play this one close. Don't let on to Maplecourt that she knows anything yet. Looks like it's going to get ugly for him. Julia also said Aventine is an egotistical ass. Not sure if that's in response to her letting him know there's a situation or a judgment call."

Morgan huffed. "Probably a bit of both. What else?"

"Julia said Cyan recommends we follow up on Lazarus's old coven. Pretty sure he's the 'Lordship' that the guys who kidnapped you referred to. I'm already one step ahead of her there. I've got a contact, used to be in with Lucy. She's in Santa Maria now. She's got information and is willing to share. Only thing is it's got to be face to face. I trust her, She's a friend."

"You didn't call Lucy about this, did you?"

"No, and I won't either. Not until I have real answers and it directly concerns her. Right now, all we have is speculation. She doesn't need conjecture and what ifs. I don't need to bring her in on this. And if I can help it, I never will." Shane's voice was rough with emotion and anger. It was clear he didn't like the prospect of having to deal with daywalkers, and he wanted to protect Lucy from them as well.

Morgan nodded in understanding. Shane had a convoluted past and was dangerous when it came to daywalkers and vampires. Shane would protect Lucy with his life. He would only drag her into a situation with daywalkers if there was no other choice. "Okay, we can do that. How soon?"

"Day after tomorrow," Shane explained.

"We can do that, but I need to get to Monterey first. We can swing by on our way out."

"That's several hours out of our way, Morgan. Can Monterey wait? We can call the job site and let them know you won't be in for a couple of days."

"We can leave a few hours early." Morgan interrupted. "It's not the job that I need to go see. I need to see someone."

## 13

H oney hadn't opened the shop for a few months. The morning crowds hung out less, looked at the art less, but they purchased the extra mugs and souvenirs more. The daytime crowds were more conservative and did not draw her into their philosophical discussions on the hidden meanings of life or the latest rock band, so there were longer periods of downtime where all she did was lean on the counter and try to not think about missing Morgan. On the days she worked with Joyce, the shop was a disco. Joyce always played her latest Turkish or Lebanese pop music.

Today the guitar thrummed heavy metal pulses to some Middle Eastern beat. Honey watched Joyce undulate her arms and roll her wrists to the music. Joyce danced constantly. If it had a beat, she danced. She managed to belly dance to everything. Sometimes she would throw in some hip-hop moves. Honey was pretty sure Joyce was not even aware she did it.

"Joyce! Turn the music down. We have incoming," Honey called as she mentally prepared for the onslaught of customers that would descend on The Corner once they exited the large group bus that had pulled up. The bus' air brakes emitted the telltale burst and hiss that confirmed they were stopping.

About twenty tourists filed in, chatting eagerly about something. Joyce and Honey mixed, blended, and poured. They plated cakes, cookies, and pastries.

They cleaned up spills and wiped down tables. The wave of consumers washed over them and left the shop empty in a mere thirty minutes. The burst of activity quickly slipped into an adrenaline slump.

"Goodie, dishes," Joyce clapped in mock excitement. "But first we dance!" She turned up the music and grabbed Honey. They spun and jumped around the tables. Honey did her best to copy Joyce's hip lifts and shimmies. Both women were smiling and giggling, enjoying themselves when a sharp commanding voice broke their reverie.

"I see you have reverted in basic public behavior, Rachelle."

The women stopped dancing.

"Oh, you," said Honey, as she swiped back her hair with one hand. She placed the other on her hip. Joyce skulked back to the office and turned down the music, picked up a stack of dishes, and headed for the kitchen.

"What do you want?" Honey's curt tone masked the panic bunching in her abdomen. The fingers at her hip dug in until she felt her fingernails bite into her skin.

"A warmer welcome, perhaps."

"Welcome to The Corner. How can I help you today, sir?" Honey said with the enthusiasm of an automaton. Her smile bit back the bile rising in her throat. She would not let Bryce see he still affected her. She controlled her emotions and if she could pretend indifference, eventually, she would be indifferent. Lana had coached her in the 'fake it 'til you make it' philosophy. *I can do this.* Her fingers found her charm. *Forza.* She could do this.

"Uh, you still wear that cheap piece of jewelry." He shook his head in distaste. "I should report you to your boss, Rachelle. You should know better than to show your insolence to me, a paying customer. I really shouldn't be surprised you are behaving this way. In public. Your professionalism was always questionable."

"Bryce, until you place an order, you are not a paying customer. Now, what do you want?" Honey kept her tone even and sharp. She focused on not letting Bryce get to her. Today she would not let that old pang of guilt seep in. Her contempt for him was actual and not faked. She would not acknowledge her fear.

"Do you remember my usual Saturday morning drink? I'll have that."

"Yeah, okay, Bryce, I told you last time. This isn't your usual coffee shop. That drink the granda-la-la-frapa-beano whipped chocolate milkshake thing isn't made here." She said tapping the counter with her index finger. "It's one of those specialty copyrighted type drinks." She pointed at the blackboard menu behind and above her, then turned back to face him. "That's our menu. What do you want?"

She hadn't realized his nose was so narrow. Before she had thought it appeared regal. Now she thought it just looked pointy. His eyes were smaller than she remembered and a harsh cold blue. Not warm and welcoming like Morgan's. Bryce's skin looked thin and delicate, not strong and manly, at all. His tan was too even, Morgan's tan had that naturally-achieved-from-outside-work coloring. Bryce's tan looked fake-and-bake. Was he using spray on tanning? Or, no, a tanning bed? *This is California. What does he need a tanning bed for?* Oh yeah, no tan lines. And, she realized, he groomed his eyebrows. They were waxed. She would have to see if Morgan did his eyebrows since he did have two distinct brows, not one. Why hadn't she noticed Bryce was disposed towards a unibrow before? She must have been blinded by the love she felt for him at the time. Her mental eyes rested on the image of Morgan's smiling face, superimposed over the reality of Bryce's face.

She registered his order and rang him through the register while not actually paying attention to him. Lana said that was a good quality for working here. Honey had never been able to master it. She always felt guilty for not giving the customer her full attention.

Honey turned and assembled Bryce's selection. Of course, he'd selected the frothiest drink they sold. Bryce was such a boy when compared to Morgan. Morgan seemed more like what a man should be. Rough, yet educated. Tough, but ready to smile and laugh. When she had been with Bryce, she thought he had been a skilled lover, but when she thought of how Morgan's hands looked, how they had felt massaging her shoulders, large and strong and warm, she wondered how much better of a lover he must be. She closed her eyes against the stinging that indicated tears were forming.

She paused before turning back to face Bryce. She handed him the drink.

Bryce put his hand over hers. Honey stared wide-eyed at his hand caressing her fingers. He was going to make her spill again.

*Red wine sloshed over the edge of the glass, running over their fingers like thin blood. Honey, tipsy, giggled.*

*Bryce said nothing, just tossed a cloth napkin at her and stood. "We're leaving. Now." He growled the word* now. *Making it clear to Honey there was no arguing. She forlornly looked at her half-eaten dinner and wondered what she had done this time.*

Honey snatched her hand away from his touch. Away from the bad memories.

"We should go out sometimes," he said. "Talk."

"No," Honey bit the reply out. What had given him the idea that she would want to talk with him? That she would ever welcome his touch again? Maybe Bryce had seen her fighting some emotion. He must have assumed it was over him.

He shot her a glare she used to consider dangerous and maybe a little bit sexy. Now she realized, it was malicious and violent. Honey focused on her breathing.

*It was just a look. He's not going to do anything to you in public.*

"I've got a project just off the Row. I'll be in town more."

Honey rolled her eyes. He had said that last time.

"Probably even more than I anticipate, since the site manager seems to have disappeared. I'll have to be the client's man on the scene, as it were," Bryce sneered.

Did Honey note a hint of satisfaction when he said the site manager was missing? Oh God. Bile rose in her throat. Her ears rang. Was he talking about Morgan? Had something happened to him? Honey blinked rapidly, dragging her focus back to Bryce. "What?"

"I said goodbye, Rachelle." He called out as he left the shop raising his cup in a pseudo salute.

"Damn it." She slammed her fist onto the counter and started crying. Why couldn't Bryce leave her alone?

She missed Morgan. She missed the security he offered. She was mad at herself for having created more of a relationship with him in her mind than what they really had. It made the hurt more hollow. It was just a stupid crush she was having a hard time getting over.

The next day Honey didn't have time to daydream about Morgan. She was too busy to do anything except, take orders, fill orders, and clean up in the lull between orders. She laughed off Lana's offer to get a restraining order to keep Bryce away from the shop. Honey felt as if she had actually overcome her fear of him during the previous day's encounter. Two years of being afraid of Bryce was now over. She had not been reduced to a pile of human jelly after keeping her cool with him. Her breakdown after Bryce left had not been caused by him but by her fear for Morgan. Honey felt exuberant over her control where Bryce was concerned. She felt completely miserable when it came to Morgan.

She counted the number of days since he'd disappeared. Sixteen days. Sixteen days of listening to his voice mail saying he wanted a second chance, and at least nine days of not being able to get a message back to him before she gave up. She had spent the first few days after their date when Morgan failed to return to the coffee shop walking past the site on Wave in hopes of seeing him. After a few days, she stopped walking past the construction site. She figured she had been obvious enough. She'd stopped and watched the workers for minutes at a time. If Morgan was there, he would have seen her. No one looked like Morgan. But no one bothered her or asked what she was doing there. When Seth told her she needed to go home, she felt like she had been going nonstop for hours.

She waved her keys at Seth as she walked out the side

door onto the loading porch. She stepped over and around the wooden palette the morning's paper cups delivery came in on. She sidestepped the coffee grounds recycling bin and nearly tripped over Big Dog's chew toy. She slogged the few blocks up the hill to where she'd parked her car. An instinctive feeling of danger washed over Honey. She glanced over her shoulder and thought she caught a glimpse of a shadow following her. She shook her head. She was tired and paranoid. There wasn't anyone there.

She got in her car and began to drive. A short time later she looked up and realized she had driven home. She just didn't remember doing it.

She jumped nervously when a shadowed figure approached her. She expected to giggle for not recognizing her neighbor.

Honey's breath caught in her throat. "Bryce. What are you doing here?" She panicked. How had he found her? Where could she go? She put her fist to her neck and grasped her talisman. *Forza*. Strength.

"So this is where you live? Rather seedy compared to what you walked away from." Bryce ignored her as he always had. He stepped closer.

"What the hell? Get away from me."

Honey retreated, stumbling as she missed a step. Bryce grabbed her arm. He held on too long and too hard for the move to be considered a gallant move to save her from a tumble. His fingers bit into her skin. She could feel bruises forming.

"Let go of me." She tried to wrench herself out of his grip, but he was stronger.

"You are still beautiful. You should come back to me. I think this time you'll know how to behave. I am in a position of real power now. Real wealth. People do what I say and what I want. I'm the one with control now. I need a woman who looks like you at my side. You should appreciate that I still want you."

"Controlling people through coercion is not power; it's bullying. I said let go," she growled the last words as she stomped on Bryce's foot and twisted.

He stepped back letting go of her arm with a toss, as if to throw her away from him

"Seriously, Rachelle, you are pitiful."

Cooly, as if nothing had happened, Bryce walked away.

Honey stood frozen, watching him until his car drove away.

Numb, she put her key into her front door.

Automatically, she fed Calliope, a small tortoiseshell calico with a white spot on her nose, who eyed her suspiciously. Then Honey collapsed in the middle of her kitchen floor sobbing. She crawled up from the floor sniffing back tears. She needed to do something normal, something that Bryce couldn't ruin. She made a large bowl of cheap salty ramen. Comfort food. It helped that she knew Bryce would hate the instant noodles for not being sophisticated enough for his pallet and for being ridiculously inexpensive.

Honey swirled a fork full of noodles as she sat on her couch. She shoved the fork into her mouth and chewed. She found the TV remote and turned on the set. Honey loved her television set. She had saved up for six months for this particular model. Almost too big for the apartment, it made Honey feel like she was having a theater experience at home. A quick review of the channels proved, yet again, there was nothing she wanted to watch. She hit play on the DVD. There was always something in the player.

Honey let the movie distract her from her reality, distract her from her fears. She mindlessly ate noodles as she watched some scantily-clad science fiction heroine kick alien butt while the love interest and screaming sidekick blew things up. She tried not to focus on what had just happened. Bryce knew where she lived.

∾

The customer in front of Honey complained that she had messed up the pastry order and the coffee tasted burned when Lana said "Morgan." It was unlike Lana to bring up any subject that would cause Honey pain. And Honey knew Lana was aware of how sensitive she was regarding Morgan. She turned away from the grouchy customer to tell Lana she didn't even have time to think about Morgan right now. Another frustrated customer's voice from further back grabbed her attention. She looked down the line. She expected to see customers grousing at each other. She did not expect the vision that took her breath away.

Morgan strode past the waiting tourists, stalking towards her. He was taller than she remembered. His eyes were trained on her face, and when she made eye contact, a large dazzling smile brightened his face. His glowing eyes crinkled ever so slightly at the edges. He had more of a tan than she remembered and his hair was slightly longer and curled behind his ears and along the back of his neck. A hint of stubble covered his jaw, drawing her attention to the dimple in his chin. He wore a leather jacket, not his usual plaid work shirt.

Her pulse raced. "Morgan," she whispered, her mouth too dry to form words.

His name barely left her lips when he wrapped his hands around her face and, never breaking eye contact, kissed her. Honey didn't close her eyes until her brain registered that Morgan's lips were on hers. They were soft and warm. She melted against him. Morgan held her face and savored her lips. Honey stopped thinking and sank into the long and deep kiss. Everyone and the coffee shop stopped existing.

Morgan did not let go of her face when he broke off the kiss. He held Honey and stared at her. He'd missed this face. He had longed to see her face like this, eyes closed, lashes brushing her cheeks, lips swollen from his kiss. He continued to hold her face when her eyes fluttered open. His body roared, wanting to claim his mate more fully.

"I am so sorry. I have been gone for too long, and I had no way to let you know what had happened. All I have are paltry excuses. I have to go away again. But not for long. I didn't stop thinking of you once. I saw your face on my eyelids when I closed them every single night. I came back as soon as I could." He coiled a finger into the tendrils of hair that framed her face. Morgan extracted a business card from the stack on the counter. "I don't want to leave you again, but I really have to go. I will be back in three days. Two days, if at all possible, and I will call you okay?" He held up the card showing Honey he now had a phone number where he could reach her.

Honey nodded. "Okay."

Morgan wrapped his arms around her back, pulling her to him. He kissed her deeply again. "I'll be back, I promise."

As he turned, he finally became aware there were actually other people in the shop. He reached into his back pocket and pulled out his wallet. He removed a hundred dollar bill. "Here." He handed the bill to Honey then added several more bills with it. "This should take care of this gentleman's order, and a few more, all right." Morgan turned toward the disgruntled man, patting him on the back, he said, "Sorry about that, buddy. Enjoy your coffee." Morgan strode out of the shop.

Morgan looked back at Honey. She still glowed.

Morgan was gone. She blinked back confusion. The man at the counter was also gone. An older lady stood there.

"Are you okay, sweetie? That was quite the kiss. Did he really pay for all of our drinks? I'll have a small decaf with a shot of chocolate, and a..." Her voice trailed off in Honey's ears. She touched her lips. Morgan had planted the most amazing kiss of her life on her in front of a shop full of customers. Then he'd whirled away and left again. "Sweetie? Can you focus after that kiss?"

Honey snapped back to full attention and the woman in front of her. "Sorry, that was a bit mind boggling."

"It looked like a real toe curler."

Honey finished her shift in a daze, reliving every nanosecond of watching Morgan walk up to her. She could picture every detail. She could remember every thread on his T-shirt, every stitch on his leather jacket, every faded fold of his jeans, the stylized swirling details on his leather boots. It was amazing how much the brain took in when, at the time, all she had focused on was his face. She relived every sensation of his kiss. The soft feel of his lips, warm and firm pressing against hers. The warmth and strength of his hands holding her face. The feeling of being claimed and comforted and protected. She remembered every nuance of his scent. She realized she had never really had the opportunity to breathe him in before. He smelled wonderful to her, earthy and masculine.

"Lana," Honey said tentatively, Lana hadn't said anything regarding Morgan all afternoon. Honey knew Lana had something to say but wouldn't until the time was right. She had to weigh her feelings over a man who hurt her friend and best employee with her feelings for a man who came in and paid for $160 worth of drinks for strangers. "Lana, if he calls after I go home—"

"I will give him your home number." The fact that she was willing to give out Honey's personal number meant that she leaned towards a favorable opinion of Morgan again.

"Thanks."

Honey spent the last hour of her shift washing dishes and bussing tables. Her mind was not in a place to deal with customers. Honey mooned with a contented grin on her face wiping spirals on a tabletop when Lana called her name.

"Honey. Earth to Honey. Wake up and get the phone!"

Honey grabbed up the towel and carried it with her behind the counter where she retrieved the phone from the cradle.

"Honey!" Morgan's warm voice came through the phone. She could hear his smile through the earpiece. "I need your phone number. I've only got the one for the shop."

Honey gave Morgan her number. "Do you have your phone on you? Let me call you right now"

"Morgan, what's..."

Her cell phone, located in her side pocket, started to vibrate. She picked it up and stared at the front. It was not a number already programmed in.

"Honey, answer your phone. It's me."

Honey put the cell to her ear. "Morgan?"

"Yes, it's me. Hang up the shop phone and keep me on your cell." Honey hung up the shop phone.

"Morgan, where have you been? What's going on?"

"Honey, I can't explain right now, but I need you to believe my leaving wasn't planned. I can tell you all about it when it's over. I know that's a lot to ask since I haven't really shown you any actions that are very trustworthy."

Honey sighed.

"I'm so sorry, Honey. I didn't mean to hurt you, and I know I did. You have every right to hate me right now, but I beg you to give me a second chance. Please."

"Morgan, I... I..."

"Be willing to say my name, sweetheart, and I'll be back as soon as I can."

Honey sighed, "Morgan."

"I'll take you out on a real date when I get back. You decide where." Honey could hear another male voice talking to Morgan in the background, muffled. "Look, Honey, I've got to go again. I'm riding so I can't call. I won't have another break for a while, but I will call you tomorrow, okay."

"I'm here all day. I'll be home after seven."

"Tomorrow I should know how long before I can come back to you." He paused. Honey could hear him saying something to the other person. "Tomorrow night, Honey."

"Okay. Tomorrow night, Morgan."

## 14

M organ sat uncomfortably in the side chair of a cheap motel room. The only place they could find was barely an upgraded roadside motel. The image on the TV flickered and changed as he flipped through the channels. Hundreds of stations available on cable, and the hotel had an odd collection limited to six channels. Cheap motel accommodations, quality hotel prices, but to not have any network news to watch was too much.

He kicked his boots off and really wanted to stretch out on the bed, while he waited for Shane to finish in the shower. If he did, he'd have to sleep in his road-dirt-covered bedding. He thought about calling Honey, but she had sounded exhausted earlier. He didn't want to wake her up if she was asleep.

Shane stepped out of the bathroom, wearing gray sweat pants and toweling off his shoulders.

"Your turn," he said in his low gravely voice. "I'm going to call my contact, so when you get out, I should have a time and place for us in the morning."

Morgan nodded.

"You think this place has pizza delivery?" Shane asked picking through the various advertisements and fliers Housekeeping had arranged on the low dresser, next to a plastic ice bucket and 'sani-wrapped for their protection' plastic cups.

"Get me one if they do. I could handle a large with everything." Morgan closed the door behind him. He should have thought of that while Shane showered. After a long day on the road, thoughts of Honey and how she tasted had distracted him.

He pulled back the grimy shower curtain, turned on the water, and adjusted the temperature. He stepped over the edge of the tub and ducked his head under the low shower head. Hot water ran over his head and down his body. Morgan closed his eyes letting the warm water sluice soap suds off his skin as he lathered his chest. Thoughts of Honey and her lips left him hard. He hadn't intended on kissing her in her workplace, but as soon as he saw her—those wide green eyes, her messy hair, the glowing aura—he had to claim her. He had to let her know his intentions. He had to taste her. He had never kissed her before, a mistake he wouldn't leave any longer.

Honey's lips had been soft and pliant. His hand wrapped around his cock. It throbbed with his want. At first, she had barely accepted his kiss, but then she had started kissing back. His hand ran over his chest, brushing a nipple. It hardened. Their lips moving together. Morgan stroked his length, each motion sharpening the memory of Honey's lips. *Stroke.*

No, he wanted her. Nothing else would satisfy his need. When he kissed her, she had tasted like coffee and raspberries. Morgan's mind began imagining the taste of her skin. She would taste cool and fruity, like a refreshing cocktail on a hot day. Her sweat would be citrusy and he would lick drops of it from between her breasts. Morgan stifled a groan. He could see her lean body in his mind's eye, slender limbs. They would entwine with his so pleasurably.

Morgan let out a ragged sigh. He turned the hot water up, it helped to ease the tension from his shoulders. His body and mind still craved Honey.

A stack of cardboard pizza boxes sat on the table. Shane was gone, and so was the ice bucket. Morgan opened the top two boxes and lifted out two slices of the one loaded with everything. Lust hungry for Honey, he would have to make do with satisfying the needs of his stomach. He lounged on the bed, clean and in sweats, eating while he waited for Shane to return. Shane had left the TV on the local news channel. Morgan tuned it out as he ate.

Shane tossed him a can of cola when he stepped back in the room, ice bucket full of sodas.

"She wants to meet late afternoon at a park on the south side of town. It sounds like she thinks she might be being watched."

"Why outside?"

"Clear line of sight, no recording equipment. There is definitely something going on with the bloodsuckers."

Morgan sucked in air at Shane's terminology. Shane never referred to them as vampires. Too much bad history there.

Their contact was late. She said she would only meet them in person. Morgan sat on a concrete bench facing a pond with a small fountain. He watched Shane circle the pond. The sun hung low in the afternoon sky.

Morgan felt a tickle of unease. Being here felt like a bad idea. This felt like a lot of effort for what potentially was only going to amount to rumor. They had better walk away knowing more than they knew right now, and that was not very much. He knew he shouldn't be sitting and waiting. It made him, literally, a sitting target. Shane, being out in the open, was even more of a target than Morgan. Trees provided enough cover for a sniper, but Morgan suspected if this was a setup, a sniper would most likely set up between the nearby houses. Yes, the meeting venue provided a clear line of sight. But for whom? No, Morgan didn't like this, but it was Shane's call. And Shane said this contact was trustworthy—a friend.

Morgan watched as a slender figure with bright pink hair approached Shane. He pulled her in for an embrace. Together the figures—one petite and lithe, the other broad and hulking—walked towards Morgan. The woman was small and delicate and she wore a low-cut, black shirt. Her skin was pale, and she emphasized her facial features with heavy dark makeup. She wore a black leather choker with a thick silver ring hanging between her breasts which created a stark contrast between her clothing and her skin. Her jeans were ripped at the knees, exposing lace stocking. She looked young, but age was difficult to determine for vampires and their kin. Daywalkers aged much slower than humans.

"Gentlemen," the woman said. "Let us walk while we discuss."

Morgan fell in step next to Shane.

The young woman began talking. "All we have are rumors. But the buzz is that someone pretty big and bad is back. Names keep flying around. But one name, Lazarus, keeps coming up."

"Lazarus is dead," Shane snarled.

"Maybe not," She said. "Vampires don't kill easily. Unless his head was cut off or he burned to ashes, there is always the possibility of coming back. There is a reason they are immortal in legend."

"I thought that's just myth," Morgan added.

"You don't know all our secrets, wolf," she snapped.

Morgan shook his head. "So we have a possible vampire overlord back from the dead. What could that possibly have to do with him wanting me to kill another wolf?"

"Do you not know his history?" she asked.

"I am well aware of the atrocities Lazarus committed against my kind. But what does that have to do with taking out other wolves?"

"Not just any wolf. The head of another family. Correct?" She glanced at Morgan questioningly. "Wolves allied present an overpowering force. That is not necessarily a good thing for my kind. Vampires are used to wanting control over your kind. Lazarus, particularly so. " She stopped and turned to face the men. "I understand your family recently negotiated a truce and agreed to potential future alliances with another family. The merging of two wolf clans could be seen as hostile forces gathering for war."

Morgan scoffed, and tossed his hands up, frustrated. "Why are vampires always so dramatic? It's a fucking business merger not a power play. I think if anyone needed to be concerned, it would be other wolves, not vampires."

She shook her head and rolled her eyes. "Dramatic? You have no idea. Lazarus thrived in chaos. If it is Lazarus, he will go straight for massive disruption. He'll be gathering forces, lining up minions. He left a lot of enemies behind. I don't know anyone who was sad at word of his demise. Most of us—" She looked at Shane. "—would like to forget that part of our lives. I know I would."

"Look," she turned to Morgan. "If they were after you as the next alpha on their list, you can bet they will attempt to recruit another wolf to take you out. Especially since you said no."

"He's not going to find wolves very helpful."

"Shane already told me he's had at least one working for him. If he can find one, he can find more. He'll go after the weak, the disenfranchised. Build their confidence, their self-worth, make them feel powerful, worthy. He'll go after the corruptible first, then the hurt, the angry. He'll build his followers from your castoffs."

She turned her gaze back to Shane, her eyes softened with old memories. "That's how he did it before. That's how Lazarus works."

"So what are you hearing location-wise? Does this guy have a base of operations?" Morgan asked, eager for some solid information.

"Nothing definite. There have always been rumors about him, but the noise is louder, more frequent." She paused and glanced around. "I doubt he's in California. At least, not yet. Too many enemies. He's probably lying low, sending in his spies and flunkies first. Did I understand Shane correctly when he said there is already a human minion?"

Morgan nodded. "A money hungry man with a history of violence towards women. The kind of man who would easily be lured with the promise of wealth and position."

She shook her head. "Damn it! Did he know much about us? Could you tell if he had bite marks? Did he seem eager to be turned? Shit, was he good looking?"

Morgan shook his head. "Maplecourt is clueless, blinded by greed. He didn't have the slightest idea there was anything going on beyond some nasty industrial sabotage and corporate manipulation. But, yeah, he is good looking enough that a vampire might consider turning him."

"Is someone going to take care of that problem?" she asked.

"Are you familiar with Cyan del Fuego?"

She huffed. "The del Fuegos have a certain reputation."

"Well, it looks like he's crossed her company, Cyan Group. We're investigating exactly what that entails. I take it we can trust Cyan to handle the situation once we hand over our findings." Morgan continued.

"You're working with Cyan?" She paused, shifting her gaze between the two men. "That might be the real reason Lazarus's men picked you up. Your wolf pact might merely be a coincidence in timing."

Morgan stopped walking. He hated that he did not know her name. Names had power, and she could be in danger just for talking to them. He understood that. Without a name, Morgan could never divulge who his informant was.

"They wanted me to kill another alpha. How could working for Cyan Group have caused that?"

"Del Fuego is a powerful coven master. He wasn't back in Lazarus's time. He stepped into the hole Lazarus left behind. Some say he created that hole. Lazarus would see Del Fuego as a threat, his first obstacle to regaining strength and glory. Lazarus could very well be going after Del Fuego by targeting his daughter, and you just happened to get caught in the middle. A wolf clan war in their jurisdiction would be a distraction. Take attention away from something more subtle, something that could do more long-term damage."

Shane huffed and stared into the sky. "Great, we have to offer protection to a blo..." He stopped speaking before he finished the word.

"Look, Shane, I understand what you are feeling and why. Remember, I was there. We're not all bad." She rested a small hand against his powerful forearm. "I know you know that. Cyan del Fuego won't need your protection. But if you can become allies with a rival wolf clan, you might also want to seriously consider allying with the Del Fuego coven."

She turned toward the imminent sunset. "Look, I know I didn't give you any answers. I wanted to see you again, remind you that some of us are your friends." She faced Morgan. "I'll keep my ears open and let you know if I hear anything." She turned to face Shane then quickly hugged him before running to an SUV in the parking lot. She gave a small wave before she disappeared into the vehicle.

Morgan stared after her. "I think that left me with more questions than answers. You?"

Shane shrugged. "What's confusing. Wolves good, Del Fuego good, Lazarus bad. It's a start. It might be enough. I've got some digging to do on Lazarus. I would have sworn that bloodsucker was dead."

"We have scattered puzzle pieces, but nothing definite. I'm going to leave it to you to keep moving forward on this. Find out what you can about Lazarus. I want Dante digging harder on Maplecourt. We need to start following up with other families. Make sure there are no loose ends for Lazarus to find. Also, we need to ascertain whether there have been any more attacks on our kind while I was gone."

"What are you going to be doing?" Shane asked.

"I have to get back to Monterey."

"That woman?"

Morgan nodded. "She's important."

"To all of this? Shane asked incredulously. "How?"

"Not to this." Morgan flipped his thumb back toward his chest. "To me."

## 15

Honey sat at one of smaller tables with her purse sitting in front of her. Her hand zipped the gold charm back and forth along the chain around her neck. Morgan said he would pick her up from work. Morgan said to please wait; he would be there. That had been hours ago.

"Honey, why don't you just leave?" Seth suggested after the first hour. "If he shows up, I'll have him call you."

"That's not a bad idea. I can go home and change. Clean up a little and meet him back here. When he comes, tell him I won't be long."

She expected Morgan would call once he realized how late he was, and it would be his turn to wait for her. She anticipated he would be waiting for her when she got back. He wasn't.

So she sat. And got mad. Mad at Morgan for disappearing on her. Mad for him being late. The longer she sat, the angrier she got. Mostly she was mad at herself for letting him jerk her around. She should have stuck with her first assessment of him—bad hair, plaid shirts, construction worker. Screw reading past the first few pages. He was not someone she should be interested in. But, damn it, she couldn't help it. His smile tugged at her heart. And that kiss—

That kiss was something that needed to be explored. Explored with tongues and hands and bodies. That kiss was why Honey sat fuming and waiting.

"I'm out. If that jerk comes in, tell him I left for Mars or something," she growled at Seth as she stormed out.

Honey grumbled curse words as she hiked uphill to where she had parked her car. Street lights flickered on. She hadn't realized exactly how long she had waited for Morgan but, obviously, she had waited far too long. For a brief moment, Honey experienced a pang of guilt, What if he had been in an accident? She shook her head. He deserved any road rash he sustained for not calling her.

Distracted by her anger, Honey had not threaded her car keys through her fingers as she normally would. She stood next to her car door delving deep into her bag. More curse words passed her lips as she rummaged in the dark pit of her purse. "Stupid lights. Can't see a damn— Uhng!"

Honey slammed against the car. Air left her lungs in a rush. Someone pushed hard into her back.

*No! No! Oh shit!* She tried to turn around, cursing whoever had hit her. She was pinned, a large kitchen knife waved around in front of her face. The arm with the hand holding the knife wore a reflective safety-yellow jacket.

Honey closed her eyes. A small *no* escaped her lips. Her attacker was heavy as he leaned into her. She tried hard not to panic. What had the newspaper said? The attacker only robbed people. He hadn't actually raped anyone. A hard knee rammed up between her legs, then pushed her legs apart. She dropped her bag. "You can take my purse. Just let me go."

"Shut up, bitch!" The voice was ragged but higher pitched than she had expected. The hand with the knife left her vision, and she heard the car door open. *Oh crap oh crap oh crap*. The back door wasn't locked. *No, no, no, no, no.*

A hand pulled her hair, jerking her head back. Her face slammed into the car door. She saw stars. Her vision blurred, sound blended into an indistinct dull roar as pain pierced her skull.

She tried to reach for her face.

*Bryce had her arm pinned to her back in a half-nelson. "Never embarrass me in public like that again," he hissed in her ear. Then her face hit the car again. He was livid. She had eaten too fast. Eaten before he took her food away and called her fat. A small belch had escaped her lips. She had giggled. He had not been amused.*

Blood trickled down the side of her face and pooled in her right eye. She tried to blink to clear her vision. The blood was new. She hadn't bled when Bryce had thrown her against his car. No, that was just a bad memory. That was another time, a different car. She didn't know the person abusing her this time.

Her assailant pulled her hair again, dragging her head back at a painful angle. Through her pain-blurred vision, she thought she saw Morgan running towards her. Her attacker shoved her into the backseat of her car. She kicked at him. She had to get away before he got on top of her. She heard a low menacing growl then a hoarse yell.

Honey turned around in the car, glancing out of the door. Her mugger fought against a large brown dog—no, a wolf. Its fangs sank into the man's wrist. When the wolf released his bite, the man grabbed his injured arm and ran.

The wolf turned his gaze to Honey.

She started to push back into the car, scrambling to get away from the animal.

Then it disappeared. Honey slowly stuck her head out of the car, arm reaching to grab the door to pull it shut if she saw the fierce beast. But she didn't. Instead, Morgan crouched by the door.

He held his hand out to her. "Honey, it's safe."

Honey took his hand and let him pull her out of the car beside him. She leaned into his bare chest. Honey opened her mouth to speak, but sobs overwhelmed her. He tugged her into his lap, and she wrapped both arms around him and hung on.

Gently, he lifted her chin to look at her face. "Head wounds tend to bleed worse than they are but, sweetheart, you're going to need stitches."

Honey sniffed. "I'm covered in blood and snot, aren't I?"

Morgan gave a small huff. "Yeah, you are."

"There goes my modeling career." She smiled weakly before dissolving into more tears.

"Shh, shh, it's okay." Morgan soothed her, stroking her back as sobs claimed her again.

Honey's breathing evened out. She sat up slightly to look Morgan in the eyes. "Why are you naked?"

"Yeah, about that..." Morgan began.

"I'm upset and delusional right now, aren't I? I really hit my head hard."

"You're upset. I don't know about delusional. We do need to take you up to the hospital to get that gash stitched up and make sure you don't have a concussion."

"You were over there then there was a big dog-wolf thing over here. Then it was gone, and you're here, and your clothes—" She glanced over his shoulder. "—are back there." She pointed to where Morgan's clothes lay scattered in the street.

"I don't think you're delusional, but you might not want to mention what you're about to see. Can you get up okay?"

Honey nodded then stood, using Morgan and the car door to help pull herself up. When she turned to face Morgan again, she was confronted by the large brown wolf that had bit her attacker.

"Oh, my God!" She recoiled against the car.

The wolf whined and wagged its tail. Honey slowly lowered herself to sit on the back seat. The wolf nuzzled her in the face, licking at her tears.

"Huh?"

The wolf turned and trotted back towards Morgan's clothes. The animal stood over Morgan's clothes. Honey blinked. The animal was gone. Morgan stood pulling his jeans on.

"Morgan?" Honey leaned back in the car, resting her head against the seat back. She could not be seeing what she was seeing. She took deep breaths, trying to regulate her pounding heart and calm her frayed nerves. The attacker had hit her head really hard against the car. She reached up to feel the cut and blood on her forehead. "Well, if this is some unconscious delusion at least I have to head wound to justify it."

Fully dressed, Morgan approached the car and leaned in to check on Honey. "Are you okay?"

"I think you might need to check me into a mental ward."

"You're fine." He picked up her bag and placed it on the seat next to her. "Why don't you rest. We'll call the police from the hospital."

Honey stared at him.

"Keys?"

She dug in her bag, then handed him a handful of keys on an oversized silver hoop.

"May I suggest you not tell anyone what you just saw when we are at the hospital."

Honey nodded. "I don't think they would believe me anyway."

Honey relaxed as best as she could on the emergency room gurney. Morgan sat behind her out of her field of vision. He had held her hand until the nurse came in and shooed him off to the corner so she could "get at her patient." The police were allowed in and asked questions while the numbing agent in Honey's forehead took effect.

Honey gave her report, although she couldn't say much. She had only seen the attacker's forearm and that stupid yellow jacket. Her necklace was missing, but nothing else seemed to have been stolen. She couldn't tell the police the attack triggered a flashback to a time when her ex had beat her. She couldn't tell them about Morgan.

Morgan gave a better statement. He had actually witnessed the attack. He had seen the mugger who looked like a strung-out kid. He appeared to be in his early twenties, of medium height and fair complexion, wearing jeans, a dark knit cap and a weatherproof, safety-yellow jacket with reflector tape. Morgan saw the man grab Honey and push her into the car. That's when a large dog came out of nowhere, jumped the attacker, then ran off again. It all happened in the blink of an eye. Concerned for her safety, he really hadn't paid attention to getting a description of the dog. Just that it had been big and brown, and Morgan considered it to be a hero since it had scared off Honey's attacker. When he reached her immediately after it all happened, she was badly shaken up, and bleeding, so he brought her to the hospital.

Morgan took the card of the investigator then took Honey home.

He had to go out of the way to pick up fast food for dinner.

"I'm not delivering very well on this promise of a better date, am I?" he asked as he handed her the paper bag full of fried food.

She sniffled and groaned. "I'm beginning to equate fast food with bad dates. You'll have to make up for it better next time. At least, they got my grilled chicken right."

"Next time, I'll do better. Promise. How's your head?"

"What head? They gave me some good drugs." Honey laughed. "I'm not going to be happy when they wear off."

She pointed at a spot for him to park in front of her building.

Morgan unlocked the outer door and held it open for Honey.

"It's an old house they converted," Honey said. "I'm in the back." Morgan followed Honey down the short hallway. She took the keys and fumbled with the lock on her door. "My cat Calliope will probably hide once she sees you. She doesn't like people much. That includes me." The door swung inward. Honey stepped in and glanced down. "Hi, baby." She cooed at a cat.

The cat hissed at Morgan as he stepped into the apartment. He closed the door behind him. The cat shot back down the hallway and into the living room before disappearing.

"That's normal," Honey said, a small hitch in her voice

betrayed her inner nervousness. She was obviously still shaken and upset from the attack.

Morgan followed her into the apartment, past the kitchen and into a small living room that comfortably fit a sofa and television. Next to a wall of windows, Honey's books shelves were covered with books and DVDs. Morgan suspected the closed door opposite the kitchen led to either a bedroom or a bathroom. Most likely both, since her home did not look like a studio apartment and nothing indicated that Honey slept in this room.

Honey kicked off her shoes and curled onto the couch. "Can you stay for a bit? Talk to me," she asked. "I don't want to be alone right now."

"Of course. I'll stay as long as you need me to. Can I use your bathroom?"

"Sure." Honey pointed to the closed door. "It's through the bedroom there. Don't mind the mess."

Morgan stepped through the door. The mess of Honey's bedroom made Morgan grin. The room was tidy. Dirty clothes were actually in a woven laundry basket in the bathroom. The only mess Morgan saw was the unmade double bed. The bed looked comfortable though barely big enough to fit him curled up against her. He shook his head. Not tonight. Not in the state Honey's nerves were in. Not with her injured head.

The bathroom was exactly where Honey said it would be. Morgan finished his need of the room, washed his hands, and stepped back into the living room.

Honey sat in the corner of the couch, knees pulled into her chest, hugging herself. She shook like a cornered rabbit. Morgan sat in the opposite corner, afraid to touch her, not certain how she would respond to his touch. She was so beautiful. But the bandage across her forehead reminded him he had failed her, had let her get hurt.

"Honey, I can go. Clearly, I'm making you nervous." She shook like a cornered rabbit. While Morgan tended to not think he had wolf tendencies, her clear display of fright aroused the fierce need to protect her.

"No," she whimpered, shaking her head.

"You sure? If you need me to leave to feel safe, I'll understand."

Tears ran down Honey's cheeks. There had been a slow, but steady trickle from her eyes since Morgan had held her in the street. She swiped at them impatiently. "Stupid, I know. I just can't seem to make them stop." She heaved a deep breath. I actually feel safe with you. I have for a long time. Just... Okay, I'm weirded out. Let me process this. But stay, please."

Morgan nodded.

"You want a drink? Do you have any wine? Will a drink help?"

Honey nodded.

Morgan left the couch and headed to the kitchen. He found a few bottles of wine on the counter. He recognized one of the labels. He smiled at the protective mother wolf looking out from the label at him. Lupercalia Vineyards. This was one of his sister Caro's specialties. He located a wine corker, tugged the cork from the bottle, and filled two wine glasses with dark red liquid. He picked up the two glasses and returned to the living room.

Honey held up a small gold object. "Look. I found my charm. It was caught in my bra."

"I don't think you ever lost your charm. Ohhh... You mean your pendant, right? That's good." Morgan handed her a wine glass. "Here. You have excellent taste in wine. This is one of my favorites."

"The chain is gone, but this is what matters." She showed Morgan the small gold piece, before taking the glass from him. Honey wrapped her hands carefully around the bowl of the glass and began sipping.

She sighed as the tangy liquid slid down the back of her tongue and she swallowed.

"I saw what I saw right?" She asked, glancing up at him, still pulled into herself.

Morgan nodded.

"How?" The question, almost a whisper, her voice small and quiet.

Gently, Morgan eased in behind her, and she curled again his chest. He wrapped an arm protectively around her. Honey didn't protest or flinch from his touch.

"We don't really know. It's genetic. We actually got confirmation about that recently. It's in the DNA, so it is passed from parents to children."

"You can't bite me and turn me into one?"

"No," Morgan chuckled low in his chest. "I'm not infectious."

He felt Honey relax more, apparently comfortable against his chest. "Do you have to turn with the full moon?" Her questions all related back to what she knew from science fiction.

"The moon has no bearing on my abilities. We used to think it was some curse or a gift from the gods. My family claims to be descendants of the Roman gods," Morgan explained between sips of wine.

"Rome, huh? I never really think of wolves when I think of Roman history. But then again, I know less about mythology than I really should. I mean, I know art history, but my focus is really more on contemporary collections. Twentieth century."

"Twentieth century, huh? What's your favorite? I'm going to hazard a guess and say it's not abstract expressionism."

Honey laughed a bit. "No, not abstract expressionism. It's mid-century realism. Actually, Frida Kahlo got me interested. Her self-portraits of pain. It was hip to like her in some of the modeling circles I traveled in. When it came time to find something else to do, I let Frida be my gateway drug into the art world." As Honey spoke, she uncurled her legs and squirmed deeper into Morgan's embrace.

"I'm a crap artist, but I love art. Although I can't draw it myself, I can understand what an artist is trying to say. I can look at a painting and feel what the artist wanted me to feel. I feel their pain, their happiness, their fear, whatever. Some of the greatest paintings ever were done out of desperation and anger. I thought working in a gallery, or a museum would let me connect people to art while I got to maintain my glamorous style, something I thought I couldn't live without. I think I was addicted to fashion." She scoffed. "Look at me now. Dressing up is wearing jeans without holes in them, a clean shirt with buttons, and shoes that aren't sneakers. I no longer have style. And now, I have facial scars."

"The doctor said it will barely leave a mark after it heals. You have a very comfortable style, Honey. One that says you are okay with who you are, and you don't need designer clothes to convince people to like you."

"I'm comfortable? I'm not sure I want to be thought of as comfortable."

"Comfortable is good. It shows you have the confidence to be yourself. It makes people at ease around you. Comfortable means not complicated."

She huffed. "I am very complicated."

"Not complicated does not mean not complex. I would say you are complex. There is a lot about you, Honey, that is very interesting. But you aren't complicated. You don't play games, and you don't bring unnecessary drama."

"I don't know. Tonight seemed pretty dramatic."

"Ah, yes, but that wasn't your drama, was it? That was foisted upon you." He peered at her. "Are you sure you're okay?"

She patted the arm wrapped around her. "Sore. Scared. Shaken up." She sighed. "I'm safe with you. Right?"

"Yes, Honey, you are very safe with me."

"Even though you can do this werewolf thing? That is what I saw, right?"

"Uh huh. We just say wolf. Werewolves have all those other requirements—bites, silver bullets, full moons. I can shift as necessary."

"Do werewolves exist? You know the ones that do have those—" Honey paused. "—requirements."

"Not that we know of. There are other things out there though. They tend to keep themselves pretty well hidden. And I'm sure there are things that I don't know about. Legends and myths come from somewhere. Who's to say that some creatures like that don't exist."

"So you can change whenever you want? And instantly?"

Morgan reached his hand out in front of hers. She watched as his hand shimmered, then began to change shape. Bones shortened and thickened, nails elongated, brown fur appeared. Just as quickly, the process reversed, and Honey was staring again at his long tapering fingers.She placed her hand on his and began petting his fingers. "Does it hurt?"

"It feels like electricity. Currents and tingles. It's not

pain, but it's a sharp feeling." He looked at her. "You are being remarkably calm about all of this."

"I am remarkably drugged up. I'm uncharacteristically calm about everything right now. I think the wine is over-helping. Do it again," she demanded. This time his hand rested on hers. When his hand shifted back, Morgan wrapped his fingers around Honey's and held her.

"Do all of you change like that?"

Morgan hummed, contemplating his answer. "Some faster than others."

"I'm sorry. I'm asking a lot of nosy questions."

"It's okay, Honey. You want to know what that was all about. I like that you want to know more about me and that I can share this part of me with you. It means I don't have to hide anything. No secrets."

"What if I have secrets, Morgan?"

"I suspect that, in time, you will be willing to share them with me. Do you have secrets, Honey?"

"I don't think I have secrets. I don't know, I might. I try not to lie since that's asking for trouble. I don't have to remember who I told what that way. Maybe secrets are like that. I don't have them so I don't have to remember what I'm hiding from whom."

"How about if you find a secret and you think I should know it, you can tell me."

"I can tell you my secrets?"

"You can tell me anything." Morgan's voice lowered with emotion as he spoke into her hair, his lips brushing the back of her head. He released his hold of her hand, and she began tracing around his fingers again.

They sat in comfortable silence for a while. Honey exploring Morgan's hand with her own, Morgan content to hold her.

"Where did you go, Morgan?" Honey asked, breaking the silence.

"I had a meeting in Santa Maria yesterday."

"No, before that. Why were you gone so long?"

Morgan shook his head. "I'm sorry. I had no way of contacting you. My phone was destroyed. I was called out of town for a meeting then something went wrong. I ended up someplace I couldn't get out of."

"Meetings? That almost sounds like keeping secrets. I thought you said no secrets?"

"That's withholding information until I know exactly what's going on. How about when I know what's going on and what happened, I will tell you. Until then, it's speculation and making up answers simply to have answers. Wouldn't you rather have the facts instead?"

"Yeah, facts are good. I thought you decided you didn't like me after that date."

"I like you very much and wanted to ask for a second chance since I botched that evening up royally."

"I thought I had messed things up," Honey confessed. She leaned over and scooped up Calliope. The cat settled into her lap. She picked up the small pendant from the table in front of her and clipped it to the cat's collar. "Keep this for me until I get a new chain."

"That was on me, and I was late this evening. I'll take you out for a real date tomorrow. I'll take you to your favorite restaurant. I'll go get a tie, if I have to."

"No need for a tie. Do you like Indian food? I'd like to go out for Indian, if you wouldn't mind."

"Indian sounds great. You aren't closing?"

"No. Lana switched hours, I open in the mornings now."

"I'll pick you up at work. And this time, don't leave until I'm there."

Honey sighed, "I'll wait for you. I get off early now. So you need to be there before five. You want to watch a movie? I'm still all nerves." Calliope jumped from Honey's lap as she leaned forward and clicked the TV on with the remote. She pressed *play* on the DVD player. The same science fiction movie she had been watching the night before began playing. Blue aliens fought for the preservation of their home world against hostile invading forces.

"Are these the blue aliens you told me were so hot?"

"Totally hot. You remembered?"

"And shapeshifters are sexy and scary."

"Yeah," Honey sighed. "And strong and protective and safe."

Honey fell asleep leaning against Morgan, halfway through the movie. Morgan let her sleep until the epic ended. She felt warm and soft as she rested against him. She fit perfectly in his arms. Morgan could hold her like this forever, but she needed proper rest. As much as he wanted to hold her all night, she really should be in her own bed.

He shifted his weight and picked her up as he stood. He toed open the door to her bedroom and began gently laying her on top of the spread.

Honey's eyes blinked open. She rested a hand on Morgan's strong forearm. "Would you mind crashing on my couch tonight? I would feel better knowing you're out there." She reached behind her, pulled a pillow to her chest and handed it to Morgan. "There are blankets in the trunk I use for a coffee table."

"Of course, I'll stay." Morgan leaned forward and kissed Honey on the top of her head, careful to avoid her battered forehead. "Sleep well. You're safe."

## 16

---

Honey relaxed in the overstuffed chair at the coffee shop, deep in conversation with Finney.

"Morgan!" Finney called out. "I haven't seen you around here for a while."

Her breath caught in her chest as their eyes met. Morgan, the man who wore work pants, a plaid shirt, and had hid his face under a scraggly beard the first time she met him, took her breath away. He still wore the plaid Honey had a hard time seeing past, but there were changes now. Under the flannel shirt, open like a jacket, he wore a form-fitting T-shirt that displayed his defined pecs. The cargo pants were gone. Now he wore jeans that showed off just how long his legs really were. His shaggy hair had grown into long curls that brushed his collar, and his chiseled jaw line and square chin were covered in a delectable even growth of stubble that made him appear sexy and fierce.

"Finney," Morgan reached out a hand to shake Finney's in greeting. "Yeah, I was gone for a couple of weeks. Good to see you again." He turned to Honey and held his hands up in a presentation gesture. "I am on time."

Honey giggled, color tinging her cheeks pink in a slight blush. "Yes, you are. Finally." She stood and slung her purse over her shoulder. "See ya' later, Finney." She grabbed Morgan's hand.

As they turned to leave, Finney pointed and asked "You two?"

Honey nodded.

"Lucky girl," Finney muttered not too quietly as they left.

"I need to feed Calliope. Mind if I drive?" Honey felt giddy in Morgan's presence. It felt as if gravity had forgotten about her. Last night he'd saved her and comforted her. Tonight she planned for a repeat of that kiss that burned her soul—and possibly more.

Honey parked across the street from her building. A small moving van blocked her normal spot.

"I have to take care of the litter box too. Want to come in?" she asked, gathering her belongings to get out of the car.

"Sure." Morgan followed her across the street.

They stepped through the outer door into the entry hall. Honey stopped to retrieve her mail.

She saw him looking at the lock. "What's up?"

He pointed at the paint chipped around the latch, exposing wood. "Honey, are these scratches new? Where they here before?"

"I don't think so. I don't remember the door looking like that."

"Hmm." Morgan pushed at the door into the building with his finger. The door swung open. He ran his finger over the latch. Honey saw electrical tape covering the catch.

Holding one hand, out he said, "Give me your keys."

She placed them in his palm.

Morgan stepped into the hallway. He stopped at the door to the front apartment. Honey watched as he ran his hands around the seam where door met jam. He knocked then tested the handle. The door was safely locked. Honey's door, however, did not appear to be in the same condition. From where she stood in the hall, she could see the door to her apartment stood open.

Honey started to step quickly around Morgan. He caught her with an arm around her waist. "Stay behind me."

Morgan walked slowly, stepping carefully as he approached Honey's door. He stopped outside the door, listening for any sound that might come from the apartment. He gently eased the door open further.

Honey started as a horse-headed figure passed her large-screen TV through the back window to a pair of arms reaching in. "No!"

Surprised, the burglars dropped the television. Honey watched as it slid, in slow motion, out the window and crashed to the ground, breaking the window on its way out. The thief who had been in her living room jumped out the broken window.

Morgan turned and bolted out the front door.

Honey ran to the window and looked out in shock, looking down at her destroyed TV lying in shattered pieces on the ground below her. "My TV!" Honey yelled, her voice full of disbelief.

Morgan returned. "I didn't catch them. They must have run behind or into another building. I thought they might have taken off in that moving van, but it's still there."

"Oh my God! Calliope!" She frantically looked around for the small cat.

Morgan helped in the search for the cat. "Where does she normally hide?"

"Behind that." Honey pointed to a shelf unit that had been knocked over.

Honey's apartment hadn't merely been burgled, it had been trashed. Shelves knocked out of place. Books and DVDs littered the floor. Her TV stand had been upended. Couch cushions were strewn on the floor. The kitchen had been equally destroyed.

"You keep looking. I'll call the police." Morgan pulled the detective's card from his wallet and dialed the number.

While Morgan described the situation to the police, Honey located Calliope under her bed. The cat was safe and still inside. Honey left Calliope to cower on her own. Attempting to hold and snuggle the cat could result in a set of claw marks down her arm, and that was on a good day. It was safer for Honey to let the cat be. Morgan stepped into her room to tell her the police were on their way, and to not pick anything up for the moment. They wanted her to start making a list of what had been taken. Honey sat, despondent, her normally tidy home had been completely ransacked.

"How am I even supposed to know what's missing in this mess?"

Morgan sat down next to her, and put an arm around her shoulder.

They sat like that until the door buzzer sounded.

Morgan got up then held out a hand to help Honey up. Hand in hand they walked to the door.

"Miss Gould?" A uniformed police officer asked, pushing on the door to Honey's apartment. "Honey Gould? Like golden hu—"

"Now's not the time for that," Morgan growled, cutting off the officer's commentary on her name.

"Yeah. Come on in." Honey reached the door as the officer and the detective from the previous night entered.

"You're having a string of bad luck, aren't you?" the detective said.

The police poked around the apartment, asking questions. Morgan pointed out that the inner front door had been taped open.

Honey stood in the middle of her apartment wiping tears from her cheeks. She told the detective everything as it had happened. Morgan checking the other apartment's door after he noticed the front was unlocked. Her door being open. The guy in her living room wearing one of those horse head masks. Everything from watching her TV fall out the window to locating her scared cat under her bed. It felt like she answered the same questions over and over again. No, she did not yet have a list of what was missing. How would she know in this mess? The obvious things missing were the DVD player and the TV. No, she didn't have expensive jewelry hiding in the bedroom. No, there was no reason to suspect that she would have been targeted. Anyone who knew her knew she had nothing worth stealing.

After what felt like hours, the police left. Honey stood, numbly looking around.

Morgan put the cushions back on the sofa, and guided her to sit. He knelt in front of her, "Honey, you need to call the landlord and let them know what happened. Okay?"

She nodded.

"Aarrggg." She covered her face with her hands and yelled, "This is so fucked!" She looked up at Morgan still standing in front of her. "And I thought last night was a bad dream. I just want to go on a nice date with you. Is that too much to ask?"

Morgan gave her a small pained grin. "I'm sorry. Does that Indian place of yours do take out? We can put in an order and eat here while we straighten up."

Honey sighed. "That sounds like a good idea, but the Chinese place delivers. How 'bout that instead?"

"Sounds great." Morgan stood and holding out a hand, he helped Honey up. "What's the number? I'll order. You call the landlord."

By the time the restaurant delivered their dinner, the landlord, a middle-aged woman dressed in expensive clothes and jewelry had arrived. The woman kept covering her mouth with long lacquered nails and fingers bedecked in rings as she took in the state of Honey's apartment. The bigger pieces that had been knocked over had been righted by this time, but smaller objects were still strewn all over the floor.

"I just don't know who can come out this late to fix these things." The landlord said as she looked at the damaged door lock and broken window. "Emergency locksmiths cost so much."

"I have a buddy from my job site who can come out and board up that window and bring a new lock for the door. The lock on the front door didn't look like it needs replacing, but I'll have him take a look. If it does, you'll want to get a locksmith in to make sure it's installed properly. And you'll want new keys for everyone in the building."

"Just send me the receipts, and I'll reimburse you. I'll find someone in the morning who can take care of that broken window."

Morgan spoke on the phone again as the landlord left,

assuring Honey that she would make sure everything was fixed.

Mentally exhausted, Honey slumped onto her couch. She picked up a Chinese food carton, a pair of chopsticks, and began eating noodles straight from the box. She stared into the empty space that had been occupied by her TV. She sighed. She faced hours of cleaning.

"Okay, Jim is bringing by a board for that window and a new door lock and some tools."

Honey nodded.

"We'll get the repairs done tonight, so you'll be able to lock up and be safe."

"Will you stay?" Honey asked pleadingly.

"Of course. I'll stay as long as you need me to."

Morgan sat, picking up another to-go container. He picked up a fork and began eating straight from the carton, as Honey did. Honey set the noodles down and selected another container. They ate dinner directly from the cartons, changing each time they wanted to eat something else.

Morgan's phone rang. He left Honey momentarily to let Jim in. Morgan helped him nail a plywood board to the window then replace Honey's front door lock. While the men worked, Honey cleaned and added missing items to her list.

"Woo hoo!" she called out in delight when she found her laptop. The thieves had not noticed her computer bag. Her MP3 player was safe too. Nothing from her bedroom was missing. She didn't have expensive jewelry, but she had a few pairs of Louboutin shoes worth hundreds of dollars. She figured the thieves began trashing the place when they couldn't find much worth stealing. Still, her TV was gone, and it would be almost a year before she could afford to buy another one of the same size. With her financial situation, it would be a few months before she could afford to purchase a new one at all. Honey finished straightening in her bedroom.

"I'm beat," she announced. "I don't think I can do anymore tonight. I'm gonna crash."

"Sure. I'll just let myself out when I'm finished in here." Morgan said, sliding books back onto a shelf.

"You said you could stay again tonight. I'd really be more comfortable knowing you're here. I don't want to think about those guys coming back. If I'm alone, I know I will."

"I'll stay."

"Thank you." She turned and closed her door.

Morgan awoke with a small warm weight on his chest. Calliope slept curled into a tight coil on top of his chest. He looked at her collar, the charm Honey had clipped to it for safe keeping was gone. He placed a hand on the cat, then slowly sat up, letting the now-awake cat jump to the floor. Honey emerged from her room. Her typically messy hair was now a riot of curls, frizz, and stray parts sticking out in every direction. She was beautiful, bed-head and bandaged forehead notwithstanding. His desire to wake next to her and see her all bed-rumpled looking up at him made him hard.

"Good morning." Her voice was low and groggy with sleep. Morgan watched as she shuffled to the kitchen. The refrigerator door opened then closed. Honey cussed, then the door opened and closed again.

Honey stood in the middle of her living room, fighting back tears. "I have to go in and open. I have no food here. I was going to make a quick cup of coffee but, apparently, the coffeemaker is gone also."

"Do you have to go in?" Morgan asked.

"At least, to open. I'll call Lana and see if I can get off early. I have too much to do here still. But I really can't afford to miss work, especially now that I have to replace all this stuff."

"Don't you have renter's insurance?" Morgan asked.

"Nope." Honey shook her head sadly. "That's money I don't have."

"I don't have to be on the site today, so why don't I stay here for you while you go to work. If you can't get off, then I'm here for when the window gets fixed. And I can keep cleaning."

Honey glanced mournfully at Morgan, "You'd do that for me?"

"I will do that for you."

The café was slammed with business. Honey barely had time to stop and text Morgan that she would be stuck at work until her shift was over. She knew Morgan would put her kitchen back together just fine, but she was worried he would be bored being at her apartment all day. Lana ran the register while Honey filled orders and Joyce maintained the seating area, keeping it clean and well stocked. They were a fine oiled machine for coffee and customer service. Honey leaned over and plated one of Lana's famous lemon bars. Drink and treat were placed on the counter under the "pick order up here" sign, Honey called out a name.

She had her back to the customers, taking care of another drink order when she heard her name.

"Honey," Morgan's deep voice rolled over her like a crashing wave. The instant thrill it gave her made Honey realize she had fallen for this guy. Fallen hard.

"Morgan!" she called out over her shoulder. "You're here. Is everything okay? Why are you here?" Concern replaced her thrill of talking to him.

"Everything is fine. I walked down to pick up my bike. I know you said you were busy, but I wanted to say hi anyway."

"Hi," she said then smiled.

"Hi ya', Morgaaan," Lana leaned over, interjecting herself in their conversation.

"Hi, Lana," he replied, chuckling. He turned back to Honey.

"I finished your bookshelves and have been avoiding the kitchen. I'll work on that when I get back. Your landlady stopped by to see how things were. She said the window guys should be there this afternoon." He raised his eyebrows. "I'll see you when you get home?"

"Yeah." Honey couldn't think. *When you get home* sounded so warm and wonderful coming from his lips.

She paused to watch him leave before finishing the order she had been working on.

"The flirt is strong in that one," Lana said.

"You like him again?" asked Honey.

"I've always liked him. I was mad at him for hurting you but, clearly, you two have worked that out. And I am grateful for him being there to stop the mugger and for helping you out with the break-in."

"Thanks." Honey blushed. Lana's opinion meant a lot to Honey. Having Lana like Morgan made Honey think she was on the right track.

The onslaught of customers did not ease as the day

progressed. Honey was running the register when a cold chill ran down her spine. Bryce Maplecourt strode into The Corner as if he owned the place. Joyce had already gone home, and Lana was across the shop. If Honey called out to her, she would just be drawing Bryce's attention. It was best to breathe deep and gird her loins.

"Hello, Rachelle." His voice felt like squeaking chalk on a blackboard. How had she ever considered it sexy?

"What would you like, Bryce?" Honey kept her tone as flat as possible, not giving away any of the panic she felt.

"A smile for starters." Bryce dragged out the words, something he did when he thought he was being charming. He wasn't charming.

"No."

"The offer to take you back still stands. You could live in the luxury you belong in, the style you were once used to." Bryce smirked. "I have a new large screen TV I think you might like."

Honey noticed Bryce's hands were covered in fine scratches. Could Bryce have been involved with her break-in? She stared blankly at him. *Show no emotion. Show no emotion*, she repeated to herself.

"You really should be more polite, or I will insist on speaking to the owner about your behavior."

Lana sidled up next to Bryce. "Can I help you?" Her purr made Bryce noticeably uncomfortable. Honey pursed her lips together to keep from smiling. Lana could be a trickster and she had targeted Bryce.

"I doubt it," Bryce sneered. "Are you another ineffectual employee here? Why don't you—" He wiggled his fingers in a walking-away motion. "—go get your manager or the owner."

"Sure thing," Lana said in a singsong voice She rolled

her head, keeping her eyes on Bryce as she turned. She took one step away, turned around, and took one step back. Her voice dropped as she asked, "Can I help you?"

Honey bit her lip to keep herself from sniggering at Lana's antics.

"Seriously are you all brain damaged? I told you to go get your boss."

Lana didn't budge, all teasing gone from her demeanor. "That would be me. You are going to stop harassing my employee." Lana stepped around behind the counter, nodding to Honey to get out of the way.

Honey didn't need to be told twice, she left for the office.

Honey pushed the button above her mailbox. Morgan had her keys for the day, so she needed to be buzzed into her own apartment. The buzzer sounded, and she pushed open the door. Morgan stood in the hall just outside of the apartment, a large grin on his face.

"Welcome home."

"Hi, Morgan." Honey sighed. It had been a long tiring day and that was the most wonderful thing she had heard all day. Morgan saying *home* to her. It felt right. Something smelled wonderful coming from her kitchen too. "Did you cook?"

She stepped into her apartment and froze.

"Well, go on in," Morgan said, stepping in behind her.

"Morgan, how?" Honey walked into her living room, dropping her purse on the floor next to the couch. Sitting on top of the TV stand was a new, large-screen television of a slightly better make and model than the one she had had. She walked around it in disbelief. Cables connected a new DVD player. A small stack of new, unopened DVDs sat on the stand in front of the player. "Oh, wow, this is amazing." She glanced up at Morgan, a large toothy grin spread across his face.

"I took care of a few extra things while I was here today," Morgan explained.

"How can you afford this?" She shook her head. "Never mind, I will pay you back. I promise. It's going to take me a while, but I will."

"It's a gift, Honey. You don't have to pay me back."

"No, Morgan. That's an expensive TV. I remember from when I got mine. I'll pay you back. And the DVD player too."

"No, really. It's okay. You don't have to pay me back."

"I insist. Bryce would do things like buy me expensive gifts then threaten to take them back. I don't want to feel like that could happen here."

"I'm not Bryce," Morgan said, his voice low.

Honey turned to him. "I know you aren't, and no offense, really, but I need to pay for this or I can't accept it." Honey swallowed. "He came in the shop today."

Morgan stopped moving, his eyes narrowed at her comment. "Why? What did he want?" His voice was a growl. "There's no reason for him to be in town. He's not needed at the job site."

"I don't know, but he said stuff about taking me back and how he's now got a big screen TV. Almost makes me wonder..."

"If he had anything to do with your burglary." Morgan finished the thought.

"Yeah but he's just..." Honey began.

"No." Morgan bit. "He's arrogant, volatile, and stupid. That's a dangerous combination. Why is he even in town?"

"Oh, he probably thinks he's some kind of hero for the client. Last time he said something about being man-on-the-scene because someone was missing." Honey gasped, covering her mouth in realization. "That was you!"

Morgan nodded, his expression grave. "Maplecourt is a number cruncher. There is no reason for him to be at my job site. Look, Honey, I don't want you talking to him. Just walk away. Never let yourself be alone with him."

"That's not going to be a problem. Lana told him his money is not welcome at The Corner and to not come back."

"I knew I liked Lana for a reason." Morgan held out the stack of new DVDs. "Maybe this will cheer you up. I noticed the movie we watched the other night was missing, so I got you a new one. Plus some other movies that seemed to be missing from your collection."

Honey flipped through the stack of movies. She held one of the DVDs up. It featured a scantily clad woman bedecked with firearms being chased by a zombie horde. "I've been meaning to get this one—" She held up another DVD, "—and this one. How did you know?"

"I sorted and organized your entire DVD collection this morning. Based on what you had here, I figured there were a few missing. Like you had all of the Evil Zombie Wars except the most recent one. Reason and deduction." Morgan tapped his temple.

"Thanks, Sherlock. But really this is too much." She indicated the TV. Inwardly, she loved it. She was thrilled to have a replacement television so quickly, but the cost of it and figuring how to pay Morgan back twenty dollars at a time made her stomach twist into knots.

Morgan grinned at her. "Hey, come see the kitchen. That

took a while, but I think you'll find everything in a logical place."

Honey stopped in the kitchen doorway. A brand new, cobalt blue, KitchenAid mixer sat on the counter next to a new Keurig single-serve coffee maker.

She turned to face him. "Morgan, you didn't." He stepped in behind her. She had to tilt her head to look into his eyes. It wouldn't take much to lift up on the toes and kiss him. "I will pay you back for everything." Her voice almost a whisper. "I promise."

"Okay, Honey, I'll let you pay me back." His smile dazzled her. "But not for the movies." He dipped his face closer to hers and held up a small box. "And not for this."

Honey looked at him quizzically. She slowly opened the box, uncertain what to expect.

"I couldn't find your pendant this morning. It wasn't on the cat when I woke up."

She tipped the contents of the box into her hand. A thin gold chain dangled from Honey's fingers. A small, round, gold pendant hung from the chain. Honey placed the pendant in her palm. A wolf paw print was etched into one side. She flipped it over and saw engraved on the back *Protetta.*

"It means protected. It was the best I could do in the limited time I had."

Tears stung Honey's eyes.

Morgan took the chain from her and clasped it around her neck. "We can work out a payment plan over dinner that will make you happy and not eat up your whole paycheck. The movies and the necklace are a gift."

"Hmmm, dinner. Is that what I smell?" She stepped away quickly, suddenly shy. She wanted to kiss him, yet she didn't want him to think her desire was only in response to his gifts.

"No." Morgan chuckled. He showed her the small pot where he had been simmering cinnamon. "It's a trick my mother taught me. She said it makes coming home more welcoming. I wanted you to feel comfortable in here after what happened."

"It worked." She smiled. "I think I might like your mother, Morgan."

Morgan's smile dimmed in brightness. "She would have like you. She died about twelve years ago."

"I'm so sorry, Morgan." Honey felt like a fool. She hadn't known.

"It's all right. She was a remarkable woman. My sister Carol is very much like her. I'm sure you'll like her when you meet her." He stepped out of the kitchen, directing Honey to follow. "Now, dinner. I believe I owe you a nice meal out at an Indian restaurant. Shall we?"

## 17

Honey felt secure and comfortable in Morgan's warm embrace. But it felt too platonic. The past few nights had been entirely too stressful, and she was more than happy he had been with her to help her cope. But now that everything had calmed down and they were watching TV, it was...well...*too* calm. He was being a perfect gentleman. Not a stray touch, not a lean too close. The only reason his arm wrapped around her shoulder now was because she had placed it there.

The movie did not engage her mentally-exhausted mind. This was not what she wanted to be doing. She absentmindedly played with her new pendant. "I'm gonna go to bed." She pushed up off the couch. "Can you stay? I feel safer with you here."

"Of course."

She heard him shift on the couch, ready for a long-term lounge. Honey closed the bedroom door behind her. She looked at her bed, then she glared at the door. Yes, she felt safer with Morgan here, but he wasn't in here with her. He sat out there on the couch. She opened the door "Morgan? Do you like me?"

He pivoted his head to look at her "Yes, Honey, I do like you."

She pulled her shirt off over her head, revealing the lacy red bra she had been wearing just for him. Last night it had been a blue set. She wasn't going to let another night go by without her sexy underwear serving its purpose. She really didn't want her bikini wax to go to waste either. "Then what are you doing on the couch?" She turned and took three steps into her room and turned to the door. She heard a thump and a step then Morgan filled the door.

She looked at him. His expression was unreadable. His eyes appeared to glow amber. The nerves vibrated in her lower abdomen then spread across her skin giving her a brief flutter of excitement.

Morgan took one long stride then wrapped her in his arms. His mouth claimed hers in a possessive kiss. His arms crushed her against his chest. She shifted her arms so that she could wind them around him. With one hand on the back of her neck, he slid the other to cup her butt. He lifted her and she wrapped her legs around him. Honey wound her arms around Morgan's head, consuming his kisses and hungrily pressing against him.

He backed up and sat on the edge of the bed. Honey molded herself around him, but she could feel his balance was off. She broke the kiss and stood up, her eyes locked with his. He lightly stroked his fingertips across the swell of her breasts. His fingers were rough from labor and so hot her skin felt as if he lit her on fire. She dropped her jeans exposing matching red panties with lace panels and straddled his lap. Morgan drew in his breath with an appreciative hiss. He folded her into his embrace and gathered her to him. His lips sought her out. He unhooked her bra and she pulled it off without breaking their kiss. With one hand on her back, the other found her bare breasts. His fingers instantly going to a nipple, rolling it between his fingers. Honey lifted on her knees and rocked her hips as Morgan tugged on her nipple and sucked on her tongue. His lips left hers and he scraped his teeth along her chin. He trailed kisses down her neck and along her collarbone. His mouth found her breast. He kissed and licked and teased her flesh.

Honey let out a groan of satisfaction. This is what she had been longing for ever since she had fallen for him, ever since that kiss. Morgan scooped a hand between her and the thin fabric of her panties, caressing her ass. His hand moved and he ran fingers over the thin fabric covering her sex. She inhaled sharply. His thumb drew circles around her sensitive peak. Honey grasped his shoulders for support and rocked against his hand. He continued to tease her breasts with his tongue. Moving the thin fabric to the side, his fingers caressed her entrance, already wet with desire. She moaned with longing as he slowly slid two long fingers into her. She lifted slightly on her knees before sinking down onto his hand. She grabbed his hair tilting his head back so she could find his mouth with hers.

Morgan pumped with his fingers, and Honey ground her hips in time to his rhythmic massage. She sucked on his tongue, trying to take as much of him into her as she could. Honey felt on fire. Morgan's touch burned, it was so hot, but she wanted more, she needed him touching her. Her soft moans began coming in rhythmic gasps as she reached her climax. She clamped down on Morgan's fingers with internal convulsions. She slowed her thrusts as her internal muscles took over, all thought beyond getting Morgan inside of her gone.

Agonizingly slow, with Honey vibrating with erotic shivers, Morgan slid his fingers from her. She rolled to the side so she lay on the bed. She pulled the sex-soaked panties off, flinging them away from her.

Honey pushed herself back and away from the edge of the bed, so that her head rested against the pillows against the wall. She panted. She needed more. She needed Morgan inside of her. "I need you." Her voice was husky with want and need.

He stood. In hurried motions, he kicked off his boots and unbuttoned his shirt simultaneously.

In one fluid sweep, he removed his jeans and shorts.

Honey was breathless with desire. Seeing Morgan aroused for the first time was as thrilling as his kisses. His arms bulged with muscle. His chest was broad, pectoral muscles visible under a covering of curling, black, chest hair —hair that tapered down below his navel to spread thick again around his manhood. His narrow waist rippled with perfectly defined abs. His legs were long, and his thighs thick and strong. Honey took it all in savoring his erection last. Like him, it was long and appeared strong, as if it too bulged with muscle.

And it was trained on her like a homing arrow.

Morgan searched his jeans pockets. He pulled out a single foil square from his wallet.

"Fuck!"

"That's the point, Morgan. I need you to fuck me. Now."

He looked up at her, "I only have one condom."

She practically cried with need. "Well, hurry up and put it on. We can get more later."

Morgan rolled the condom down his length then crawled on the bed towards her.

Honey grabbed at him. He couldn't come close fast enough.

When he was above her, she wrapped her legs around his back pulling her hips up to his. His tip teased her folds, swollen with need. Without any more preamble, Morgan drove into her. Honey gasped loudly and joyously. Her frenzied need of him pushed him to the edge of his control. Morgan consciously slowed his rhythm. Purposefully stopping to focus on her breasts again, sucking and laving her nipples.

Morgan slowly pushed into her and held his hips against her. Honey frantic with need continued to rock against him. "Why did you stop?" she panted.

"One condom," he said, pushing up on his arms to gaze down at her. She ran her hands down his chest and stomach to where they were joined. She toyed with the curling hairs about his shaft. Slowly, he pulled back. She stroked the sides of his thick anatomy as he unsheathed partially. Morgan growled deep in his throat. "Want to make this last. That's not going to happen if you do that."

Honey smiled wickedly at him then moved her fingers back up his chest. Morgan drove back into her and began sliding in and out with a slow tantalizing rhythm.

Honey gave up trying to focus and grabbed his arms as she came around him again. Her spasms were too much for Morgan to handle. His hips moved faster, replacing the slow pace with a hurried pounding. His own orgasm burst forth. Together they moaned in ecstatic bliss.

After a few moments to catch his breath, Morgan rolled onto his back, bringing Honey with him so she lay across his chest.

She traced her fingers across his strong jaw and teased his lips.

"What took you so long to come to me?"

"What do you mean?" He stroked his fingers up and down her spine.

"You've spent the last two night holding me and sleeping on my couch without making one single move, barely even a hug."

"I didn't want to take advantage of you. You needed compassion, not passion."

"And tonight?"

"I was clearly being a fool. I am so glad you set me straight." He wrapped a curl of her hair around his finger. "I've wanted to touch you for so long."

"I'm so glad you got the hint."

Morgan gathered her close for a kiss. It was gentle and giving, not like the all-consuming kisses they'd shared during their lovemaking.

Honey, spent, laid her head against Morgan. She felt the rise and fall of his chest as his breathing calmed. Comfort and contentment lulled Honey to sleep.

Morgan sat on the edge of the bed, his jeans were around his waist but not yet buttoned. He bent over to tie his work boots.

Honey groggily draped across his back. "You aren't leaving, are you? I thought you said you could stay." There was a touch of hurt in her voice.

Morgan picked up her hand and kissed her palm before turning to face her. He brushed the hair from her face "Condoms. I'm going out for condoms. Now that I've had you, I need more." He leaned down and claimed her mouth. The kiss was full of need and desire.

"There's a 7-11 on Lighthouse. My keys are on the hook. Don't keep me waiting." she sighed, "You've given me ideas."

Morgan leaned in for another prolonged kiss then left.

Honey wanted to throw the alarm clock across the room when it startled them awake the next morning, but she couldn't reach it to smash it into silence. Morgan blindly hit at the clock until the annoying jangling stopped. She and Morgan had gotten very little sleep the night before. She started to roll out of bed. Morgan threw a strong arm over her and dragged her back against his chest. He began nuzzling her neck. "Where do you think you are going?"

"You know—work. I have to open." She squirmed trying to escape his hold.

"Keep moving like that and you won't be going anywhere for a while."

Honey pushed her hips back and ground her ass into Morgan's leg. "Promise?"

Morgan flipped her over and found her mouth with his. His tongue plunged between her lips, seeking to bury as much of him in her as he could. He knocked the alarm clock off the bedside table in his blind search for a foil pack.

"Damn." He broke the kiss and leaned over the side of the bed. The paperboard box of condoms had been shredded in last night's hurry to access the contents. Foil wrappers were strewn everywhere. Some were open, others had been tossed aside for not opening fast enough. Morgan found one, ripped it open with his teeth. In one swift motion, he sheathed himself then buried his cock to its hilt in Honey. She gasped with the suddenness of it but physically was more than ready to accept him.

Once Morgan started touching Honey, she felt like a drug addict craving her next fix. She had to have all of him at once. An entire night of Morgan and she still felt frantic with first-time need. Honey rocked against Morgan as he pounded into her. This morning wasn't about touching and exploring so much as confirming they needed each other. Morgan's orgasm seized his actions first. He stopped buried deep within Honey. She continued to pump against him as he held against her. Her orgasm followed shortly thereafter, clenching down on Morgan and making her head spin.

"Oh, wow. I am not going to be able to function today." Honey rolled out of bed. Morgan collapsed across the space she abandoned. He groaned.

"Don't you have to go to work?"

"Yeah, but they don't expect me until later." Morgan made himself comfortable against the pillows.

Honey squinted in mock anger at him "Bastard." Morgan grinned, exposing all of his perfect white teeth. They gleamed against his tanned face.

"You can stay, but you're buying me lunch later."

Her legs wobbled under her as she made her way to the shower.

"Honey! Honey, Did you hear me? You have a call. Someone wants to ask about gallery space."

Honey blinked. Joyce's friendly face swam into view.

"Oh, right, phone. Thanks."

Honey couldn't focus. Her mind kept wandering back to the hours of bliss she'd spent in Morgan's arms the night before.

She hung up the phone then stared at it. She had no

idea what she had just agreed to. Someone wanted to show her their work, hoping for a gallery showing. Honey couldn't remember the artist's name or even when she said she could meet them. She shook her head. They would show up when they showed up. She would have to wing it.

"Where is your head today, kiddo?" Joyce asked.

"In heaven," Honey's ability to focus only lasted seconds before her eyes hazed out of focus, and she began sighing contentedly to herself.

"Oh, yeah? Heaven? Heaven's name wouldn't happen to be Morgan, would it?" Joyce asked.

"Yes, it would."

"I'm glad things are going well for you. I take it he is as skilled as he is good-looking." Joyce chuckled

"A lady never kisses and tells." Honey chided, her fingers wrapped around her pendant, the pendant Morgan had given her.

"You aren't a lady, and your blush tells all. It's okay. It's kind of cute. You are *so* smitten." The bell over the door chimed. Joyce turned to see Morgan walk in. She turned back to see Honey, her eyes shining as she gazed at him. "You can't hear me anyway. Just don't make me hose you two down."

Honey turned her attention back to Joyce, "Excuse me?"

"Go take a break! Geez." Joyce had been right. As soon as Honey saw Morgan, she couldn't hear the world around her.

"Thanks!" Honey ripped off her apron, slipped her hand into Morgan's, and was out the door before Joyce could respond.

"How's work today?" Morgan asked.

Honey noticed he hadn't dressed in work clothes today. "You have made me stupid. I can't think straight. All I can think about is you."

Morgan stopped and pulled Honey into his embrace and off the sidewalk. "All I can think about is you too and kissing you again."

His lips softly slanted against hers. A sweet kiss, tentative, tasting. Honey responded, opening her mouth, slipping her tongue between his lips. The kiss deepened, and they were lost in their embrace.

Morgan broke the kiss and looked into Honey's green eyes. He was lost, and he knew it. His heart pounded in his chest. He wanted to possess her completely now that he had claimed her, yet he knew he had to proceed carefully so not to frighten her off. Too overbearing and Honey could interpret his actions as the opening gambit of an abuser. Yes, he wanted Honey all to himself but never at the expense of her mental wellbeing.

Morgan stroked her cheek with his thumb.

He would have to find an apartment around here so he could continue to woo her properly. The Airstream was not adequate nor appropriate for the job. Besides it wasn't finished, and the couch was godawful uncomfortable. Honey deserved a better bed for when she would stay with him.

"What are you thinking?" Honey asked.

"I was thinking how beautiful you are." Morgan's voice was soft as he continued to stare at her.

"As much as I want to stay right here just like this, I only have thirty minutes, and my fat ass needs food." Her words indicated the need to move, but she didn't. She stood with her arms wrapped around his waist, staring back into his eyes.

Morgan stepped back, slipping his hand from her back around her shoulder so they could begin walking.

"What are we eating?"

"Hamburger and fries. I don't have the wherewithal to juggle tourist crowds." Honey turned them so they began walking in the opposite direction. "There's a fast food place a few blocks up the hill."

Morgan nodded. "I'm familiar with it. I didn't think you liked fast food."

Honey laughed. "It's not my favorite date food. But yeah, I do actually eat fast food on purpose, just not all the time, I have to keep my fat ass in check."

Morgan stopped walking. A look of concern crossed his brow. "Why do you say that?"

"Say what?" Honey turned to look at him.

"Fat ass. You don't have one. As a matter of fact, you barely have any body fat other than those." Morgan stared greedily at her breasts. "You are built like an underwear model. You realize that, right?"

Honey sighed. "I should be built like an underwear model. I was one." She began walking again, dragging Morgan along by his hand. "You already know more about me. I don't want to scare you off, but it looks like you are going to learn even more."

"I want to learn all about you, Honey. If you're not comfortable, I'll understand, but..." he paused.

"No, no secrets, Morgan. My ass is fat—" She sighed. "—in comparison to what it was at the height of my modeling career. I am huge. *In comparison.*" Honey emphasized the last words. "I have an eating disorder, but I'm actually a good healthy weight now. My doctors have said so. But I didn't use to be. Uhm, I have severe body dysmorphia issues."

"Dysmorphia?"

"Yeah. I don't see what other people see. I'm mostly better, but from time to time I slip."

Honey stepped up to the counter and ordered a double hamburger, fries, and a large soda. She stepped aside to allow Morgan to order. He ordered twice as much food as she had, then paid.

She slid into a hard plastic booth, placing the tray of food down in front of her.

"So when I was modeling, I lived on water, cigarettes, and a carrot or two a week. Oh, and vodka. At first it wasn't like that but, eventually, I was literally skin and bones. I became obsessed with being thin. If you couldn't count your ribs while looking in the mirror you were considered too fat. Of course, stylists and photographers only praised me for being so thin. Thin and elegant. The thinner I got the more contracts I got. I ignored the foul breath—cigarettes and gum masked that. The loose teeth I chalked up to eating hard foods, like celery. The celery I ate usually came with a Bloody Mary. I drank calories before I'd eat calories." Honey took a large bite of her burger, barbecue sauce smeared across her cheek.

"The *me* of back then would never eat one of these. I would have rather been dead. Of course, I practically was. So there I was dying and not realizing it. My periods stopped. Instead of seeing that as a warning my body was sick, I saw it as a bonus. No bloating. No pesky accidents. My hair started thinning drastically, but since I worked for designers who preferred their models in crazy wigs, it wasn't a concern."

"I was living in London when my mom showed up. She had seen some of my most recent photos and flew over to bring me back to the States. She faked a reason, saying I had to come home. Said my brother was in a coma. So, of course, I flew home with her. It never occurred to me that if my brother was in a coma, Mom would have called. She wouldn't have flown to personally escort me home. My higher order thinking skills were being affected by my condition. When I got home, my brother was there. He was fine. No coma. They were all waiting for me. I basically walked off the plane and into an intervention.

"It took it a while to kick in. I fought against it at first. I was a successful model. This was clearly backlash to my fame and choice of lifestyle. Mom took me to several therapists. The last one was brilliant. She started showing me these pictures of famine victims. I could see those poor women were starving. They were nothing but skin and bones. Their elbows and knees looked crazy huge compared to the rest of their arms and legs. I remember wondering how they could even move because there was no sense of muscle.

"The therapist asked me if I thought their bodies were beautiful. I said I thought they were sick and needed help. Nourishment. I said they looked like they were dying. That's when she unveiled her little deception. The bodies were all me. I didn't recognize my own body. She had a Photoshop artist take a few of my pictures, change the skin color, and put different heads on them. Some of the pictures were flipped. I hadn't even realized they were the same poses used over and over again. That's when it hit me. I was starving to death. I was that dying body.

"Up until that moment, my body dysmorphia was so bad I could not see that my own body was damaged. I began taking daily pictures and hiding my head so I could see my body. I got onboard with the nutrition program and began gaining weight. I used money I saved while modeling to go to school and get healthy.

"I still have issues seeing myself properly. I have to actually work at it. So I'm not trying to be vain if I take a picture in a mirror, I need to remind myself. It's a tool to keep me healthy."

"Honey, I..." Morgan paused not sure what to say.

"So I slip. I forget to eat, and I say I have a fat ass. It's a weird kind of ownership. Like how some African Americans use the n-word with each other. It causes everyone else to flinch, but for them, it's power and ownership. Definitely not appropriate for anyone else to use that term. So for me, I can call out my ass fat, but no one else can."

Honey finished the last of her fries and continued as Morgan watched her. "I was really good for several years then I had a hard, fast slip backward. Uhm...Bryce started commenting on my weight. Saying things like I was gaining a little too much weight and how I was so much prettier in my modeling pictures. I fell back into the binge and purge habit. That's a hard one to break. Bryce would harass me if I wasn't eating, and then after I would eat, he would comment about my figure. He would take food away from me if he thought I had eaten too much."

"Bryce is a dangerous asshole."

Honey chuckled. "That he is. I was secretly in therapy while I was with him. The binge and purge confession to my therapist opened the door so I was able to see his abuse. I've been good for a while now. Lana has been crazy supportive."

They left the restaurant and began walking back towards the café.

"Honey, I will support you however you need me to. I don't know how or what, but you tell me what you need and I will do it."

"Really? Okay, first, don't pick on me for having to go to therapy occasionally."

"Never."

"I might need a reminder to eat but also don't be afraid

to call a halt if you notice I'm hitting a binge, because the binge/purge habit has been a really hard one to recover from. And by binge, I mean a *binge*, not a big meal. You know what a binge looks like?"

Morgan shook his head.

"A binge doesn't involve a meal. It's random weird foods. Nothing balanced. It's when I start eating things I don't normally eat, like sour gummy worms. I don't typically eat those. I'm a chocolate kind of girl. So foods I don't normally eat and constant eating in huge quantities. Salt-sweet-salt is my typical pattern. I haven't binged in almost two years," she said proudly. "You still want me?" Morgan snaked his arms around her waist, pulling her close. "I think I will always want you." The mating glow shimmered gently around her. She was his, and he had no intention of letting her get away.

Honey smiled at Morgan. "I keep telling you these horrible things about me then you say something like that. You're not running away screaming or calling me crazy-train."

"I turn into a wolf, sweetheart. I think I can handle a girl-friend with some food issues and an asshole for an ex."

She rested her hands against his chest.

"You said girlfriend."

"I said girlfriend. Is that okay with you?"

"That's very okay with me!"

Morgan leaned against a mound of pillows he'd propped against the bedroom wall. Honey sat in front of him. He lightly traced the lines of her tattoo. Green tendrils of vine tracery scrolled over her skin. The outlines of pink lotus petals grew over most of her back. Her skin was smooth like silk under his fingertips.

He wanted to offer for her to have the ink work finished. In time, he would. Right now she would refuse. She thought she still owed him money for replacing her television and other items that had been stolen. Money didn't matter. Only Honey's happiness mattered. His finger wandered up her spine. He traced the moon below her neck. When this piece was finished, it would encompass her entire back—an extreme close-up of a lotus blossom under icons of the phases of the moon, framed with vines. For Honey, it symbolized growth and becoming who she was meant to be. To him, it was beautiful artistry on the most beautiful canvas of Honey's perfect back.

Honey hunched over her phone. This posture stretched the skin of her back over her bones. Morgan let his fingers trail down her spine, slaloming between the vertebrae. He stretched his hand and began tracing her ribs. A few were emphasized by her posture. Stupid how an entire industry would call a body this perfectly proportioned fat. *She's perfect.* Hell, even if she did put on weight, she would be gorgeous. Morgan smiled. He would love to see her big and round with his baby, and if she stayed big after the birth, he would just have more Honey to love.

Honey squirmed. "Hey, that tickles." She batted at his hand.

Morgan reached around her and pulled her back against him. "Who are you texting so fervently?"

"Lana. It's work. I'm trying to get her to change my schedule. She wants me to work through my regular days off. By the time I have a day off again, it will have been almost two full weeks. But since it's two different pay periods, there is nothing I can do about it."

Morgan reached around and took the phone from Honey. He set it deliberately on the nightstand. His hand stroked the skin on the side of her neck and down her arm.

"Hmmm." Honey leaned into his touch. "Hmmm."

"Don't worry about work. Lana wouldn't do that to you without reason."

"But that means we don't get the same days off." Honey began pouting. "Hard to spend all day in bed with you if I'm at work."

Morgan snorted. "It's hard to spend all day in bed when it's this small."

"Are you mocking my double bed? It's bigger than that couch you sleep on in the trailer."

"Touché." Morgan began kissing the skin along the top of Honey's shoulder. "This bed is barely big enough for the two of us. I'll get a larger one when I find an apartment."

Honey shifted so she could face Morgan. "An apartment?"

"I need a place down here. I can't live in the trailer for much longer in the condition it's in. Dante needs to pick it up and take it back to the yard in Sonoma, so it can get worked on. It's barely habitable as it is. I certainly can't have you there. While I could make love to you on that couch— hell, I could make love to you anywhere—you deserve better." Morgan brushed a stray curl back. "You need your space. You don't want me here all the time. So I need an apartment."

"Is your job moving you here?"

"No," Morgan shook his head. "You're here. I'll figure the job thing out."

"I'm here?"

Morgan chuckled. "Yes, you're here. You're my girlfriend, and I want to be with you. That means moving here."

Morgan cupped the back of Honey's neck, pulling her in for a kiss. Her lips were soft and pliant against his. Honey shifted her weight and straddled Morgan's lap.

"And you're going to get a big bed?" she asked after they broke off the kiss. She began twining her fingers into the hairs of his chest.

"The biggest one I can find, so I can keep you in it for days at a time."

"What would we possibly do in bed for days at a time?" Honey teased.

Morgan leaned to the side, locating a condom pack. "Go through these in bulk." He held up the foil square.

Honey took the pack from Morgan and tore it open.

Honey lay staring at the ceiling, listening to Morgan shower. They had spent the entire evening making love. Morgan made her body tingle in the most amazing ways, even when he was no longer touching her. *He's moving here to be with me.* Butterflies twirled in her stomach, not with trepidation, but with happy excitement. She knew where her emotions were regarding him. She needed her brain to agree and her lips to be willing to say the words. Clearly, Morgan felt the same, otherwise, why would he be moving?

The shower stopped. Morgan stepped into the bedroom, a blue towel wrapped low around his hips. Water dotted and sparkled along his arms, and the hairs on his chest lay in wavy wet lines against his tawny skin. Honey's desire for him skyrocketed. She had a need to lick all the water droplets from his body.

"Where should we go find food?" he asked, toweling his hair off.

Honey took him in with her eyes. "Do we need to eat? Could we maybe do that again? I suddenly have an urge to give you a tongue bath."

Morgan chuckled. The towel around his waist hit the floor. "I don't need convincing."

He crawled onto the bed and hovered over her, pressing her back against the mattress.

His tongue trailed up Honey's body from her navel, between her breasts, and up her neck.

"Hmm, tongue bath sounds like a wonderful idea," Morgan growled.

Honey stretched to reach Morgan and licked his neck. Hooking her legs around his, she managed to exert force so that Morgan rolled. His back lay against the mattress with Honey on top.

She lowered her head and began licking the drops of water from his broad shoulders. He tasted of clean skin and fresh water. Her licks began alternating with small sucking kisses and gentle bites. Honey's mouth found Morgan's nipple. He audibly inhaled.

Honey looked up, admiring his sculpted face. His eyes were closed, and his lips held the slightest grin. She kept her eyes on his face as she lowered back down to his other nipple. She sucked it into her mouth. His closed eyes fluttered as he hissed again. She replaced her mouth with her fingers, twirling the sensitive nub. She kissed a trail down his chest. Licking when she encountered a stray droplet of water. Her hand left his nipple when she reached his navel. She teased around the edges with her finger before flicking it with her tongue. His erection jumped and pulsed, kicking her in the shoulder. Honey paused to glance at the engorged flesh. She smiled to herself, noting that Morgan really liked having his bellybutton toyed with. She returned her attention to his navel, gently biting his abs just below the indentation.

Morgan groaned in pleasure as Honey laved and sucked.

Honey worked her attentions lower on his abdomen. When she encountered the thatch of hair above his manhood, Honey bypassed that skin and began licking and biting Morgan's inner thigh.

"Tease," Morgan breathed.

Honey looked up. Morgan watched her, his hazel eyes glowed amber.

"Your eyes are glowing."

"Because of what you are doing to me," Morgan moaned.

Honey repositioned herself to be between his legs. Never breaking eye contact with Morgan, Honey slowly licked up the underside of his manhood.

His eyes seemed to flare brighter.

"Those are your wolf eyes." Honey closed her own eyes before taking him into her mouth.

"Ahhh," Morgan let out a ragged sigh. "Strong. Emotion. Ahh"

Honey slowly pulled up, pressing her tongue against Morgan's cock in her mouth. Just as she reached the spade-shaped head, she lowered her mouth again. She pulled as much of Morgan into her mouth as she could. Not all of him would fit, and Honey couldn't open her throat. She pulled her mouth up and off Morgan before grabbing him with a firm fist.

"I think," she said as she slid her body down his length, "I want to feel you a bit before." Flesh against flesh was almost too much for Honey to resist. She wanted to make love to him without any barriers. Honey quickly removed herself. "Oh, that's nice."

"And dangerous." Morgan slid a condom over himself.

"That feels entirely too good to me. Best not tempt that one."

"What? No control?" Honey asked as she slid back down Morgan's length.

"Not with you." Morgan thrust up into her. "With you, all control is gone."

Honey rocked against Morgan, riding him until she couldn't control her muscles.

Morgan held her hips, following Honey to orgasm.

Honey collapsed across Morgan's chest. "I think I lose all control with you too." Her fingers toyed with his now, mostly dry, chest hairs. "You were saying something about food?"

Morgan chuckled. "What's food?"

## 18

M organ slid into the back of the dark limo and nodded his head in greeting to the beautiful woman sitting across from him. "I'm surprised to see you here. I expected a phone call." He eyed a well-dressed man in a sharkskin suit and black sunglasses seated beside her. Morgan wondered briefly if he was Cyan's lover or her body guard or both.

"Monterey is lovely this time of year. Of course, it is always lovely. Delivering this gives me a chance to take a much needed, long weekend. Visit my properties." Cyan del Fuego's sultry good looks and accent hinted of exotic locations.

She handed Morgan a thick envelope. "Your investigator has been most thorough. These are copies of the financial documents he requested that he could not access online. You were right, Bryce Maplecourt is a fool. Not only is he transferring funds offshore, he thinks we're Mafia of some kind. And he has a file of *questionable*—" She flipped her fingers in air quotes around the word questionable. "—business dealings of ours. I'm not going to ask how your investigator, your cousin, I think he said, no...?"

Morgan nodded.

"Well, I won't ask how your cousin is finding his information. As he said, it's not admissible in court. But we won't be using lawyers in our dealings with Mr. Maplecourt."

Morgan gave the contents of the envelope a cursory glance. "You know this information could have been delivered to my office. There was no need for you to drive all the way down here."

"But then, we couldn't have had this little chat. I thought you would like to know that my father is taking this threat of Lazarus returning very seriously. He was a dangerous man before his supposed death, especially to our kind. He did political damage that vampire councils are slowly recovering from. He set us back decades." Cyan shifted, crossing her legs.

"My father has a network in place. We will soon know about any movements Lazarus plans to make even before he does."

"Have your father's contacts located Lazarus?"

"Not yet. We know where he has been. It is only a matter of time before we know where he is. From what I gathered, Lazarus's intent is to start an all-out race war."

Morgan nodded. "He's not going to get it. My sister has been reaching out to all the wolf families she can identify, alerting them. Needless to say, we tend to stay hidden even from our own kind."

"I am sure it is a daunting task, but one your sister is well capable of handling. I have met her. There is a place for her at Cyan Group if she ever grows bored with handling your family's business affairs."

~

Calliope mewed at Honey when she opened the door to her apartment.

"Hi, Calliope. What now?"

Calliope only greeted her when she wanted something —either more food or when the litter box hadn't been cleaned to her requirements.

The cat followed Honey into the living room, vocalizing her discontent. Honey sighed. She placed the large box she carried on the couch then looked at the cat. She didn't want to play twenty questions with her pet. It was always a frustrating game that usually took more than twenty tries to find out what the cat wanted. A hiss as Honey reached for the cat's ears indicated that Calliope did not want to be scratched behind the ears. One down, nineteen to go. Honey cleaned out the litter box, still Calliope mewed. She made sure the cat had fresh water and a freshly-opened can of food. Honey found a few of Calliope's mouse toys, picked them up, and replaced them with other mouse toys from the toy box. Just as Honey was about to scream with frustration, she eyed the container of catnip. Honey poured out a small pile of the dried herbs in the middle of the kitchen floor.

"That's all I got, cat. I have no idea what you could possibly want."

Calliope rubbed against Honey's ankles and began purring. "Really, cat? You just wanted to see me jump through hoops for you?"

In reply, Calliope rolled over in the pile of catnip.

Honey shook her head. The cat drove her crazy, but she couldn't imagine life without her.

Realizing she stood in the middle of the kitchen, she

decided to fix herself a quick bowl of noodles. She checked her phone again. No messages from Morgan all day.

Then again she hadn't texted him either. She decided she didn't want to play games with him. She didn't need to wait to see who would text first. She typed out a quick message while the noodles boiled.

She stood, draining hot noodle water into the sink when her door buzzer sounded. Stepping over the cat, blissed out in the middle of the floor, she reached the opening buzzer by her front door. She opened her door and watched Morgan stride in.

Tension and tiredness left her body when she saw his smile.

He slipped an arm around her waist and kissed her. "Hello, beautiful. Did you like your present?"

"My present?" Honey asked, leading Morgan into the apartment.

"You should have gotten a delivery today. Didn't you get it?"

"This box? I still haven't managed to open it."

"You need to come here and open it."

"Okay, fine." Honey wiped her hands on a dish towel and using a steak knife, slit the tape where the box had been sealed. Inside the delivery box was another smaller, thinner box. Honey slipped a gold ribbon from the new box and opened it to reveal a pile of teal fabric and white tissue paper. Carefully, she found the top of the fabric and lifted. Sheets of tissue paper fell away as a full-length, elegant gown emerged from the box.

"Oh, this is gorgeous." Honey held the dress up to her figure. The bust line was pleated and twisted, allowing the gown to flow like a column of aqua silk. Honey lifted her gaze to Morgan. "This is designer. Thank you! Why?"

"You'll need it this weekend. Those meetings I said I have are a family wedding. It's formal."

"But how?"

Morgan chuckled. "I got a lot done that day you left me here to clean up the kitchen."

"Wow," Honey twirled, looking down at the dress she still held against herself. "But I can't go." Honey felt like crying. She knew she had started whining. She was tired, and the thought of having to miss a weekend alone with Morgan because of work broke her. Tears escaped her eyes. "I have to work, Lana won't let me off." Honey swiped at her tears. "She's being a real bitch about too. Oh, Morgan, this dress is beautiful, but I don't think I'll be able to wear it. I can't accept this."

Morgan pulled out his phone, tapped in a number, then handed it to Honey.

She glanced at the phone. "Hello?"

"Gotcha!" Lana's voice cackled at the other end.

"Lana?" Honey was confused.

"I had you work extra so you could take off. Morgan already arranged for you to have the time. I front-loaded your schedule so that you didn't have to worry about losing hours. Everything is all set. I'll swing by in the morning to pick up Calliope. You go have a fun weekend."

"Seriously?"

"Seriously. Make sure you come back to work next week, okay?"

Honey laughed. "Of course. Why wouldn't I?"

She handed Morgan his phone back.

"You sneak. You planned this" He nodded. "I knew you wouldn't agree to take off for a long weekend. Lana said you never take vacation time, and you only ever call in sick when you are too ill to move. So I knew I would need a little subterfuge to get you to come away with me."

Morgan followed Honey back into the kitchen. She handed him a bowl of noodles before filling her own. Honey slurped up the food, hungrier than she realized she had become. "So what's the plan then?" she asked between bites.

"Long weekend at my family's home. They are somewhat old fashioned, so you will need to pack a least one nice outfit in addition to the dress for the actual wedding. The rest of the time, what you normally wear is fine. It's inland, so dress for slightly warmer weather."

"Were you really looking at apartments today or were you off being sneaky?"

"I took care of a few things, but yes, I looked at apartments."

"Find anything?" Honey was hopeful. She liked the idea of Morgan staying and not having to leave town when the construction job was over.

Morgan shook his head. "I looked at a few places, but they had no personality and small bedrooms. I wasn't joking when I said I'm getting a big bed." Morgan took the now empty bowl from Honey.

"I am so tired right now." Honey yawned and stretched out on the couch. "When do we leave for this long weekend?"

"Tomorrow. I have a few errands in the morning, then we're on the road."

"So not early?

"Not early."

"I can sleep in?"

Morgan chuckled. "You can sleep in."

∾

The front door buzzer sounded. Honey groaned into her pillow. She wanted to sleep. This was early. Too early for someone sleeping in. The buzzer sounded again. Honey secretly hoped Morgan would be up and take care of whatever it was.

Morgan wasn't there. She rolled over and glared at her alarm clock. It was after ten, not as early as she thought. She slid out of bed and shuffled to the front door. Honey grabbed a sweater to put on over the tank top and knit character pajama pants she slept in.

"Yes? You buzzed?" she spoke into the intercom.

"It's Lana."

Honey pushed the unlock buzzer to allow Lana in then leaned out her front door.

"I'm here to pick up Calliope. Is she all packed?"

"Morning," Honey mumbled. "I don't have her ready yet. Sorry."

Honey shuffled into her living room. She paused and chuckled.

"I thought you said she wasn't ready," Lana stated, staring at the trunk Honey used as a coffee table.

Set on top of the surface were Calliope's cat carrier, food dishes, and a shopping tote with cat toys and food.

Honey picked up a note she found on top of the cat carrier. "I didn't. Morgan must have taken care of this before he left this morning."

*I'll let you capture the cat. I'll be back around noon – Morgan*

Honey smiled then folded the note. She glanced up to look at Calliope's favorite spot in the window. She wasn't there. "Okay, now I just have to find Calliope." It wasn't a large apartment, but she was a small cat and had many hiding places.

"I've got her."

Honey turned to see Lana holding the cat, scratching her behind the ears. She shook her head. The cat that liked no one loved Lana.

Lana eased Calliope into the cat carrier with skill and dexterity. The cat curled up on the blanket and lay down contentedly.

"Seriously, cat? She fights me on everything, and you show up and she's sweet as pie." Honey looked at the cat. "You do this on purpose, don't you? You want people to think I'm crazy. I'm on to you. I know your game." Honey poked a finger through the crate door. Calliope rubbed against her and purred. Honey sighed and scratched her cat.

"She knows she's going to Camp Lana and not the vet."

"Yeah, but the vet is Maggie, and she loves Maggie."

"All animals love Maggie, except when she has a needle in her hand."

Honey laughed and picked up the cat carrier. She picked up her keys before following Lana out to her car.

"So do you know where Morgan is whisking you off to?"

"No. Do you? All I know it's his family's home and a wedding."

"You're meeting the parents?"

"I'm meeting his sisters, I know that much. His parents died a few years ago. So this is probably the same thing. Meeting the family. I hadn't really thought of it that way. Oh crap."

Lana patted her on the shoulder. "Oh crap, nothing. You're awesome, Honey. Besides, it doesn't actually matter if they like you or not. It only matters that Morgan likes you and you like him."

Honey nodded. But she knew that the support of family could really help or hurt a relationship. Her parents had loved Bryce. Her mom had even talked her out of leaving him more than once. She actually hadn't told her mother where she went when she ran away from Bryce, just in case her mother passed that information along. It wasn't until she had been able to tell her parents why she left Bryce that she trusted them with where she had settled.

How would they handle Morgan? Honey knew that some of her superficial bad habits were the result of how she was raised. Her mother would probably think he was nice enough, but she might not accept him as being good enough for Honey because of his job. Her father might be a little more accepting, simply because he came from a blue-collar background and grew up around uneducated, but skilled laborers. Then again, that might actually count against Morgan. She knew that uneducated part had been a big reason they had been so set against her modeling.

As if she could read Honey's mind, Lana said, "Just because you're meeting his family doesn't mean you have to introduce him to yours until you're ready. Besides, they live out of state. It's a valid excuse to put it off for a nice long time."

Honey nodded in agreement.

"Have fun at Camp Lana." Honey said into the cat carrier, as she slid it onto the back seat of the car. She leaned in and ran the seat belt through the handle and buckled the cat in. "Thanks again, Lana. How much time do I have off work?"

"You aren't on the schedule until Wednesday at eleven."

"Nice."

Honey waved as she watched Lana pull away. She started climbing the front steps making a mental list of what she needed to get done and approximately how much time she had. It was probably eleven by now. Morgan would be coming back for her soon. She needed to shower and dress and pack. Her stomach grumbled. "And eat. I need to eat," she said out loud.

Honey stepped into the shower when the front door buzzer sounded. *Crap!* She wrapped a towel around herself and padded into her hall.

"Morgan?" she asked into the intercom.

"It's me, Honey." His deep voice sounded funny through the speaker, but it still gave her a thrill to hear him say her name.

She buzzed him in and opened the door. She waited for Morgan inside the door, not keen on having any neighbors see her with a towel wrapped around her.

He stepped in carrying a black suit bag.

"You're not dressed."

"No, but I am packed. Just jumping into the shower now."

"Hey, I'm not complaining. Only observing." Morgan followed Honey into her room. She continued into the bathroom.

Morgan glared at the bed which was covered in bags and clothes. He shook his head, his idea of taking advantage of Honey's state of undress thwarted by the state of the bed. In a large sweeping motion, Morgan scooped the items from the bed and made a pile on the floor. He heard the shower water turn on. Honey was not yet in the water. "Come in here a second, Honey."

She stepped into the bedroom holding the towel in front of her. "Yes?"

Morgan reached for her and tugged the towel from her

grasp. "You don't need this right now." Morgan pulled her to him and claimed her lips with his.

An hour later, Honey walked into the kitchen, toweling her hair. Morgan handed her a cup of coffee. He leaned back against the counter, his hair still tousled from their lovemaking. Honey reached up and brushed it behind his ears with her fingers.

"I am so glad to be here with you and not at work." She sipped her coffee. "Coffee at work is better, but the company isn't."

"I'm glad to hear that." Morgan wrapped his arm around her waist and held her close. "I'd hate to think that's a service you offer to anybody."

"Only regulars who don't like Lana's lemon bars."

Morgan took the coffee cup from her hands and placed it on the counter before he wrapped her in both arms and began kissing her. "I take it I'm the only person who doesn't like those." he asked between kisses.

Honey giggled. She leaned into Morgan's long body. She fit perfectly as if they had been made for each other. "What time do we need to be there?"

"Tonight."

"So no hurry?"

"No hurry, but we are going to need to get going if we want to get lunch and still get there tonight. I'm tempted to take you back to bed though." Morgan began nuzzling Honey's neck.

"Won't we be able to do this once we are there?"

Morgan gazed into Honey's eyes. He fingered a stray curl by her temple. "Possibly not. My family is very formal, and there are going to be lots of guests around."

"Maybe we can run away after the wedding?"

Morgan smiled, showing large even teeth. "I like the way you think."

Honey kissed him on the chin. Morgan moved his head so she could reach his mouth.

"Ahhh, we need to leave, or it will never happen. And I cannot miss this wedding. JoJo will never forgive me."

"JoJo is your adopted sister, right?" Honey asked as she stepped out of Morgan's warm embrace. She would have rather stayed, but he was right. They needed to leave or they would end up back in bed.

"Yeah, she became my legal ward, after my parents' death. She's my sister where it counts." Morgan tapped himself in the chest, over his heart. "She's pretty much everyone's favorite."

"She like you?" Honey asked as she made a claw shape with her hand and curled it like she was scratching at something.

"No, she's not like me. She's not wolf. Her mother worked for my family when she died. Mom refused to let JoJo be taken from the only family she'd ever known."

"Oh, how sweet. So she was raised with you?"

"I was a teenager when all of that happened. She was raised closer to some of my cousins, but I was always around."

Honey laughed, "I bet you're the one who helped all the younger kids get into trouble. Instigator."

"Were you there?" Morgan grinned.

"I'm right. You were a troublemaker?"

"I was a teenage boy. What do you think?"

"I'm right, I'm totally right." Honey answered smugly.

Morgan picked up his suit bag and Honey's duffle bag. "Ready?"

Honey slipped on a jacket and picked up the garment bag containing the dress.

She followed him outside towards a parked truck. Morgan had said he was picking up his car this morning. This was a truck. A square, boxy, old pickup truck, color blocked with areas of flat, patternless color. The hood was a pale blue color that created a stripe along the top of the door and along the top of the bed of the truck. The middle section was mostly white with large areas of rust. There were a few areas where the rust had been sprayed over with gray primer. Another stripe of the pale blue ran the entire length along the bottom of the truck. The vehicle had to be at least thirty years old, if not older. Technically, it should be considered a vintage vehicle, but to Honey, it was a rusty, old, beat-up truck. Honey thought a truck is not a car, and this was an old truck. The squared-off cab was large but clearly had no extra room for hanging their garment bags. Honey looked at Morgan and gave herself a mental shake. She was going away for the weekend with him, not his truck.

She glanced into the bed of the truck. More rust.

Without saying a word, Honey turned and walked back into her apartment building. Once inside her apartment, she leaned against the closed front door. "I can do this. I can do this. Don't judge. It's just a truck. Don't judge. Don't judge. Don't judge." Honey talked herself out of a panic attack. "I'm going away with Morgan, not his truck." She groaned and pushed off the door.

She returned to Morgan holding some towels in her hand.

"I thought you changed your mind there for a second." His brow creased with concern.

Honey smiled. She couldn't admit how close to the truth he had come. She held up the towels "To put under the bags. That—" She nodded towards the truck bed. "—doesn't look particularly friendly."

"Good thinking." Morgan smiled as he took the towels and spread them out in the truck bed. He laid the garment bags down first then placed Honey's heavier duffle bag on top.

"All set. Shall we?"

Honey nodded and climbed into the truck. She reminded herself over and over, Morgan was not his truck. The truck did not define him.

## 19

H oney shifted in the seat trying to get comfortable. "I have a confession, Morgan." She held on to the pendant at her neck. Her stomach roiled with nerves. *She was going away with Morgan, not his truck.* "I like you."

Morgan kept his focus on the road. "That's hardly a confession based on this morning's activities. I like you too."

"I mean, I really like you. I like *like*—" Honey emphasized the word, drawing it out, "—like you. Like, might not even be the right word for it. I more than like you."

"You aren't going to use that other L-word, are you?" he smiled. Just a small twitch of upward movement at the corner of his mouth. Honey recognized that smile; it meant Morgan wanted to play. It was an incredibly sexy expression. Honey wanted to slide across the cab and begin licking where his lips curved, but her nerves kept her on her side of the truck. *Was Morgan ready for the L-word? Was she?*

"No. At least, not yet. But—" She shifted so she could see him more easily. "I think I easily could." She stared at him. Morgan said nothing. He continued to smile that little playful grin and focused on driving. "You aren't freaking out."

"Why should I? You're saying something I want to hear." He finally glanced at her, flashing a large smile. "It's encouraging."

"Encouraging, huh?" She sat back. "Okay, then. I hope it's still encouraging after I tell you all of this."

"You were born a man?" Yep, he was playing with her.

"No. I was not born a man. All original parts, thank you very much."

"Because if you were, I'm basically okay with that. What you do with what you've got— Damn." He scratched at the stubble on his chin as if thinking hard. "Okay, not a man. A serial killer?"

"Morgan!"

"You're a mutant that shoots knives from between your knuckles."

"Will you shut up." Honey shook her head at him. She needed him to be serious for a second "I'm shallow!"

"That's your big confession? You're shallow?"

"Would you let me finish, ya' big oaf!"

"Sorry."

"I'm shallow. I used to judge men based on their outward appearance only. Not just looks, but grooming too. The clothes they wore and how they wore them. What cars they drove. Who they knew. Not what they knew, but who. What their job title was. And mostly the size of their wallets."

"Hmm-mmm." Morgan acknowledged what she said with a nod.

"Personality, height, size, skill weren't even in my top five"

"Not judging a guy by how big he is isn't such a bad

thing. I mean I'm told it's not what you've got but how you use it," he smirked.

"That's just it, Morgan. I stayed with crappy lovers who didn't have a clue how to make love to anyone but themselves because they looked a certain way or drove a certain car."

"What is it you are trying to tell me, Honey?"

"I'm saying I really like you. You are different for me from any guy I have ever dated."

"I would hope so." He glanced at her out from the corner of his eye, before returning his focus to the road.

"I'm not only talking about that wolf thing you've got going on. It's everything else. You are kind. You took care of me when I needed it. You paid for all those people's coffee because you might have inconvenienced them for a minute or two. You replaced everything in my apartment. You wear plaid shirts. I'm saying I never would have dated a guy who drove a rust-bucket of a truck, let alone go away to meet his family for a long weekend in one. So I'm apologizing now if I say or do something shallow or snotty or arrogant or just plain fucking stupid. I'm learning to not judge people based on their appearance. Lana has really helped me with that, but I know I've got a ways to go yet. I've got years of superficial bad behavior to get over."

"Fair enough. But you do actually like me. I'm not some experiment in slumming or trying out the rough-and-ready laborer?"

"I am completely infatuated with you, Morgan. I didn't plan on it, but I am. And what you do to me in bed. Damn!" Honey sighed. "This isn't about money—having it or not." She motioned in the space between them. "I just need you to know that in my past, it always was about money, and designer labels. So if I am a complete idiot this weekend, I'm sorry. I don't mean to be, but I can be an ignorant ass at times."

Morgan drove them into an unincorporated neighborhood, not quite country but clearly not suburbs. It looked very much working class, even though the yards were large and so were the houses. Morgan pulled into a steep driveway. He followed the long drive up the hill to behind the house. Honey could see several outbuildings, a large garage, and the top of a pool slide behind a paneled fence. The yard was full of cars. Cyclone fencing encircled the entire property.

They really weren't that far away from the peninsula. It had barely taken them an hour to get here. Honey thought if this was his family home, they could have easily driven here every morning for the weekend.

Morgan honked and a short broad Hispanic looking man came out of the large garage. He wiped his hands on a greasy looking rag as he approached the truck. "Put it over there," he said, indicating a space between a couple of broken-down cars. Morgan got out of the truck and clapped the man on the shoulder. "Thanks Jorge. This saved us some time."

"Sorry, she wasn't ready earlier, Mr. Palatine. She's all gassed up and ready for you." He lifted his arm and signaled to someone with a flick of his wrist.

Honey hovered around the back of the truck. She had expected Morgan to introduce her. This was his home, right?

"Honey, I'm glad you told me your feelings." A slick black car purring like a contented feline rolled to a stop in front of her. It looked like the love child of a jungle cat and a shark in car form. Morgan escorted her to the passenger side. He opened the door for her and indicated she should sit. He leaned in over her. "I'm glad you feel the way you do and that money isn't involved." Morgan closed the door.

Honey watched, confused, as Jorge helped Morgan move their items from the back of the truck to the trunk of the sleek car. Honey barely heard the thump and click of the trunk, then Morgan slid into the driver's seat. He shook hands with the man named Jorge, closed the door and began driving.

Honey stared in shock, her mouth agape. This was the kind of car that defined luxury, and she didn't even know its make.

"The truck wasn't mine. Jorge lent it to me because this, my car, wasn't ready yet. I didn't want to waste another two or three hours waiting for it to be ready, drive back to get you, and then head north. Picking it up here saved us a few hours."

Honey was still in shock at being in the car. Everything was tan and black leather. She reverently stroked the dash in front of her. "What is this thing?"

"It's a Maybach. They don't make them anymore." Morgan's tone indicated that he liked his car but not so much that he was impressed with himself for owning it.

"Uhm, this is a really expensive car, isn't it Morgan?"

"Yes, it is. That's not going to be a problem, is it, Honey? You said what we have isn't about money, and you said that thinking I was a poor construction worker. Now you know I'm not, it's still not about money, is it?"

"How? I'm sorry. I'm still trying to wrap my brain around this. You are or you aren't a construction worker?"

"I am a structural engineer, a foundations specialist. I run Seven Hills. I am also the CEO of the parent company Truria. My family owns the company. Has for a very long time."

"Wow, okay." Honey glanced at the interior of the car then she looked at Morgan, still in awe of the turn of events.

"So you are a construction worker, but you actually don't need to be." She spoke slowly, clarifying for herself at the same time.

"Right. I like to get hands-on at the beginning of a project. It helps the other guys know who I am, know they can talk to me, and lets them see I know what it is they are actually doing," he explained.

"That's why you haven't needed to go into work early the past few days and are dressing differently" Honey couldn't take her eyes off the interior of the car, as if it verified the words Morgan said.

"Right. I'm transitioning at this point. Now that the project has moved on past the installation of the base foundation, I can pull back and let Jim—he's the site manager—take over for me. I'm mostly there at this point for the client."

She tilted her head to watch him. Was he going to shift into another beast? First a wolf, now rich tycoon? What else was Morgan hiding? "But what about that job you did in Pacific Grove?"

"That was helping out a buddy. They had some guys call in sick with the flu. I was available. He had a time crunch. He needed the concrete poured at a certain time, and they needed help getting the forms set up properly."

"Morgan, I still really really like you. But..." She paused thinking about her phrasing. "But since you have money, could I help you buy some different clothes? I mean, I really hate those plaid shirts."

Morgan roared with laughter. "Sure, but those are work shirts. They are cheap, rugged, disposable. If they get messed up, no bother. I only had work clothes in Monterey. I hadn't planned on being social. I certainly hadn't planned on meeting you."

"See I told you I'm shallow."

Still laughing, Morgan said, "If it makes you feel better, no plaid at all this weekend. And if you don't approve of the rest of my wardrobe, I will let you take me shopping."

Morgan's driving skills and the smooth ride of the car made the trip feel as if they flew. They crossed the Golden Gate Bridge before she felt like enough time had passed at all.

Morgan continued north on Highway 101. He exited, and they drove into the golden, water-starved hills of Northern California.

The car snaked its way up a long grade deep into wine country. Honey watched as acres of grape vines slipped past her window. She felt as if the vines and hills around her were moving while she sat still.

A brick and iron gate indicated the entrance to a drive. Small solar lamps lit a path on either side of the driveway, guiding the car towards more lights. They rounded a bend and Honey gasped. Oak trees that sparkled with lights framed an elaborate brick and stucco entrance to a large, three-story facade. The car circled around a small circular drive then stopped.

Honey stared, mouth open. The building extended out to either side. This wasn't a house, this was a large, mission-style mansion.

Morgan exited the car and opened Honey's door. She put her hand in his offered one, and stood. She gaped at the entryway. Large, round, terra cotta pots filled with succulents stood like sentries on either side of a brick walkway.

Low wood steps led to a deep wide patio. Columns and arches repeated the length of the front patio. Honey noticed a ramp to the right zig-zagging from the walk to the patio.

"We're here," Morgan announced.

"This isn't a house, Morgan. This is a resort."

"This is home. It's a house, not a resort."

"No, this isn't a house. A house is—you know—three bedrooms, two baths, a garage or a carport. Single level. Maybe even one of those old Victorian two-story houses. No, this—this is a fucking mansion."

Morgan snickered. "Definitely more than three bedrooms and two baths. But it is home."

"And you live here all by yourself?"

"No." Morgan shook his head. "Extended family lives here. I have rooms, and yes, I mostly live here. But, definitely, not all by myself."

One of the large wooden doors swung open. An older man in a wheelchair followed by a middle-aged woman emerged from the mansion.

"Morgan," the man roared as he wheeled down the ramp to greet them. "You're back in time."

"Remi…" Morgan motioned Honey to his side. "This is Honey Gould. Honey, this my Uncle Remi."

Honey offered her hand, expecting Remi to shake it. She was caught off guard when he turned it and brought it to his lips.

"A pleasure." Remi's voice boomed.

"Nice to meet you." She turned, expecting to be introduced to the woman who had opened the trunk and had begun removing items from the car.

A small group of teenage boys burst out of the front door. They jostled for position. The winner of the race stopped in front of Morgan. "Can I put her in the garage?"

Morgan tossed him the keys. "One scratch and I'll hide ya'."

"Yeah, yeah, yeah," the kid said as he slipped into the driver's seat and started the engine.

The other boys started to shuffle back into the house.

"Oh no, you don't." The stern tone of the woman's voice stopped them in their tracks. "Take those things up to Morgan's rooms." She pointed to Morgan's bags. "And you can put those in a guest room." She pointed to Honey's bag and handed over her garment bag to one of the boys.

"Which one?" Clearly, the prize had been to park the car. Delivering bags was a losing chore.

The woman raked Honey up and down with a judgmental look then glanced out of the side of her eye at Morgan, "Let's put Miss Gould in the Blue Bird Room."

Honey heard Morgan grumble.

The woman turned on Morgan, pointing at his chest. "I have a house full of guests and kids. I expect you to follow the rules. She'll be on the same hall as JoJo's bridesmaids."

"Jinx has run this house for almost twenty years," Remi announced. "We follow her rules."

"Those were the rules of the house when I started, and since no one has officially changed them, I follow them," Jinx replied.

"No one is going to change them," Morgan added. He turned to Honey. "I think I mentioned that my parents ran a school?"

Honey nodded.

"We have a small private school on premises. Mostly for extended family and others with our—" Morgan gestured in a circling motion, "—family trait. The rules Jinx is referring to were put in place to keep the kids in line and to prevent underage hanky-panky."

"The family is traditionally Catholic," Remi added.

"I don't know anyone who's been a practicing Catholic for years," Morgan continued.

"Your grandmother," Remi cut in.

"Well, anyone except for Nan. She's a holdout of times since past."

"You did say your family was rather formal. This just fits," Honey contributed to the conversation.

They followed Remi up the ramp. Jinx waited for them at the top of the stairs. "Jinx, if you would show Miss Gould to her room, Morgan and I have some matters to discuss."

"Is that what I'm in time for?" Morgan asked. He turned to Honey and cupped her elbow, holding her arm for a moment. "I'll come see you before you go to sleep. Okay?"

Honey expected Morgan to lean in for a kiss. She was disappointed that he hadn't. Of course, she realized, his family might frown on public displays of affection between unmarried couples.

"Okay." She watched Morgan follow Remi down a wide hallway.

"Miss Gould," Jinx spoke getting her attention. Her arm stretched out to indicate Honey should follow her in the designated direction.

She followed as Jinx led her up a flight of stairs and through a maze of hallways. Honey had never been in a private residence so large. They passed by an open sitting room space with overstuffed chairs and couches. It resembled a luxury hotel lobby with conversation areas more than what Honey thought of as a living room.

"So you run the house?" Honey asked nervously. "Are you like a butler?"

Jinx chuckled. "I am exactly like a butler, but my official

title is Head Household Manager. I also act as personal assistant and caregiver. I manage all household staff."

"Household staff? The house has a staff?" Honey was amazed. This was the type of home she had only ever seen on television.

"This place needs a staff. Not counting the children who are here for the school, the family that lives here requires cooking and cleaning. There is also the garage staff. We do have a few—uhm—what would be called 'footmen' on the Continent. We call them personal assistants here. They help out where and how they are needed." Jinx explained.

"Wow. So how big is this place?" Honey asked.

"Plenty big, but I don't think it's big enough for this weekend. The wedding is being held in the courtyard out back. Tonight we are full of guests."

Honey looked around. She was astounded at just how silent it was. "But it's so quiet. I wouldn't know anyone was here."

"Good sound proofing. For a family with sensitive hearing, that is vital. Also, I have regulated all partying to the other side of the south wing where the dorms are located. They are as far away from the rest of the house as possible."

She stopped in front of a paneled door, turned the knob, and pushed open the door. "Here we are." Honey wondered how she'd ever find it again since it wasn't labeled like in a hotel. Jinx stepped into the room with Honey following. The furnishings were dark maple, the walls covered in dark blue floral wallpaper with blue birds in amongst the designs. It was a simple, guest bedroom. She noticed a small pile of folded towels had been set on the bed in anticipated need.

Jinx indicated light switches and outlets. "These lights are on the wall switch. The bedside table lamp has a switch here." She reached under the lamp shade and snicked the light on.

Honey glanced around the room. Her bags were already on the foot of the double bed, not the large bed she had hoped to be sharing with Morgan this weekend. Then again it was beginning to look as if she would not be sharing a bed with him at all the next few nights.

"I'll show you where the bathroom is." Jinx stepped back out of the room.

*Definitely not a hotel.* She didn't even get her own bathroom. The bathroom she did get was larger than expected but covered in makeup bags and curling irons.

"JoJo's bridesmaids are not the neatest young ladies," Jinx said, indicating the mess, the tone in her voice wasn't as neutral as Honey thought Jinx wanted it to be. She sounded judgmental and aggravated.

The bathroom featured a bank of two sinks in front of a large mirror. Opposite the sinks were three doors. Two of the doors led to commodes and the last door led to a small shower room. The design allowed for more than one person to use the facilities at the same time without appearing like a public restroom or locker room.

"There is another bathroom at the other end of the hall." Jinx indicated. "But this one is closer to your room. I'm afraid you'll have to climb over JoJo's entourage in either one."

Jinx guided Honey back to her room.

"Great thanks." Honey nodded. She knew she was being deposited back at her room.

"Good night, Miss Gould. Breakfast will be served in the morning. I'm sure Morgan will help you to locate that when the time comes."

Honey closed the door after Jinx left. Definitely aggravated.

Now what? She looked around the room, her hand nervously sliding the pendant back and forth. No television. She couldn't remember if she packed any books. Probably not. Honey had anticipated spending all of her time with Morgan. There was a small dresser. She opened the drawers. Empty. It was a guest room with no reason for there to be anything inside. She began unpacking her duffle bag. She placed her toiletries in the top drawer of the dresser. Everything else she left in the bag and placed it on the side chair. She unzipped the garment bag carrying her dress. She unfurled the length and noticed that it had gotten a little bunched. She opened the closet and found a garment steamer in the otherwise empty space. Honey hung the dress then began examining the steamer. It was simple enough. Water reservoir, switch, and wand. And the ubiquitous warning label that steam was hot and could burn.

Honey depressed the lock button and pulled the reservoir off the unit. She knocked then entered the bathroom, quickly filling the plastic container. Back in her room, she pushed the container back onto the machine, plugged it in, and clicked it on. She sat back and waited. It had been a few years since she had used one. She knew she needed to wait for steam to begin rushing from the wand end. As soon as steam billowed out of the end, Honey gently guided the wand up and down the folds of her gown. The little wadded up wrinkles relaxed and fell away.

Honey clicked the machine off and unplugged it. She pulled the water tank and padded back down to the bathroom to empty it.

Morgan leaned against her door when she returned.

"I don't think I can invite you in," she said tartly, sashaying past him into the room.

Morgan leaned against the open door. "I'm sorry. House rules. At least, for the first visit."

Honey reassembled the steamer.

"So where can a girl get a drink around here?"

Noise. Honey finally believed there were other people in this large mansion. Morgan led her down a series of hallways and staircases. The hall they were in opened onto a large open den full of people. Honey noticed mostly young adults and older teens.

A few people called out to Morgan. He waved. A large screen television was set up at one end of the room with what looked to be a fairly intense video game competition happening based on how many were gathered around watching and the cheers and groans coming from them.

A pool table occupied the center area. An equally intense game took place there but with fewer audience members.

Honey followed Morgan through the room to a wet bar. A double door refrigerator proved to be well stocked with a variety of drink, and frozen snacks. Morgan grabbed two beers and a bag of chips from the counter.

He nodded to Honey, indicating she should continue to follow him. They walked out onto a long patio. Honey noticed a few pit fires and several different groups. Morgan led her to a secluded bench where they sat. He twisted the top from a beer and handed it to her.

"This is quite the place," Honey said.

"Yeah, it can be crowded at times. Of course, it's not

normally like this. Most of these people are only here for the wedding."

"Most?" Honey asked

"Some of the kids inside live here because of the school. But, yeah, people are here for the wedding. Not that many actually live here full time." Morgan began ticking off his fingers. "My sister Caro and her husband, their kid. Kids. My sister Julia has rooms, but she mostly stays at her place in San Francisco. My grandmother, Remi, Aunt Karen, Dante, Ari, Shane. JoJo, but I don't know if she's staying or going to find a place with her new husband. Joe lives over the garage. A few teachers live here. Last count I think we have five staff members who live on the property. I have no idea about the school. Not counting the school or staff, I think twelve or fifteen of us live here with any regularity. Of course, there were more, but people grew up and moved out. As this generation has kids, there will be more again."

"That's a pretty big household," Honey admitted. "I couldn't imagine living with my entire family all together. But then again, I also could never imagine living in a house like this."

Morgan chuckled. "The only reason I can imagine living in a single-family home is because of what I've seen on television. No, this place is great. It's big enough you don't have to be around anyone else. Did you notice how quiet it was upstairs? You really can't tell there are people here unless you are in the same area as the rest of them."

Honey watched as lights from the distance fires flickered across Morgan's profile. "You like it here, don't you?"

"Of course. It's home." Morgan turned to gaze into Honey's eyes. "You think you could like someplace like this?"

"I think..." She paused, searching his face. "...I would like any place as long as I am with you."

Honey closed her eyes and leaned into Morgan's kiss. This kiss felt different. This one felt as if her emotions had clarified, and her heart and her head were in agreement. This kiss felt as if Morgan poured all of the same emotions into her as she was pouring into him.

Honey opened her eyes and looked into Morgan's glowing ones. She wanted to say something, but words would ruin the moment. She returned her lips to his. She couldn't speak, but she could kiss. And the kisses felt like they were communicating just fine.

Morgan held Honey's hand all the way back to her room.

"So are you going to show me where your rooms are?" she teased.

"It's probably safer not to." Morgan chuckled. He pointed vaguely off to his left. "I'm over that way."

"That's not helpful," Honey complained.

"No sneaking off trying to find my room tonight. I'm going to be on lockdown too. It's not particularly fair, and I am particularly annoyed by it. We are consenting adults."

"In a house full of impressionable children..." Honey finished for him.

"True. And we are unwed, consenting or not."

"Your Catholic upbringing bites you in the butt." Honey snickered.

Morgan scoffed. "I still don't have to like it."

Morgan stopped outside of Honey's door.

"Is this me?"

Morgan nodded. "This is you."

They stared into each other eyes for a long time. A door snicked open. A giggling blur of blond and pink scurried past them down the hall and disappeared into the bathroom.

"I'll come get you in the morning. The wedding is at one.

I'm sure everything will be a flurry of activity until then." Morgan leaned in for a kiss. They both paused and watched the blur of blond giggle race past them and disappear behind a different door.

Honey kissed him quickly. "I hate this by the way. I've gotten used to waking up in your arms."

Morgan grinned. "I've gotten used to you too. Good night, Honey."

## 20

Honey opened her door and headed towards the bathroom. She knocked then opened the door to find a gaggle of young women with their hair in large round curlers clamoring for the mirror.

"Oops. Sorry," Honey muttered.

"Oh, it's okay," one of them called out.

"The potty is open," another one said.

"Christie is still in the shower, so you'll have to wait."

"Will there be any hot water left?"

Honey stood in silent amazement of the hive-mind conversation. The curlers and the makeup reminded her of being backstage at a low-budget runway show. The only difference was the lack of clothing racks. There had been many times Honey had to do her own makeup and hair. The memories flooded back. They were good memories, and they brought a smile to her face.

The bathroom door shot open, and another young woman leaned in and yelled that breakfast was almost over and everyone had better have eaten already. Honey stood back as the group in the bathroom squealed in unison, became a flurry of activity, and ran out the door. She could only assume they were headed off to make sure they ate. Honey leaned in and turned off a faucet that had been left running.

She returned to her room after taking care of her morning ablutions. She'd decided that a late morning shower would probably be best, and the bathroom might actually not be so chaotic. After dressing in jeans for the morning, she picked up her phone to text Morgan. She'd just pressed send when a knock sounded on her door.

"Morning, beautiful," Morgan purred and leaned in for a kiss. "Ready for this?"

"What—breakfast? Definitely. I'm going to need to come back here for a shower and to get ready later. I'm trying to decide when the best time will be to have access to the bathroom. I'm sharing with a bunch of bridesmaids."

Morgan huffed, "Sorry about that."

"No, you're not. You're laughing at my pain." Honey sneered teasingly as she followed him down the hall.

Morgan stopped and pulled her into his embrace. He played with the curls by her ear. "I am genuinely sorry you have to share the bathroom with JoJo's crazy friends." He stood holding her, gazing into her eyes. "Next time we visit, you'll stay with me. I promise."

Morgan's intense gaze left Honey breathless.

"Okay," she muttered.

"Come. Food." Morgan took her hand and led her off.

They walked into a large white and stainless-steel kitchen full of activity.

"Nice to see you this morning, Morgan." A slightly round, older, woman called out as she chopped a pile of peppers and onions

"Good morning, Connie," Morgan called back. Honey stopped as Morgan continued into the fray.

"Breakfast is in the big dining room this morning," Connie announced

"You're going to make us eat with the masses?"

"Us?" Connie turned from her task. "What us? All I see is you nosing into my refrigerator."

Morgan closed the door of the large, walk-in refrigerator. He walked over and placed an arm around Connie's shoulders. He held out his other hand to Honey. "Connie, this is Honey. Honey, this is Connie, queen of the kitchen. She makes the best guacamole and salsa. She also makes a mean blueberry waffle."

Morgan's affection for this woman was clear in his praise of her cooking and the expression on his face. Honey held out her hand to Connie. Connie took her hand and covered it with the other. "Now tell me about Honey."

Morgan leaned down and whispered conspiratorially to Connie, his eyes on Honey. "Honey has my heart."

Honey blushed. She felt a sting of tears in the eyes. Her heart welled with joy. She felt the same about him, and he had actually voiced it.

"That's all I need to know about her," Connie said. "Nice to meet you, Honey. I look forward to getting to know you."

Honey nodded, still in a blissed shock at Morgan's confession.

"Now get out of my kitchen. You want food, you get to eat with *the masses*." Connie flicked her fingers in air quotes. "I've got too much work to do, and the caterers are about to invade." She pointed out the door. "Go."

Morgan chuckled.

"Hey, Morgan." Honey stopped him outside of the kitchen.

He stopped and turned to face her. "Yeah?"

Honey swallowed. All of a sudden her throat felt dry. She hoped she could speak without choking up. "You have my heart too."

Morgan stepped in close. His eyes flared gold. He took Honey's hand and kissed her knuckles. His smile dazzled her.

"Come on. Let's get some breakfast."

Honey felt as if her face would crack from her smile. *This is what in love feels like.* It was a very good feeling.

Breakfast was served buffet style. Honey was astounded at the quantity of food prepared, but it made sense when she saw how much Morgan ate. A few others also had their plates piled high. Honey did not shy away from taking her fair share of bacon.

"What?" she asked, chomping on a piece.

Morgan laughed. "You. You're not afraid of food. I know you told me you've had issues in the past, but you are clearly not afraid of food. And I thought you said you didn't eat pork."

Honey smiled. "This isn't pork. It's bacon. Bacon doesn't count."

Honey didn't have access to a full-length mirror. The small mirror in her room was all she had to use. It wasn't worth her neck to try to get into either bathroom with the various bridesmaids running around. She decided a minimalist approach to hair and makeup would serve her purpose. She did put more cosmetics on than she normally wore on a daily basis. This afternoon, she added shimmery gold eyeshadow and lip gloss with a hint of color. She didn't want to call attention to her forehead. She slicked her messy curls across her brow to hide the bandage and pulled the rest into a low loose bun, leaving a few tendrils of golden blond curls to frame her face.

She slipped the dress over her head and smoothed the fabric past her hips. The dress fit as if it had been made for her. The bodice, gathered into small tight pleats, swirled between her breasts. Layers of sheer aqua-colored silk fell in graceful waves to the floor. Thin shoulder straps kept the column dress in place. From what she could see of herself, she looked pretty good. Maybe not as good if she had had a team of stylists putting her together but still pretty good.

She slipped her feet into a pair of Louboutins. If there were an appropriate time and place to wear these shoes, this was clearly it. All of the clothes from Honey's modeling days no longer fit. Anything she had that had continued to fit, she'd left in her closet when she ran away. She had taken a few pairs of her beloved shoes. Designer shoes were her weakness, even if she could no longer afford them.

There was nothing for her to do but wait. Morgan had already indicated he would be by when it was time to head down for the ceremony. She had expected that Morgan would have to wait for her and not the opposite.

She perched on the edge of her bed, phone in hand. She accessed her favorite game app and lined up colorful gems. A deep voice told her she was doing great. She continued to match gems in the game while she waited for Morgan.

A loud thundering passed by her door. Honey stepped out to see what had caused the sound. She caught a glimpse of pink and yellow fluff disappearing around the corner. She smiled to herself. The bridesmaids. They were all over-the-top dramatic and silly, she thought. Probably the heightened anxiety of being in a wedding. She could only imagine if the bridesmaids were out-of-control, how insane the bride must be. Honey shook her head and returned to her video game.

Lost in concentration of beating the next level, Honey almost missed the soft tap at her door.

The knock repeated.

Honey stood, smoothing the fabric around her hips before opening the door. She hoped Morgan would find her beautiful. Hoped he would see past the bandage that she was constantly aware of. She felt beautiful every time he smiled at her, and in this dress, she thought she might actually look as nice as he made her feel.

Honey opened the door. Jinx stood there in a long black gown with a plunging neckline. A simple row of pearls draped over her prominent collarbone. The necklace reminded Honey that she hadn't put on her jewelry.

"Morgan sends his apologies, and he asked me to escort you down."

"Is everything okay?" Honey asked as she slipped her earrings on. She slid stacks of pink and gold Indian glass bangles over her wrists. She left the single pendant as her only necklace.

"Everything is fine. He just needed to take care of something."

Honey sighed, Jinx seemed exceptionally cryptic this afternoon.

Honey followed Jinx through different halls and down different stairs than she had traversed previously. She was definitely not going to learn the ins and out of this house in a weekend.

They continued into the courtyard. Many guests were already seated. Jinx leaned over and said something to the usher. Honey recognized him as the young man who won the race to park Morgan's car. He nodded to Jinx's instructions.

He approached Honey. "Miss." He stuck out his elbow for her to take. Guests were already crowding the middle section on both sides of the aisle. Honey expected him to deposit her somewhere in an empty section towards the back, but they kept walking. He stopped at the front row, indicating for Honey to sit.

"Oh, I'm not family," she whispered to the usher.

"You're with Morgan, right?"

She nodded.

"So you're here. Third seat in please."

Honey felt awkward and conspicuous as she took her seat. She knew no one around her. The people in the row behind her, she assumed, were Morgan's family whom she hadn't met yet. Remi rolled up the center aisle. The usher removed the chair to Honey's left. Remi positioned himself next to her.

"Hello, Miss Gould." Even when speaking quietly, he had a large voice.

Honey smiled and nodded in greeting. "Do you know where Morgan is?"

"Apparently, JoJo had a moment of panic this afternoon. Originally, she planned to walk herself down the aisle. She conscripted Morgan into participating in this event."

Honey nodded as if she understood. She didn't. Did this mean Morgan was now one of the groomsmen? The processional music began before she had a chance to ask.

Music that had been quietly playing in the background suddenly grew louder, transitioning into a traditional processional march. Honey watched as two small girls in white dresses, with layered tulle skirts that made them look like white puff balls, tossed small purple flowers as they walked up the aisle. The scent of lavender reached her as the girls passed. The flower girls were followed by a rainbow brigade. The bridesmaids were each dressed in a different color, creating a pastel spectrum effect. They wore yellow, peach, pink, lavender, and pale blue dresses in a puffy style similar to the flower girls. The groomsmen wore black tuxedos with color coordinating vests and boutonnieres. The couples separated and lined up, flanking the sides of the small lectern where a priest stood. JoJo's groom approached the priest, and the groomsman in blue stepped closer to him. Honey guessed he must be the best man.

The music swelled into the *Wedding March*, and everyone stood to watch the bride make her entrance. Honey didn't know what to expect. Based on JoJo's choice of bridesmaids, she almost expected to see someone in a frivolous and flamboyant dress. She caught a glimpse of a small, delicate, young woman with waves of dark hair in an elegant white gown with long lace sleeves. The high waist and bell-shaped skirt reminded Honey of a 1950s movie star.

Before Honey took in any more details, her eyes found Morgan escorting his sister down the aisle. Honey felt her mouth go dry. She knew her attention should be on the bride, but she could not take her eyes from Morgan. He was better looking than any model Honey had ever known. Standing next to the petite JoJo emphasized his height. The cut of the tuxedo emphasized his broad shoulders.

Honey caught Morgan's eye, and he smiled. She could see by his expression that he felt honored to give JoJo away. Sparks of gold flew from his eyes.

They reached the front of the aisle. The groom and the priest stepped forward. Morgan took JoJo's hand and placed it in that of her husband-to-be. The priest mumbled a few words. Morgan nodded and said his reply then stepped back next to Honey. Honey wrapped her arms possessively around Morgan's arm. She leaned in. He smelled nice, clean like fresh rain on a dry forest floor.

Honey's mind drifted as the ceremony proceeded. She thought about what she would wear if she were the bride. Something classic. Simple. She decided on one bridesmaid, Lana. Lana would probably wear a tux. That would be really quite sharp looking, she thought, all black and white. Honey, framed by people in tuxedos while she wore a cream colored dress with a tea length skirt. So handsome in the tux he currently wore, she decided Morgan could wear it again. Honey blinked back to reality as she realized she was imagining marrying Morgan. She leaned her head against his shoulder. Who else would she marry? He hadn't said he loved her, exactly. No, he said she had his heart. That was pretty darned close.

JoJo leaned forward and kissed her husband. Everyone burst into cheers and applause. The wedding party walked back down the aisle. The bride and groom were followed by their rainbow entourage. Guests began pouring into the aisle, following them out.

Morgan grabbed Honey's hand and headed in the opposite direction. "Come on. We'll meet everyone later"

"What are you doing?" Honey laughed.

Morgan glanced over his shoulder. "Avoiding that crush."

"Won't you be expected to be there, having given away the bride and all?"

"That was nerve-racking. But I couldn't say no. She was a crying mess when a few of the bridesmaids dragged me off to see her. Her big plan was to do that on her own with a picture of her mom in the bouquet."

"Her mom's picture? How sweet."

"Apparently, she was fine with it last night at the rehearsal, but she flipped this morning. I'm sorry I couldn't meet you, but Jinx explained everything, right?"

"Not exactly. She said you sent her to bring me down to the wedding and that was it. No explanation."

Morgan humphed, blowing air through his nose. "Sounds like Jinx hasn't decided if she likes you or not."

"I think it's probably not."

"I'll talk with her."

"Is that really necessary? So what if your head butler doesn't like me. It's not like I'm going to live here."

Morgan paused, looking at Honey. "I'll have a talk with her."

Honey realized they had circled around the outside of the crowd and approached the reception party area from the opposite side. They stepped out from between planters and past the DJ, out onto the dance floor, heading towards the reception tables.

People dressed in formal attire mingled about the tables. Morgan began introducing Honey. She lost track of names and faces began blurring together. More than once Morgan left Honey standing alone as he was pulled into more detailed conversations. Honey spent her time looking around at the people and the back side of the mansion. A row of columns and arches created a covered walkway and trellises supported flowering vines over a separate patio area. The opulence of the setting and everyone's elegant dress made her feel as if she was in a living magazine spread. This was almost too perfect to be real.

Honey watched as JoJo dragged her new husband to different groups. She may have been dressed more sophisticated than her bridesmaids, but she exhibited the same exuberant and flighty enthusiasm. She plowed into Morgan.

He caught her fierce hug with a huff of air. Honey couldn't make out what they said to each other from where she stood, only squeals and excitement. Morgan turned to Honey and held his hand out for her. She approached him taking his hand. JoJo hugged her unexpectedly. Then scampered off, pulling her new husband along.

Honey had to laugh at the brief, excited exchange. "Is she always like that?"

Morgan sighed. "Fortunately, no. She'll be back to normal in a month or so, after all the adrenaline and excitement wears off."

A server with a tray of champagne strolled by. Honey lifted two flutes, handing one to Morgan. "I've met so many people already that I don't know who anybody is. I hope there isn't a quiz later."

"Come on. I want to introduce you to my other sisters." Morgan led the way towards a very pregnant woman. Honey could tell by her features and coloring that she was clearly Morgan's sister. She had the same aquiline nose and curling dark hair, only longer. Only her features were softer, feminine. "Carolyn, I'd like to introduce you to Honey."

Carolyn awkwardly pushed herself out of the chair she was in before offering her hand to Honey. "Nice to meet you. So you're the woman Morgan met in Monterey?"

Honey nodded.

"Good, good. Have you met Julia yet? She's our younger sister. A bit of a powerhouse these days."

"Powerhouse? You don't mean anything like JoJo, do you?" Honey wasn't sure she could handle more intense exuberance.

Carolyn laughed. "No, not like JoJo at all. Julia is more business power. Intense. JoJo is like a ball of kinetic plasma, zapping from grounding rod to grounding rod. Julia has her nose into a big project these days, so she might be a little abrupt."

Honey smiled and nodded. She didn't know what else to say. Meeting new people was not something that came naturally to her.

She felt at a distinct disadvantage. Everyone she met had known Morgan for years. She felt as if she constantly walked into conversations already started. Everyone continued with the conversation, expecting her to be able to keep up, but she was hopelessly behind. Morgan was clearly distracted by the conversations he kept getting pulled into. Honey didn't know what else to do but follow him around. She watched Morgan smile and talk or have a serious face and talk. More than once he seemed to huddle in close and speak quietly with a few other men who would leave and return. This party was turning into a boring, lonely event.

Honey wandered around admiring different dresses. She thought maybe she could find a snack or even a place to sit and people watch. There were certainly enough people here to keep her occupied for several hours.

A young man with an easy grin approached Honey. "Bride or groom?" he asked.

"Pardon?"

"Bride or groom? Who are you here for?" He gestured broadly toward the party.

"Oh, right. Bride."

"Great!" He stepped in closer. "So how do you know JoJo? Are you another relative? It seems like everyone here is related in one way or another."

Honey laughed. This guy should have been hitting on one of the bridesmaids. Maybe he was working his way over to them. "No, actually I don't know JoJo at all. I just met her today, in fact. I'm here with Morgan, her brother. He gave her away this afternoon."

"Oh, Morgan." His grin disappeared, and he took a few step backwards away from Honey. "Well, nice to meet you. Enjoy the party."

*Hmm.* Morgan must have quite a reputation. Honey figured the guy would have at least looked around for Morgan and continued hitting on her when he didn't see him. She had not expected him to scamper away like a frightened rabbit. She found the canapes and other finger foods and sampled a few delicacies before deciding she wasn't really hungry. Honey continued to look at the selection to see if anything did appeal to her.

"You're Honey right?" a voice behind her asked.

"Yeah." Honey turned.

A friendly looking man with a square jaw and sandy blond hair approached her. He stuck out his hand "I'm Jake. Caro sent me."

"Who?"

"Carolyn. She sent me to find you. She saw you on your own and wanted me to invite you back to our table. I'm Caro's husband"

"Oh, okay. That's nice. Thank you."

Honey followed Jake back toward the tables.

They approached a table where Remi and a little old woman sat. The woman was petite, wrinkled, and shriveled with age. She wore her thick, snow-white hair pulled back into a rather severe bun.

"You know Remi, right?" Jake said in lieu of introductions.

Honey nodded in agreement before taking a seat at the table. "This is Nan. She's Caro's great grandmother. That would make you Remi's grandmother, right, Nan?" Jake raised his voice when he addressed Nan.

Nan muttered something not particularly intelligible.

So this was Nan, the old Catholic grandmother. "Hi." She said as she sat down at the table with Nan and Remi.

"I'm going to go find Caro. I'll be right back." Jake wandered off into the party in search of his wife.

Honey tried to think of something to say to Remi. She didn't want to sit there in awkward silence. "Uhm, so how are you related to Morgan? I'm a bit confused. He says pretty much everyone here is related, so big extended family? Lots of cousins? How does this work?"

"Lots of cousins and distant cousins. Some of the family Morgan mentions are family by choice not by blood. I'm actually Morgan's cousin once removed, not his uncle."

Honey looked at Remi with a puzzled expression.

He clarified for her, "I'm his father's cousin."

"Oh, okay." Honey nodded, her conversation gambit depleted.

"If you'll excuse me, Honey, I see Jinx. I need to speak with her regarding the aftermath of these festivities." Remi's electric wheelchair whirred into life as he backed away from the table.

Honey was left alone with Nan.

"It was a lovely ceremony." Honey started. Nan sat nodding her head slightly. She didn't seem to be reacting to Honey's words, just rocking slightly. Honey tried again, a little louder, "Nice day for it. Great weather. Of course, it's probably always great weather up here. Not like Monterey and Pacific Grove that gets fogged in all the time." Honey watched Nan. Not a flicker of recognition. She stopped trying.

Honey let her gaze drift over the party, her focus drawn

to a group of teenagers on the patio a level above where she sat. A group of boys was gathered around one girl. At the next table over, another girl sat alone. Honey watched a tall boy, the one who had been her usher, sit down and start talking to the lonely girl. One by one more of the boys moved to the other table.

Honey began to feel sorry for the girl who had been abandoned, when the process began again with the boys drifting from one girl en masse to the other. Eventually, it appeared the groups evened out with each girl having a small collection of admirers.

"At least, they have admirers," Honey pouted.

"Ain't no one gonna sniff around you."

Nan had spoken.

Honey turned to her in shock. She hadn't thought the old woman could talk.

"Excuse me? What's that supposed to mean?" The old woman was right. No one had bothered to try to talk to Honey since that one guy in the blue suit. Honey wanted to know what did Nan know about it.

Nan muttered something and returned to her nodding, rocking motion.

*Great.* Nan is some kind of complaint oracle. Only hears when people are bitching about something and only provides insults without insight.

Honey slumped in her chair. She contemplated heading back to her room, but she didn't know how to get to it. Stupid oversized house. Stupid party. Stupid Morgan.

## 21

Honey watched as Carolyn waddled over to her and Nan.

"Having a good time, Nan?" Carolyn asked.

Nan rocked and nodded.

Carolyn held her hand out to Honey. "Walk with me. It's the only thing that eases my sciatica these days."

Honey stood. Carolyn looped her arm through Honey's and led her away from the tables away from the party.

"How soon are you due?" Honey asked, a note of concern in her voice. Carolyn did appear to be uncomfortable and ready to pop.

Carolyn looked around, straightened her posture and her baby bump seemed to retreat. "Oh, geez, not for weeks and weeks." Honey noticed her gait evened out. Carolyn walked smoothly no longer waddling. "That was just for anyone who might have been paying attention, like Nan in one of her lucid moments.

"I can't believe my husband actually abandoned you with her. He should have kept you with him. He didn't 'cause he's afraid of Morgan." Carolyn shook her head.

"Remi was there for a bit, but he left to talk to Jinx. Not that his conversation was much better than Nan's."

"Remi is a good teacher and lecturer. He can talk when he has something to say."

"Wait. Afraid of Morgan? Why would your husband be afraid of Morgan?"

"Not so much afraid of him as afraid of Morgan thinking he was flirting with you or something."

"Why on earth would Morgan think your husband would flirt with me?" Honey was genuinely confused. "He wouldn't, would he?"

Carolyn continued to stroll calmly. Honey noticed they had reached the covered walkway. "Jake can be a little flirty. That's how he is; he doesn't mean anything by it. It's more Morgan being possessive."

Honey scoffed.

"Has anyone talked to you today when Morgan wasn't around?"

"Now that you ask, no, not really."

"And they won't because of Morgan."

Honey shook her head. It didn't make any sense. Not that she wanted anyone other than Morgan to talk to her, but she usually did get hit on a few times whenever she went to a big party. Today felt unusual. "Your grandmother said something like that. Said no one would sniff around me. I thought it was an odd thing to say."

"That's Nan. She says things in the meanest way possible if she bothers to talk at all. Don't let her fool you. If she doesn't want to be bothered, she goes quiet. But she's got a wicked sharp tongue, and she knows what she's saying." Carolyn's tone was laughing, sarcastic, but there was truth in her words. "No one will bother you, especially since it's known you came with Morgan."

"Is Morgan the golden child or something? Why be on eggshells around him so much?"

Carolyn turned. She and Honey were now facing the party. Hundreds of people seemed to be enjoying themselves laughing, drinking, and dancing.

She sighed. "How much do you know about Morgan?"

Honey looked at the other woman's profile. She really was striking, with the same eyes as Morgan. Honey wondered if the glowed the way Morgan's did.

"You have the same eyes. His eyes, they glow. Do yours?"

Carolyn nodded. "They glow and for the same reasons."

"So you...?"

Carolyn laughed. "I do, and this one in here—" She placed her hands around her pregnant belly. "—will as well. So you know about us?"

Honey nodded.

"Do you know about pack structure? How there is always a clear leader and the rest play a dominance game?"

Honey nodded again. "Yeah, alpha wolves. Then usually a beta and down the line in pecking order."

"Okay, so then you need to know Morgan is this family's alpha."

Honey stopped nodding and stared at Carolyn. "How? I thought oldest, strongest. Remi is clearly the oldest and is very domineering."

"Remi does have a commanding presence, but that has more to do with years of running a school full of children with poor impulse control than with alpha traits."

"Morgan is the alpha?" Honey still didn't fully believe what she heard. "Shouldn't he be assertive and lording over everyone, controlling everything? I thought that was the role of an alpha male."

"Morgan is different. It's what makes him such a

wonderful head of this group. He knew he would have the job someday, but he had expected our father to live a good long time. We all had. He took over after the accident that killed our parents and our uncle." Carolyn shook her head, silent for a moment before continuing. "He took over as alpha before he was ready for it. The job came with a lot of family and business responsibilities. Morgan had always been a decent manager, so he did what he did best. He delegated. It's what he's good at. He didn't try to run every aspect of the family businesses or the family or the school. He lets Remi run the school without any interference. Morgan is good at being a structural engineer, so he continues with the construction business. Julia is good with overall business affairs, and he lets her do most of that, even though he has final say.

"Our family has more alphas than we have ever had because of Morgan. We have a female alpha for the first time. Julia is amazing, and she's really been able to shine and come into her power. His unique way of ruling the roost has seemed pretty hands-off, but he is consulted on everything. Ultimately, he makes the big decisions. It's no excuse for ignoring you, but that's what he's been doing all afternoon." Carolyn pointed to where Morgan stood in the midst of a group of other men.

Honey noticed Morgan was slightly taller than the rest, but all of the men were tall, good looking, and broad through the shoulders. They were all probably built like body builders under their suits.

"Are you an alpha?" Honey asked.

Carolyn snickered. "No, and I wouldn't want to be one. It's a lot of work. Managing a toddler and a baby is going to be plenty for me. I don't need to deal with the constant competition and proving of myself that some require."

"Is Morgan always having to compete?" She didn't like the thought that she might be a pawn in one of his competitions.

"No, he doesn't. No one even challenges his authority, except for maybe Julia, but that's more sister-brother than alphas butting heads. The younger wolves, they compete a lot." Carolyn pointed to a group of young men and what appeared to be a tower of shots. "It's a natural male trait to begin with. It just seems emphasized in those who are also wolves."

"What about the girls? Don't they go in for the competition?" She had a hard time believing that only male wolves would engage in competitive tendencies. Honey knew models who could be cutthroat.

Carolyn rolled her eyes. "Mean girl syndrome can be tough with our kind. And, yes, they do engage the guys." The two women watched as the yellow and the lavender bridesmaids joined the men with the tower of shots. It was clear they were there to drink, not to flirt.

"Is everything a competition around here?" Honey asked.

"It is with the boys and some of the girls, especially after they hit puberty and are trying to figure out their position in the scheme of things."

"Like the boys with those two girls I saw earlier."

Carolyn nodded then continued "Exactly. Some of the adults saw what was going on." She indicated a large bald man built like a bodybuilder dancing with a teenage girl. "Did you notice there were three girls and one was almost completely ignored?"

Honey shook her head, she had only seen two

"Well, that's who Shane is dancing with now. Shane is one of our big guys around here. He's actually an alpha in his own right." They watched as the music ended and Shane bowed to the girl before escorting her off the dance floor. Before she could even turn around there were several boys clamoring to dance with her. "See how the boys now think they need to dance with her, when before they wouldn't even talk to her."

"So Shane is basically messing with the girl?" Honey asked.

"Oh, no. Shane is messing with the boys. They were clearly being rude. By dancing with her, Shane put her on their radar."

Honey sighed. "Well, at least she is getting to dance."

"Why are you talking to me and not dancing, Honey? Clearly, you would rather be dancing."

Honey nodded. "Well, Morgan's been off conferencing with others." She scoffed. "And here I thought he was taking me away for a romantic weekend." She turned to Carolyn. "You know I've been shuffled off to a little guest room, and I share a bathroom with a flock of squealing bridesmaids. I don't even know how to get back to my room without someone walking me there." She spread her arms, gesturing her frustration. "I'm not dancing because I've been ditched."

Carolyn squinted in annoyance, "My brother can be thickheaded at times. He's too busy minding business when he should be minding you." She made a clicking sound with her tongue against the roof of her mouth as she plotted something. "Come with me."

She directed Honey towards a good looking young man who was blatantly flirting with the female bartender.

"Dante, we need your assistance."

Dante stood. He was tall and clearly related to Morgan. Similar build, similar coloring. He was younger, with more refined features, prettier compared to Morgan's ruggedness.

Honey thought he could be a younger brother, but she only knew of Morgan having sisters.

"Honey, this is our cousin Dante," Carolyn introduced them.

"Honey, how sweet." Dante took Honey's hand. He leaned in then paused. "You're Morgan's." His hazel eyes made contact with Honey's green eyes, and he kissed the back of her hand. Honey felt the gesture was slightly sleazier than gallant, as she noticed he hadn't finished his thought. Morgan's what? Girlfriend? No, he simply left it at Morgan's...

"Yes, and he is being neglectful. We need your assistance in fixing that." Carolyn explained.

Dante looped Honey's arm around his elbow. "And why isn't he here with the beautiful Honey"

"He is off playing family politics. It's a wedding. He should have eyes only for her."

"So how are you planning to get him to dance with me?" Honey asked.

"That's easy. You're going to dance with me." Dante grinned, exposing a mouth full of bright white teeth. "He'll hate it."

"Make sure you bump into Shane. A little more competition should put Morgan straight for the rest of the night," Carolyn added to the plot.

"As long as he doesn't try to dump me on your grandmother again. No offense, but..."

"None taken," Dante chuckled in good humor, "She's an old bat. You really want to make him sweat?"

Honey nodded. Dante turned to Carolyn, "Find Roman Aventine. That'll set Morgan straight."

"Roman's here?" Carolyn's laugh was almost a maniacal

cackle. "Dante, you are an evil genius. I'll go find Roman. You two…" She pointed to the dance floor.

"Who's Roman Aventine?" Honey asked as Dante led her to the dance floor and swept her into his embrace.

"Roman is friendly competition. The Aventines are business competitors, as well as another family like ours. You know about us, right?" Dante squinted at her, confirming she had been told.

Honey nodded.

"Roman is their family's version of Morgan. Except their Primary Alpha is Roman's father. Just as Morgan and Carolyn's father would have been if he were still alive."

Dante smoothly guided Honey around the dance floor. About halfway through the song, they were interrupted by the bodybuilder Shane.

Shane's voice was deeper, gruffer, "I understand the lady needs my assistance."

Dante stepped back from Honey and gave her hand to Shane. "Shane, Honey. Honey, Shane." Once the brief introduction was made, Dante sauntered off. Honey expected he went to find another girl to flirt with.

Shane was a completely different physical type than Morgan or Dante, yet he was still extremely good looking. Powerfully built with broad thick shoulders, it was clear he had massive biceps bulging under his tuxedo jacket. He had a nicely shaped head, which was good, considering he was bald. His eyes slanted slightly downward at the edges, and he had broad, high cheekbones.

"You're the girl from the coffee shop," he stated. "Morgan is clearly being a fool. He had us drive all the way to Monterey to see you for five minutes and now…" Shane shook his head as he moved Honey with unexpected grace and fluidity.

"Yeah, was that you with him that day?" She didn't continue with the day that Morgan finally kissed her. "And now?"

"And now he's left you alone long enough to dance with Dante and me."

She laughed at this, as Shane stepped into a twirl.

They stopped in front of a tall blond man. "I believe, there is a damsel in distress here." The man's voice had a slight upper-crust New England lilt to it.

"Aventine." Shane drew out the name slowly. "Are you helping or are you hindering?"

"I am here to help the lady. And if it annoys Palatine, all the better." He turned his focus to Honey, "Roman Aventine at your service." He held his hand out to Honey.

Roman Aventine was easily as tall as Morgan, but with his more slender build, he appeared to be taller. He had piercing blue eyes, and his blond hair was cut short. Honey was impressed that all the good-looking men she was suddenly getting attention from were there to help her regain Morgan's attention.

"Honey Gould," she said as she took his hand. "Thank you, Shane." She grinned at him, enjoying the subterfuge.

"Honey Gould, gold as honey, I will warn you Palatine is not going to like this. So, to piss him off properly, I'm going to hold you a little tighter than propriety dictates."

"Oh," Honey squeaked when Roman pulled her tightly into his embrace.

"I will probably get punched for this, but really, the man has it coming. Carolyn explained he's been ignoring you this whole afternoon. How unseemly of him." The music had switched to something slow and Roman gently guided Honey through simple dance steps.

"You're doing this for me even if you know Morgan

might punch you?" Honey was a bit confused. Why would this man risk getting hit.

"Dancing with a beautiful lady is totally worth that moment of pain." Roman's face was close to Honey's. To the casual viewer it would appear they were an intimate couple and not strangers who had only met moments before. "And trust me, even if he does deck me, his pain will be deeper than mine when he sees us together." He chuckled malevolently.

"So I take it you and Morgan are..." Roman was whipped away from Honey.

Morgan's fist bunched on Roman's shoulder grabbing a handful of suit fabric. "Enemies," he growled.

"Adversaries," Roman corrected. "Took you long enough, Palatine."

Morgan, caught off guard by Roman's last remark dropped his grasp on the blond man's jacket. Morgan looked at Honey, she stood with her arms crossed, an expression of disappointment on her face.

"If you won't dance with her, I will. She's a lovely dancer." Roman continued.

Morgan shot him a glare then pulled Honey into his arms.

Morgan began swaying to the music, Honey tucked into his embrace, head resting on his chest. "Aventine's right. That took me too long. It should never have happened."

"What? Rescuing me from dancing with handsome men?" Honey smiled. Their plan had worked.

"No, leaving you alone so that you ended up dancing with other men. I should have been dancing with you the entire time. I'm an idiot. Dante had to tip me off. And then when I saw you with Aventine, I about lost it." He kissed the top of her head. "Do you have any idea what you were doing to me?"

"Completely," Honey giggled. "Carolyn and Dante plotted the whole thing. Make you stupid jealous so you would stop ignoring me."

"Sometimes I can actually admit my sisters are smarter than me. This is definitely one of those times. I was ignoring you, wasn't I?"

Honey nodded her head, brushing the side of her face against the fabric of his tux.

They stopped dancing. "Forgive me?"

Honey looked up at him, his gaze intent on her face. "You'll have to make it up to me for the rest of the evening."

"I can do that." He leaned down and kissed her lightly. "You have my heart, and I'm a fool."

"This sounds like a promising start."

"Have I told you how breathtakingly beautiful you are?"

"No. Keep going. You're making good progress."

Morgan pulled her firmly into his embrace as he glided with her across the floor. In her heels, she was almost as tall as Morgan. Her cheek rested against his.

"Morgan," she began.

"Hmm-mmm?"

"You more than have my heart." Honey swallowed. She continued to lean into him. "I love you."

Morgan stopped dancing. Pulling his cheek away from hers, he tucked a finger under her chin so that she opened her eyes to look at him. "Why does it sound like there's a but coming."

Honey laughed in reply. "There is. I love you but don't leave me alone again. I felt completely abandoned."

He kissed her temple, "I'm sorry, sweetheart. That was stupid, and I won't leave your side for the rest of the night."

He paused. His expression momentarily went blank, and gold flashed from his eyes. "You love me." His mouth spread into a wide grin, exposing all his teeth.

Honey's own grin spread. She nodded as Morgan lifted her off her feet and spun her around. Morgan slowly lowered her, so her feet were back on the dance floor. "I love you. I love you too." He cupped her face in both hands and kissed her.

After watching the cutting of the cake, Morgan led Honey along the covered walk, and away from the party. "This trip hasn't gone the way you were expecting, has it?"

"Not exactly. I thought—" Honey paused, "—oh, I don't know what I thought. I made up something in my head. I made up several somethings in my head. This is none of them."

They stopped. A couple locked in an amorous embrace were leaning against the doorway they had been headed towards. Morgan cleared his throat. Honey recognized Roman Aventine, the tall blond she had danced with earlier. She did not recognize the woman. She looked familiar with the same dark hair and eyes as Carolyn and Morgan, but her nose was shorter.

"Julia?" Morgan asked.

"Palatine!" Roman Aventine said, a little loudly in surprise.

"Uh. Hi, Morgan," the woman he called Julia said.

Honey watched as Morgan's gaze slid back and forth between the two. She expected there was a story here.

"Right," Morgan said with a sigh. "Julia, this is Honey. Honey, this is my sister Julia. You met Aventine earlier." His introduction was clearly distracted by the activities they had come upon. "So you and...?" Morgan asked his sister while pointing at Aventine.

"This isn't what it looks like," Julia began.

Morgan's eyebrows shot up. Honey knew what she thought it looked like. How could it have been anything else, unless these two weren't supposed to be kissing each other?

"Not what it looks like?" Aventine's voice was sharp as he questioned Julia's excuse.

"Roman, please." Julia sounded aggravated, as if she had had enough of his behavior.

Morgan steered Honey away as the two engaged in a bickering match.

"What was that?" Honey asked.

"I think that was my sister making out with our business competitor. The one she professes to dislike greatly."

"Methinks she doth protest too much?" Honey asked.

"It certainly looks like it. I can't say I saw that one coming. They'll make one hell of a power couple if it happens."

"You don't seem terribly upset. I got the impression you didn't like him."

"I don't like him dancing with you." Morgan paused and nodded. "Our families have a formal truce. We are partnering on a new venture, so why not an alliance of marriage."

"That sounds so medieval."

"It does, but if that is the beginnings of something, why not? Julia deserves to be happy. I just never expected it to be him." Morgan led Honey through a different door into the house.

Honey followed him through the game room they had been in last night. She began to recognize places, but she still had no idea how to get around in the house. Morgan continued to lead her through hallways and up a flight of stairs. He opened a set of double doors, and they emerged onto a balcony tucked into a corner where one wing of the mansion met the main house. Wrought iron balustrades surrounded them on two sides.

Honey gasped as she looked at the view. The party continued below them. Spread out in front of them was a vista of rolling golden hills and grape vines. The late afternoon sun cast long shadows. The light made the hills glow.

"This is gorgeous, Morgan." She tilted her head to look up into his face. His gaze was on the rolling hills.

Morgan glanced over at Honey. His glowing eyes reflected the color of the hills. He wrapped his arms around her so that she could lean back against his chest. Honey sighed, happy to relax into Morgan's strength.

She turned, lifting her face to kiss him. She pressed her lips to his then Morgan deepened the kiss, sliding his tongue through her lips to fully claim her. He broke the kiss long enough to scoop her into his arms before he began kissing her again. Without breaking their kiss, he nudged the door open enough to let him pass through.

Honey wrapped her arms around his neck and watched his steady gaze as he carried her down the hall and into her room. He kicked the door shut behind him and placed Honey on the bed.

"I thought no sneaking off to my room?"

Morgan began removing his tie. "We're not sneaking. I'm just not leaving."

## 22

Honey snuggled into the warm cocoon of Morgan's embrace. With her eyes closed, she inhaled his warm masculine scent. She lightly stroked the arm around her.

They'd slept entwined in her double bed. Obviously, a larger bed was not necessary.

They had made love several times. Morgan had clearly planned for the evening's activities. They exhausted every condom he had stashed in her bag. She huffed in amusement. She hadn't even noticed he had done that.

She was in love with this man, and he said he loved her. It was scary and thrilling. Everything was about to change in her world. As long as she had Morgan, she thought she could handle anything that came her way.

The smooth even rise and fall of his chest, his breath on her hair, lulled her back to sleep.

Honey woke to a sharp knock on the door. She didn't want to move. She was much too comfortable. The knock sounded again.

Honey unwrapped herself from Morgan's protective arms and tossed on a dressing gown.

Jinx stood impatiently on the other side of the door. "Would you let Morgan know he's expected in the dining room for a meeting at nine." She turned on her heel and left. She clearly did not approve of having located Morgan in Honey's room.

"I heard," Morgan groaned. He picked up his watch from the side table. "Seven-thirty. That's enough time for a shower and breakfast." He sat up. He scooped his shorts from the floor and pulled them on.

Honey stood with her arms crossed as she watched him pull his slacks on and slip his long arms through his dress shirt sleeves. Morgan tossed the rest of his clothing items over one arm and picked up his shoes.

Morgan leaned down for a kiss. "Meet you in the breakfast room in half an hour?"Morgan leaned down for a kiss.

"I don't know where that is, Morgan." Honey stated dryly, moving her head to the side not letting him kiss her.

"Right," Morgan exhaled through his nose. "Sorry. I will come back for you in half an hour." He leaned in and kissed her. "I love you. We'll move you into my rooms tonight. And I'll make sure you get a proper tour of the house this afternoon."

"Morgan, the only door I've been through more than once is that one right there. And the only place I know how to get to and from is the bathroom. I am at a distinct disadvantage here, and I really don't like being woken up by that sneering woman. I just want to be able to get from one place to another without thinking I'm going to get lost and not knowing anyone if I do get lost. It's annoying, okay." Her tone was terse.

"I know it is, sweetheart. And I've been lousy about it.

But I will fix this. I want you to be comfortable here. It's really not the labyrinth you think it is."

"I'll talk to Jinx. She'll make sure you can get around."

"No, she won't. She clearly doesn't like me. She is being passive-aggressive towards me. She could have told me you were walking JoJo down the aisle yesterday. Instead, she was so cryptic about it. And you didn't see the look on her face just now. She disapproves of me for having you spend the night in here. It's my fault you aren't in your own bed." Honey felt herself starting to cry. She wiped at her cheek and looked at her wet fingers. "I want you to show me around, not the staff."

She sat abruptly on the bed.

"Ya' know, five minutes ago I woke up, in love, in your arms, happy. And now I'm feeling very insecure because I don't know where I am here without you. I am so out of my league, I almost like you better as a poor construction worker. I can't keep up with this." Honey gestured indicating everything. "You live in a house with staff."

Moran sat, wrapping an arm around her shoulders. "Don't say that. Come on. We'll move your stuff now. You can shower there. I won't leave you. And I will make sure you know where everything is."

Honey sniffed. "Draw me a map?"

"I'll draw you a map. I love you. Come on. Throw some clothes on." Morgan stood and began tossing items into the duffle bag sitting on the side chair. Honey helped him stuff the rest of her belongings in the bag then she followed him down a series of halls.

Honey was surprised when they entered Morgan's rooms. The living space was a large open floor plan. Columns and an archway divided the living room from the bedroom area. Honey noted the large king-sized bed. She placed her items on one of the brown leather couches.

Honey was amazed. "This is bigger than my whole apartment, and it's inside of a house."

Morgan led her into the oversized bath. This was not a bathroom designed for multiple-person use but a spa-like luxury bathroom. A wide counter under a large mirror held only one sink. A large jacuzzi tub occupied one corner. A walk-in shower took over the opposite corner. A half wall protected the toilet from appearing to be in the middle of it all. Morgan leaned into the shower, spinning knobs to start the hot water. "You shower first." He stood in the doorway and pointed back out towards his living room. "I'll be in there. Don't worry. I'm not leaving you alone." He pointed back out towards his living room.

"I have a better idea. Why don't you join me?" Honey teased.

"That sounds like a beautiful suggestion, but I'm expected down stairs by nine. That won't happen if I get into that shower with you this morning."

Morgan held her hand all the way down to the kitchen. He made it a point to show Honey exactly where they were in relation to other locations in the house. Before they reached the kitchen, he showed her the breakfast room, a separate non-formal dining area where he usually ate his meals when not on the big table in the kitchen. Connie greeted them as they entered the kitchen. "Good morning, Honey, Morgan." Honey noticed the frenzied activities of the morning before were gone. The kitchen was still bustling, just not frantic. Connie and a couple of assistants were preparing breakfast food in large trays.

"Breakfast around here is usually whatever you make yourself." Morgan began explaining. He reached into one of the trays and pulled out a triangle of french toast.

"You can cook in here unless there is some big event or I've been requested to make a big meal, like today." Connie continued for him. "You can't cook in here if I'm too busy. Or if I have decided you aren't allowed in my kitchen."

Morgan chuckled. "Yeah, I was banned for a full year because I ruined a pan."

"No, you were banned for setting fire to my kitchen and almost burning down the house."

"It wasn't that bad," Morgan grumbled playfully.

"Oh, yes, it was. We had to scrub the walls and ceiling and repaint. Those scorch marks would not come off."

Honey laughed at their good-natured banter.

"Did you miss the big breakfast on the back patio?" Connie asked. "It's not as grand as yesterday's. Not as many guests, but we still have a house full of people."

"You know I always come into the kitchen first. I don't go looking for food to be set up." Morgan snatched another slice of the fried bread and handed it to Honey. "Come on. Let's go find this food."

Morgan led Honey out through the kitchen, past the breakfast room, and through sliding glass doors onto the back patio. This was a different patio than the one Honey remembered. This one was clearly set up for outdoor cooking and dining. The large brick grill looked more like an outdoor kitchen than a simple grill. Foil trays of the food from the kitchen were lined up along the grill buffet style. Connie was right. It wasn't as elaborate as the day before, but there was plenty of food.

Several guests sat around with paper plates on their laps enjoying their breakfasts. Honey noticed a few were wearing sunglasses and nursing large mugs of coffee. She expected they might have partied a little too hard the night before.

After breakfast, Morgan showed Honey how to get from the kitchen to the games room.

Loud groans and cheers from the group surrounding the large screen television grabbed Honey's attention. A group of teens played a kinetic video game. A camera on the television sensed the players' movements and translated them into in-game actions. The game intrigued Honey. It looked like fun.

She stood watching the competition. She didn't realize how physically energetic video games had become. Large yellow letters announced game over. The group groaned as a younger boy danced around excited with his win.

"Want to play?" Morgan asked.

"Sure."

The kid who had lost the last game focused on the television screen with a controller in his hand.

Morgan said behind him. "The lady wants to play. Set her up."

"The lady can wait her turn," the kid said. One of his compatriots started slapping him on the shoulder, making him turn around.

"Oh, crap. Sorry," he said when he saw Morgan. "Yeah, she can play my turn." His focus on Morgan, he handed Honey the control wand.

"I have no idea what I'm doing," she admitted to the younger boy she stood next to.

"It's easy. You move the way it tells you to move."

Honey read the prompts as they were displayed. The premise of the game seemed easy enough. The execution was an entirely different matter. She felt like a marionette with spastic strings as she tried to mimic the movements of the demented rabbit-like creature on the screen. She was breathless with laughter by the time *Game Over* displayed.

The boy next to her repeated his victory dance until he caught sight of Morgan. He stopped moving and stared wide-eyed at the taller man. "Sorry" he squeaked, before dropping his controller and backing out of the room.

"What did you do to that kid?" Honey asked as they left the room.

"Went a little alpha on him."

Honey stopped. "Show me," she demanded.

She took a step back when Morgan's face changed. His eyes blazed gold, his brow grew thicker, cheekbones sharper, teeth a little longer. Morgan flashed an angry menacing visage, then his face returned to normal. Morgan's handsome chiseled features almost looked soft in comparison.

"Okay. That's frightening. You did that to scare him on purpose."

"Of course, I did. I have a reputation to uphold. Right now, winning a video game is going to rank that kid among his peers. I didn't want him to think a victory against someone who has never played that system before is going to count. And I particularity didn't want him to think winning a game against my girl means anything. Think of it as a stop gap measure, preventative ego maintenance."

"Well whatever you want to call it, it's scary as hell, and I hope to never be on the receiving end of that face." She placed her palm against his cheek. "I like this face much better."

Morgan placed his hand against hers and turned into her hand, kissing her palm.

"Carolyn was telling me they are always in competition," Honey said tilting her head back towards the game room.

Morgan nodded. "Always. Especially the younger ones. They are continually trying to prove themselves. When they go off to college, it will be about grades, scholarships they don't need, and school rankings. Once they graduate, they typically let their job status be the competitive ranking. The ones you don't see competing are either submissive and they don't really care or they are very dominant and don't feel the need to compete."

"So, you weren't one of the competitive ones?"

"Are you kidding? I was in the middle of it all. Constantly, trying to top the kid next to me. Being dominant as a kid has more to do with self-esteem and ego than actual dominance. Not feeling the need to compete to show your strength doesn't automatically translate into being a strong adult. It helps, but it's no guarantee."

Remi wheeled toward them. "There you are, Morgan. You are expected in the dining room."

Honey looked at Morgan, a moment of panic crossed her face.

"Miss Gould, I understand you like art." Remi began. "While Morgan is in his meeting, I thought I would show you the family's art collection."

"Go on," Morgan said. "Remi won't let you get lost. And he's right. I think you'll find our collection interesting. I'll come find you when I'm done."

Morgan leaned in and kissed her cheek. "I love you," he whispered in her ear before turning and disappearing behind a set of large wood doors.

≈

Morgan closed the dining room doors behind him. He felt like he was segregating his life into time with Honey and everything else. He needed to find balance. He needed to start letting Honey into the rest of his life. That or take her and run away and give it all up. That was an intriguing thought. Definitely, something he could reasonably consider. Turn around right now, go grab Honey and whisk her away from it all. He would definitely be able to spend his time focusing on what was important.

*Honey.* She had become vital to his very breath, and he wasn't sure he had made that clear to her yet.

He blinked and focused on the others in the room. This looked like a war council. His gaze slid from Julia to Shane to Joe. Everyone's face was grim. Not a smile in the bunch. Dante wasn't happy, but he looked more like he had yet to go to bed from last night's revelries.

"Are we waiting on anyone else?" Morgan asked.

The consensus in the room was they were all present.

Morgan pulled out the chair closest to him and sat. Julia slid over a hand-written agenda. Take it from Julia to have even an impromptu meeting organized. Morgan looked over the list. Nodding to himself.

"All right. Fill me in."

Shane nodded to Julia, confirming he was first up on the agenda. "Cyan del Fuego has been more than cooperative. Del Fuegos have taken lead on the entire Lazarus investigation. At this point, we're providing them support."

Morgan nodded. "Do we have a solid connection between Lazarus and the gents who picked me up?"

"Nothing we could prove in court, but it's him."

"Speaking of court," Dante groaned. "Those documents from Cyan Group are pretty damaging for your friend Maplecourt. I've already identified the offshore account he's been siphoning funds into. I just need to connect a few dots, then we can hand him over to Cyan with incontestable evidence."

"Good," Morgan growled. "Anything else you found out about him? Anything?"

"Give you a reason to eviscerate him before handing his carcass over to Cyan del Fuego?" Dante's eyebrows lifted above his sunglasses.

"Exactly."

With a scoff, Dante slid a file across the table to Morgan. "These are old, but I thought you might want to see them. They will make you angry. They certainly pissed me off, and I'm not in love with the girl."

Morgan opened the folder to a stack of color photographs. Honey, the wind whipping her hair, looked sad, dejected. Walking next to her, a glaring Bryce Maplecourt.

"The guy who took these recognized her and thought he could sell them for one of those *where are they now* articles. He didn't."

Morgan slowly sorted through the photos. Honey and Maplecourt were arguing. The progression of images laid out the events like a storyboard. The last few shots were of Maplecourt hitting Honey. Morgan crushed the last image in his fist. It showed Honey cowering before raised fists seconds before they would hit her.

"The photographer said he could have sold these, but he kept them in case Honey ever needed them. Then when she just disappeared, he hoped she had gotten away from the guy."

"And he kept these?"

"Yeah. He's got something against men who hit women.

He said if these could damn the man in the photos, I could have them for free."

"It's damning enough for me." Morgan breathed heavily through his nose. He itched to show Maplecourt what it would feel like to be on the receiving end of a pummeling.

Morgan closed his eyes to refocus. He looked down at the agenda. The next topic read 'Smith.'

"Remi left with Honey. Does that mean he found out nothing on our Smith?" Morgan asked.

Julia pushed a piece of paper over to him. "Here's Remi's report. It looks like this Smith used to be a Kawasaki. They had some falling out apparently over a woman and money."

"Isn't that what it's always about?" Joe scoffed.

"His family had been keeping tabs on him but lost track of him about five years ago They were appreciative that we reported a sighting. Apparently, they wanted to bring him back in. We didn't tell them of his premature demise. From what Remi wrote, its sounds like they hinted at him being a fugitive and not some prodigal son."

"And if this Smith was a fugitive that would have given Lazarus leverage against him."

"It had to be pretty good leverage."

"We'll never know."

Shane cocked an eyebrow at Morgan. Morgan coolly eyed him back. "Him or me. I chose me."

"Anyway—" Julia cut in "—from what Remi reported, the Kawasakis are open to working with us if vampires are involved."

"If vampires are involved and we start creating alliances with other families, that's really going to look like we are making strategic maneuvers for some kind of war," Dante interjected.

"That's why we have to be smart about this. We have to find out exactly what's going on." Morgan responded.

"Isn't that what your friend in Santa Maria said? Us making nice with the Aventines would have been reason enough to piss Lazarus off?"

"She also said it could be a gambit of his to distract the Del Fuego coven from his real intentions. We aren't the target. We're a tool. It's in our best interest to build strategic alliances with other wolves, especially regionally, and to formalize our relationship with the local bloodsuckers," Shane announced.

Everyone stopped and stared at him. "I'm not saying I will like it. I'm saying it's the smart political move. Look, if Lazarus is somehow actually back from the dead, there are going to be as many unhappy bloodsuckers as wolves out there. Enemy of my enemy is my friend." Shane looked around at everyone as they continued to stare at him. "Hey, not all bloodsuckers are bad. I will deny that if you try to quote me on it."

"We need some talented negotiators and natural ambassadors," Julia said.

"Speaking of ambassadors, how are relations going with Aventine?" Dante waggled his eyebrows at Julia. She shot him a loaded glare.

"Actually, having Aventine with us on this is going to be very beneficial. Roman is a very skillful negotiator and has a growing reputation that's almost the polar opposite of his father's. While his father hasn't stepped down officially, he hasn't taken an active interest in their business or family since his wife got sick. We can use him to our benefit. Besides Carolyn, is about to deliver, and she would be the person we have best suited for that role."

Morgan nodded his head. "We need calm wolves with

business know-how for negotiating with vampires. Let's give that to Remi. He'll know who would be best suited for this kind of job. Heck, if we have to train someone for the job of vampire ambassador, he'll know who we need to groom."

Julia leaned forward to address the group again. "Now about establishing connections with other families. Remi opened the door for me with the Kawasakis, and I've had promising email correspondence with a family out of South Africa and some other more local families. Now that we have this DNA evidence situation, this outreach initiative needs to be stepped up." She rapped her knuckles on the table. "We need to find out who we have north of us. See if the Nevada group will talk. They like to pretend they don't exist. What's our end game? I think it's changed. Before it was a matter of being formally aware and acknowledging each other, but now I think we need to consider spear-heading the foundation of some kind of alliance."

"That's exactly what needs to happen. We also have to find and bring in all our Smiths. At least, make them aware that this now exists," Morgan added.

"This DNA situation," Julia said, "has us concerned on two fronts. We need to be able to access the database infor-mation so we can keep our information safe, and we need to start educating, not just the Smiths, but other branches of the family." She pointed at Dante and Joe. "That's what I've got these bozos working on."

"I resemble that remark," Dante smirked.

"Seriously, though," Joe interjected. "We've been working on filling out the family tree with Remi, Dante's mom, and Nan as much as either of us can get out of her. We have missing branches. So far I have confirmed and traced back everyone who has been through the school. Fortu-nately, that's not a lot, and their genealogy lines are clean.

We're compiling a list of who and when family lines seem to have broken or ended. The plan is to contract PIs and lawyers for remote groundwork as needed, and pound the pavement for whatever is left."

Dante continued. "Fortunately, someone started keeping really tight records a few years back and made sure they passed that task on through the years. Julia asked me to start organizing our methods into easily followable chunks. I'm guessing that's so we can share a step-by-step process with others as we build alliances?"

"Exactly," Julia interjected. "I want us to be able to show to other families, in good faith, that we are serious about information sharing and containment. Just as Aventine shared the discovery with us, we need to share our processes with others."

"Yeah, I've got a contact at Aventine Industries." Dante pulled a notepad from his back pocket, and flipped it open. "Winters. Dallas Winters. Apparently, he's doing the same kind of thing as Joe and I. We are supposed to get together at some point and compare notes on our processes—what's working and what's not."

"Good." Morgan turned toward Julia. "Now how is our attempt at acquiring labs and getting a hold of database information progressing?"

"I'm stalled. I have a list of labs we can be ready to move on, but the board won't budge until they hear your recommendation as CEO."

"Do you have the list for me to look at?" Morgan asked.

"I emailed them to you, but I can get you printouts after we're done here."

"Good. That'll work. We need to get moving on that. Anything else?"

"Yes. I'm jumping into this genome information business

as hard and as fast as I can. I've got a list of conferences a mile long that I need to analyze to see which one will get us up to speed fastest, as well as which ones I need to attend and where."

"Is it time to spin this into a new company or are we good keeping it under the umbrella of Truria?" Morgan asked.

Julia pursed her lips. "My thoughts are that it stays under Truria for now. I want to acquire existing companies and bring them in, not start from scratch. I have no plans to become the head of a genomics company, but I do need to know enough to ensure we have the right people on the board and running those operations."

"Have we gotten anything from Aventine on this?"

"They are closing on SeaQuence, that lab you visited. Also working on an outreach program," Julia pointed vaguely at Dante and Joe again, as she flipped through a yellow legal pad covered in her handwritten notes. "They're already on that. Lab acquisition and just learning more regarding the whole genomics thing." She flipped to another page. "Yes. Your driver, the one you said was shot. He doesn't exist. There are no records of a car being sent for you. No missing person report. Nothing. The receptionist at the lab doesn't keep those kinds of records, and my note here says she just doesn't remember. And I quote 'People go in and out all day. You can't expect me to remember them all.' A real quality witness with that one."

"Nothing?" Morgan asked incredulously.

"Nothing. And, no attempts or threats against Roman Aventine."

"It might have been an isolated incident. Maybe. With two of Lazarus's flunkies out of the picture, maybe it's thrown him off his game."

Morgan nodded. He wadded up the paper agenda in front of him. "Anything else?"

Shane nodded to him. "What's your status right now?"

"Honestly?" Morgan asked.

"Honestly."

"I'm not sure. I feel like I've dropped the ball on a few things. Ever since I met Honey, I feel like I'm messing things up with her."

Shane chuckled. "She's your mate isn't she? That's what's throwing you off."

Morgan sighed. "She is. Now to not scare her off. My first priority is to wrap up this project in Monterey. I can step away and not be on location; however, I am actively looking for a place down there. I'll have to work remote for the time being." Morgan stood, indicating he was done with the meeting. "I still want us all on a security alert. Julia, you have active bodyguards?"

She rolled her eyes and nodded.

"Good. Make sure you don't ditch them." Honey was his priority at the moment, but his family was his life. He couldn't be there to protect everyone at the same time. He had to trust each one of them to do what they did best— take care of themselves and get the job done.

## 23

"Morgan told me you studied art," Remi said as he led Honey into a part of the house she hadn't visited before.

"Yeah, I studied Art History and Museum Gallery Management. I thought I would work in some exclusive gallery when I started. It seemed like a good fit, you know, former model in a gallery of art. It sounds so superficial now. Of course, by the time I graduated, I really wanted to work in the Modern Art Museum. Now I sling coffee."

Remi slowed down so that Honey could walk next to him. "I thought Morgan said you ran a rather bohemian gallery space. Did I misunderstand?"

She scoffed. "It is very bohemian. I am in charge of the rotating art show that's on display in the coffee shop where I work. Not exactly what I'd call being a curator or anything."

"Curating smaller shows counts, Honey. Don't discount the work you do because it isn't as grand as your expectations."

They turned a corner and Honey stopped. Her jaw

dropped as she pointed at the painting in front of her. She smiled in disbelief. "That's Finney's!"

"Yes, that is one of our newest pieces. I'm not sure it's the investment our purchasing agent thinks it has the potential of being. Of course, I think our purchasing agent was coerced into buying it by Julia. She's trying to convince Jinx to let her put it in her office. Says it speaks to her. Jinx seems to think Morgan wants it. I don't know. It doesn't strike me as Morgan's style."

So much for intrigue and subterfuge. It wasn't obscure royalty who'd purchased the painting, but Morgan. And she thought he didn't like abstract expressionism. Lana was right. There was so much more to Morgan than Honey ever would have guessed just by looking at him wearing a plaid work shirt.

"What is Morgan's style?" Honey asked, realizing she didn't really know a lot of the little details about Morgan. She knew how he made her feel and that was enough.

"Why, he prefers mid-century realism. He has an original Diego Rivera hanging in his suite. Has he not shown you yet?" Remi asked. "His first degrees are in Art History and Architecture. He liked to make big art when he was a child. I honestly never expected him to continue on to build buildings."

Honey laughed to herself. No wonder Morgan knew about abstract expressionism. He must have found her to be very entertaining when she spouted her praise of Frieda Kahlo when he had an original Diego Rivera.

Remi continued, "Of course, with his family already owning a small construction firm, it makes sense looking back that Morgan would take what he had and combine it with what he loves. He's turned Seven Hills into the foremost earthquake-proof foundation experts in Northern

California. He works with top architecture firms and gets to tell other designers what will and won't work."

They turned another corner into a wide gallery space. Honey caught her breath and stared in amazement. The space wasn't large, but the art it held was impressive and very old.

Honey was inexplicably drawn to a small painting in an elaborate gold and black frame. The painting delicately portrayed the Virgin Mary, a baby Jesus, and an angel. Honey covered her mouth in awe. Mary had blond wavy hair, a round face with delicate features, small mouth, small chin. The baby Jesus figure, pudgy and pink, smiled happily. The cherub was equally pudgy, but his expression was more knowing, worldly. All three figures were crowned with a barely visible arch of a halo. The quality of the paint made it appear as if the figures glowed from within. The paint application appeared practically smooth with nearly invisible paint strokes. Age had crackled the paint in areas, but overall the image was well preserved. Clearly, this painting had been cared for its entire long existence.

"She's a beauty isn't she?" Remi asked. "She pulls everyone in their first time here."

"God, this is from the Renaissance, isn't it?" She looked to Remi for confirmation.

"That is the Renaissance. It's credited to Raphael."

"Raphael? *The* Raphael?" Honey turned her gaze back to the painting. She slowly eased forward, so she could examine it more closely. "No wonder we still study him today. This is unreal. There are depths within depths. This area right here—" she indicated with her finger a space just beyond Mary's shoulder. "—there are color shifts in here that are practically subliminal. I could look at this for hours and still not truly see it. I can see how people spend years studying one painting. I never really understood that. Of course, I've never been this close to a masterpiece before."

"Haven't you been to Italy?"

"Yeah, but that was before I paid attention to art, really. I mean we saw stuff, but whenever I was there, it was to work not to study art. I feel like I wasted my time over there now. This is amazing."

"Well, we have several pre-Raphaelites you might be interested in as well." Remi backed up indicating to Honey she should move on to admire the rest of the collection.

As she turned, a medium-sized bronze sculpture at the end of the gallery caught her attention. Her hand instinctively went to her charm. She reverently walked up to the statue of the large wolf. She-wolf, Honey corrected herself. The wolf stood on all four paws. She appeared to have whelped recently. Her expression was one of concerned awareness, jaws slack and ears pricked forward. Waves of longer fur created repeating patterns around the head and neck of the sculpture.

"Capitoline Wolf. She's beautiful. Didn't I read something where they found she isn't Etruscan as they originally thought but a medieval work? This is really detailed for a replica. And it's amazingly old." Honey inched her face closer to look at the detail work in the fur pattern.

"The one in the museum is medieval. It's the replica. This one is the original. And it is Etruscan. It's been in our family since it was first commissioned."

Honey's head snapped to Remi. "What? How?"

Remi chuckled, a low rumbling sound. "How much do you know about ancient Rome, Honey?"

"Not a lot," she confessed.

"Sit." Remi indicated a low bench in the middle of the gallery, a few feet from the wolf statue. Honey sat so she could continue to look at the sculpture. "What do you know about her," Remi asked, nodding towards the statue.

"The Capitoline Wolf. Etruscan. Bronze. Uhm, Art History don't fail me now," she muttered to herself. "She's the mythological wolf that suckled Remus and Romulus, the twin founders of Rome, right?"

Remi nodded. "Very good. What else do you know about Remus and Romulus?" He was using his teacher's voice. Honey noticed a subtle difference in intonation and inflection.

"Nothing. Didn't one of them kill the other?" she asked.

"The story of Remus and Romulus is more than the founding myth of Rome. It's our family history."

Honey raised her eyebrows at Remi, not quite in disbelief, but questioning surprise.

Remi's lecture voice was soothing, and it drew her in. "Numitor, an Etruscan king of the city-state Alba Longa had a beautiful daughter. Rhea Silvia attracted many suitors, including the gods themselves."

As Remi spoke, Honey conjured up pictures of men in tall sandals and short togas. All the buildings looked like temples of white columns. She knew it wasn't historically accurate, but it was the picture in her mind.

Remi continued to tell the tale of how Rhea Silvia's father's jealous brother, Amulius, wanted her and the city for himself. When Rhea Silvia refused him, Amulius took over the city, throwing Numitor in jail. Rhea Silvia continued to refuse Amulius's advances, so he sentenced her to live as a Vestal Virgin. But she was no virgin. Rhea Silvia's lover was the war god Mars.

Honey imagined a lithe, beautiful girl dressed in diaphanous cream and gold robes, with the elaborate hairstyle of seven braids of the Vestal Virgins clinging to a large tawny-skinned man. The Mars in her imagination wore red, had bulging muscles, and a big black beard. Rhea Silvia and Mars. She was beautiful, he was strong. As the story continued, the movie in Honey's brain also continued.

Rhea Silvia became pregnant with Mars's children. For breaking her vows of celibacy, she was sentenced to death. The twin sons she gave birth to were also sentenced to be killed. Amulius, afraid of the wrath of the war god, had them thrown into the river, thinking they would drown or the elements would be the end of them. The river god Tiberinus saved all three and brought them to the banks in the swamp at the base of the Palatine Hill.

Because of his love for her, Mars turned Rhea Silvia into a wolf so she could fight and hunt for her survival. She cared for her children as both human woman and as wolf, until they were found by an Etruscan farmer who took them in. He married Rhea Silvia, who now went by the name Acca Laren'tia, and raised Remus and Romulus as his own.

Remus and Romulus grew, and when they reached puberty, they also had the ability to change into wolf form. They became fierce warriors and battled to take the city of Alba Longa back. Successful in reclaiming the city, they released their grandfather from prison. Numitor wanted to grant them rule over Alba Longa, but they refused. They wanted to start their own city.

Honey pictured isolated hills with temples on top. She did not picture the city of Rome at all, a city she had visited more than once during her days as a model.

Remi's deep voice continue. "Remus wanted them to build on the Aventine Hill, Romulus, the Palatine Hill. History calls it an argument. It really was a bloody battle over the location of their city. Romulus won, defeating Remus in a fight of wolf dominance."

"So Romulus killed Remus?" Honey asked for clarification.

"Yes, Romulus killed Remus. Rome is named for the former. The family is named for our origins at the base of the Palatine Hill," Remi explained.

"The other hill—you said Aventine. Didn't I meet someone with that name yesterday?"

"You're talking about Roman Aventine. Yes, he was here. His family goes back as far. They are the descendants of Remus. The current generation is attempting to forge a peace accord and work together. I'm not sure how well it will work. If their alpha begins to pay attention again, it might fail."

"So —" Honey paused, thinking. "—you're descended from the god Mars? I thought Morgan told me the wolf thing was genetic."

"Isn't your lineage genetic?" Remi asked.

"Oh, right. Good point. Wow." She slowly shook her head from side to side. "If the Palatines and Aventines can trace their history this far back, how many other wolf families are there? Or are you the only wolf families?"

"Not at all. What we have been able to find out is every culture that has a wolf-to-human shifting myth has, or had, a family line with the trait. Palatines and Aventines moved throughout Europe. Unfortunately, the family didn't always keep track of offspring. Most families, clans, or packs, whatever they refer to themselves as, tend to not advertise. We are aware there are groups all over the world, but we don't have much interaction with them. I think Julia is working to build some information network among the different alphas. That involves a lot of work. Locating the families. Gaining their trust enough to confirm they are wolves."

Remi folded his hands in his lap. "I admit, I like the old ways. We kept to ourselves."

Honey thought about this for a minute. Wolves in hiding, not letting the outside world in. This was a family that if they gave you their trust, you must have done something to earn it.

"But you know about the Aventines."

"We've known about them since the very beginning, just as they have about us. It's not exactly the same as going into a different country and asking where their wolves are."

Honey chuckled. "Yeah, talk about being in the closet. I guess that explains why you're such a tight family and the school."

"Exactly. Children don't start turning until they hit puberty. That's when you find out if you have the talent or not. Not all of us turn, but we all keep the secret. Teen years can be difficult enough as it is. Add on top of that the competitiveness and fight for position within a large extended family. Our children develop increased speed and strength as they come into their wolf. This can lead to problems with the general population. Our children frequently get into trouble in school and in general. We found that by providing a learning environment that knows how to deal with their gifts, we can keep them in school where they need to be and provide them with proper training. Our children are well educated. When we started the school, we set up a foundation so that all the students who complete high school level work with us can go on to the college of their choice. In the school, we are able to focus their energy and competitive nature on knowledge and learning. We've had the school for almost forty years. Since its inception, our graduates have all gone on to complete their educations and have successful careers. I'm teaching the children of children I taught when we started."

"What grades do you teach? You said high school. When do they start here?" Honey asked.

"They start when they need it. Our first official grade is the sixth grade. Up until that point, younger students are individually tutored on an as-needed basis."

Remi's phone buzzed. He picked it up, looking at the display. "Speaking of the school, there seems to be an issue I need to go handle. I can leave you here to commune with the rest of our collection? Shall I message Morgan to come find you in the gallery?" Remi began tapping into his phone before Honey replied.

"Yeah, that's fine. I think I need some time to really absorb everything you told me anyway. This is as good as any place to be alone with my thoughts."

Remi nodded, and wheeled out the way they had come in.

Honey sat and stared at the wolf. She couldn't think much past the fact that she looked at something made thousands of years ago. It was the same feeling she got when she viewed Egyptian artifacts. There was an artist who made something they wanted to share with the world, to create a tiny part of themselves to live forever in a work of art, and it worked. No one knew who the artist was. Had he been happy? Was being an artist fulfilling? Here was part of him in front of her. If she was bold, she could even touch it. Was this really a tangible connection to Morgan's family history?

No wonder he said he was familiar with the Capitoline Hill. Here she sat face to face with the Capitoline Wolf. *Wolf.* The mark on her pendant was fitting. It was almost too much to take in. Honey tried to look around at the other works, mostly paintings. She couldn't focus on anything beyond the wolf. Her eyes kept returning to it. Her mind kept thinking about it. Mars, the god of war. Wolves. Remus and Romulus, Rome. Genealogy was something this family had clearly tracked for centuries. Clearly, they knew how far back. Were there emperors and Caesars in their history? She wondered how far and wide were their connections.

Hell, Morgan wasn't a rich tycoon; he was some kind of wolf prince. Honey looked around. Her head started to pound. Her stitches throbbed. She felt lost, drowning in thoughts about history, lost in the house again. She needed Morgan. This was too much to handle on her own.She fished for the map he had drawn out. It didn't include this part of the house. Overwhelmed, tears slid down her face. She breathed in through her nose and out through her mouth, purposefully focusing on her breathing in an attempt to not let panic take over. She shoved the paper back into her pocket and wrapped her fingers around the pendant. A gift from Morgan, a talisman of strength.

She slowly walked out of the gallery. She remembered turning to see Finney's large painting. She reversed her steps. She focused on *in through her nose, out through her mouth*. The hall looked familiar. She turned around to look at it from the perspective she had first walked down it. Yes, this looked like the right direction. Another turn, another set of double doors. Finally, Honey found herself next to the dining room Morgan had disappeared into. She let out a sigh of relief.

A large couch was in front of her. She decided to sit and wait. Just knowing she was closer to Morgan, she felt better.

The door to the dining room opened, and Honey heard the mutterings of different conversations winding down. She turned when she heard the click of heels walk quickly past behind her to see Julia.

Dante and another man left the room next.

Honey recognized Shane's gruff voice. She didn't see who he talked to immediately. "There haven't been any incidents since you were abducted. I think it might be a null threat at this point, but we are still following up with that daywalker intel."

Honey's eyes widened. Someone had been abducted? Who?

Morgan stepped out of the room following Shane.

"What does he mean abducted?" Honey blurted out.

"Oh, man," Shane muttered. He clapped Morgan on the back. "I'll leave this one to you. Sorry about that, brother."

"Honey," Morgan approached Honey, his arms out to her. "That's not really what—"

"No," she cut him off. "Shane said *abducted*. What did he mean? When?"

Morgan cupped his hands around the backs of her arms. "I don't really have that information."

Honey shrugged out of his grasp. "Morgan, remember no secrets. And you damn sure have information if you were the one abducted. I need to know now, or I think I need to leave now."

Honey paced back and forth in front of the leather couch. Morgan sat in the middle, slowly explaining his disappearance weeks earlier.

"So you didn't go camping?"

"Not on purpose anyway. As far as we have been able to ascertain, there have been no other threats. It appears to have been an isolated incident.

Security on everyone in the family increased as soon as

they realized I was missing. No one knew about you, so you have been safe. I've been guarding you personally since I got back."

"I'm in danger?"

"No, I don't think you are. I've had heightened awareness since my incident. I don't want anything to happen to you, so I've been watching out."

"Are you saying that what's going on between us is just body-guarding to the extreme?"

Morgan stood. Placing himself in the path of Honey's nervous walking. "Not at all." He wrapped his arms around her and pulled her in close. "I'm in love with you. What grew between us has nothing to do with me being abducted. If anything, that made me take decisive action and stop acting like a stupid kid with a crush."

"Then what's going on?" Honey pleaded.

"I'm going to kiss you," Morgan announced.

Honey let him claim her lips. She relaxed against their softness.

She sighed. "That's not what I meant. I meant with that other thing Shane mentioned."

"That's still all being investigated. One of the men who abducted me was what we call a 'daywalker.' We followed up to see if there are any rumors circulating in their ranks."

Honey nodded in understanding. "Wait. What's a daywalker?"

"They're related to vampires."

"Are you kidding me? Vampires are real?"

Morgan nodded slowly. "Maplecourt's involved."

"Bryce knows you're a werewolf?"

"I doubt it. He doesn't seem to have much of an imagination. He was oblivious to clues right in front of him. I think he thinks it's all about money and control and the mafia.

He's put himself into a dangerous position. I'm very serious when I say I don't want you near him."

Pain pierced Honey's skull. She pressed her fingers to her temples, trying to squeeze her skull back together without touching her stitches. "I'm getting a headache. This is too much. You're a werewolf, descended from fucking Mars. You were kidnapped and shot. Bryce is somehow in the middle of all of this. And now vampires. I think my brain might be done. I need to eat something. I need a drink. I need..." Honey's eyes rolled up and she slumped against Morgan.

"Honey!" He patted her face. She was non-responsive. "Honey?" He felt her pulse. It beat steady, and she was breathing. Morgan scooped her up and carried her to his bed.

Honey's eyes flickered open. "What?"

"You passed out. You need to rest."

Honey slept. For the first hour, Morgan sat and watched over her. When he realized she would sleep for a while, he headed to the kitchen to make arrangements for an early dinner to be served in his rooms. Honey was still asleep when he returned.

There was a knock on his door.

Julia stormed in. "Okay, this is the information I found." She dropped a stack of printouts on the low coffee table.

Morgan glanced to check on Honey.

"Am I interrupting?" Julia didn't sound the least bit sorry if she was.

"No. Honey's taking a nap, that's all."

"Well, the board has my hands tied on this one. They won't do anything until you give approval. It's frustrating Morgan. I'm doing the work. I'm making the recommendations. And they won't wipe their own noses unless you tell them it's okay."

"What do you want me to do to change that?"

"Put me in charge. Let me run the damn company. I already am anyway." From the tone of her voice, Morgan knew it wasn't a suggestion.

Morgan knew Julia was right. His focus was on the construction company, not the parent corporation. He knew he was thinking small since his area of interest was just a small part of the whole enterprise, but he also knew where his heart truly lay.

"You got it. Let's draw up the paperwork. I'll step down. Make me a consultant, so I'm not completely out of the picture."

"Smart decision." She nodded sharply.

"Of course, that's what I do—make smart decisions. You have been running the company. I've been a figurehead. I'm in the way, so let's put you in a position to really do what you do best. Now tell me what's in those papers I'm not going to read."

Julia laughed. "A list of potential labs for purchasing. Aventine has almost closed the buy-out on SeaQuence. We're going to need access to more than one lab, and we are going to need to be able to conduct genetic research outside of a commercial lab. It's easier to purchase an existing lab and staff than to build one from scratch. I thought you might want to look at the prospects." She glanced up to Honey's sleeping form. "Mate, huh?"

Morgan cocked his eyebrows and nodded.

"Well, try not to be distracted for too long. We do need your focus back here." Julia pointed to the papers on the table. "Shane is digging up something that sounds like it could be nasty. I hope your mate is tough. She's jumping on board in time for a bumpy ride."

"She hasn't agreed to come along for the ride yet. That's why I'm moving to Monterey for a while."

"Morgan, we're really going to need you up here with all this going on. Is moving now such a good idea?" Julia asked, concerned.

"It's where she is. I have to be where she is."

"Bring her up here."

"I don't think it will be that easy. I don't know if she would give up her job and her life down there to live with me."

"Morgan, your brain has turned to rocks. Marry her and bring her home."

Morgan kissed Julia on the cheek. "You're brilliant."

"Of course, I am." Julia picked up the papers she dropped earlier. "You don't need these, so I'll keep them. When do you head back?"

"Tomorrow. I have to wrap up a few things at the site before I hand it over."

"I'll have the papers drawn up this week. I'll overnight them for signing."

"Sounds good."

Honey rolled over and opened her eyes. Morgan sat across the room looking at her. She pushed into a sitting position. She smiled at his intense gaze, shapeshifters were definitely sexy.

"I had the weirdest dream," she announced. She had dreamed of temples and togas, and Mars, the god.

"Let me guess. Werewolves, Rome, and vampires?"

"Shit, it wasn't a dream, was it? What happened?"

"You passed out, sweetheart. When was the last time you ate? You simply checked out for a bit then fell asleep." Morgan sat next to her. "Are you going to be okay?"

Honey nodded. Her reality had taken a sudden shift, but she would be safe with Morgan and all of his various talents.

"Are *we* going to be okay?"

Honey put her hand on Morgan's arm. "Of course, we are. Why wouldn't we be?"

"You had said it was too much."

"Too much all at once, but I think I can adjust. I accepted that you can do the wolf thing with great calmness. I think I was owed that little freak-out over the rest. Did you say Bryce was a vampire?"

## 24

Honey leaned against the counter at work. The scent of coffee filled her senses. She could taste it in the air. Since returning to Monterey, life had returned to normal. She toyed with her pendant, daydreaming of vineyards and mansions. She could almost believe the past weekend hadn't happened. Almost. Thinking back on it made it seem a bit too glamorous, a bit too fantastical.

Like in a lovely dream, her working-class, construction worker boyfriend turned out to be more than he appeared. Perfect pecs, perfect abs, and, of course, insanely wealthy. And a werewolf. But not just any werewolf. An alpha.

It had to be a dream, an extension of some delusion left over from the head injury. They had not left her apartment in a rust bucket of a truck that magically turned into a sleek luxury car. They didn't arrive at a beautiful expansive mansion. But for the life of her, Honey could not picture anything else. The wedding with the crazy bridesmaids and having to share a bathroom with them—that made perfect sense. Was completely logical. So did the family frowning upon unmarried couples sleeping together. Maybe that disapproving butler person had really been Morgan's mother, and she didn't like Honey.

No, that couldn't have been Morgan's home. It had to have been a resort in wine country. She had gotten lost in the hotel. That's what it was.

There were real parts though. They had spent an extra day strolling around in the country, just she and Morgan. They had sneaked off into some vineyards and walked for hours. If it had been a real fairytale, there would have been horses. A horseback ride between rows of grape vines. Honey decided she should see if she could add that little tidbit into her mixed-up memories.

And then, of course, there had been the passing out from mental overload. Clearly, she had been hurt worse than they realized when she was mugged. Everything with Morgan had been so normal up until that point. It was only after she hit her head that things got weird. Maybe she hit her head again, giving her a real concussion. Maybe there had been horses and she had fallen off. A second head injury would explain the crazy dreams of wolves and vampires and Roman gods. But would that explain Morgan saying he loved her? She didn't want that part to be a dream.

No, that was real enough too. After all, she'd woke up with him in her bed this morning. He had smiled that big toothy smile of his. They had dressed for work and did morning things like eat breakfast together. He had even said he loved her this morning before she left for work first.

"Did you hear?" Seth interrupted her daydreaming. "They caught your guy."

Honey looked at Seth, confused. "My guy? Who? Morgan?" Honey looked at Seth, confused.

"Wait. You and Morgan? When did that happen?"

"Where have you been, Seth? Yeah, me and Morgan. I went away for the weekend with him."

"Duh, I know that. I meant that jackass who mugged you. They caught him."

"Really? Good." Honey sighed. "How?"

"Idiot wears that stupid yellow jacket everywhere. Some cop saw him in line at a bank or something and recognized him from a description, and that yellow jacket."

Honey tentatively touched the bandage on her head. The stitches were out now, but she kept the angry red line covered as it still needed to heal. "Oh, wow, that's a relief. I wonder if they'll need me to be a witness or something. You think I should call the police?"

"Naw, they'll call you if they need anything. The radio said this ends a streak that was growing more and more violent."

Honey worried that he may have hurt someone worse than her. She didn't want to think about that if he had raped someone.

"They said he had just gotten out of jail, so the attacks violate his parole. You know who's going back in for a long time. There's probably an article in the newspaper about it."

"At least he's off the streets now."

The tinkling of the bell over the door interrupted their conversation, one that had brought Honey back to reality. Reality that was coffee and tourists and sweatshirts with Cannery Row stenciled across the chest. Reality that was a construction worker boyfriend who was allergic to chocolate and drank Orangina. Reality that was a bed that was almost too small to fit them both, but they didn't care as long as they could be together. Honey realized she was going to be okay with this reality, and her fantasy weekend could be a happy delusion.

A line developed at the counter. Honey turned her focus to pouring coffee and plating pastries. When it got busy like this, the only way to survive was not to look at the line but to focus on one person at a time. Make that one person feel special for the few moments she had to serve them.

It was also why Honey didn't notice Bryce's sneer until he stepped up to the counter. Honey flinched. Seth had disappeared. She felt stuck. There was no one to trade places with, so she didn't have to speak to Bryce.

"What no friendly smile, Rachelle?"

"You aren't supposed to be in here, Bryce." Knots formed and untied, twisting in her stomach. The fight or flight response in her winding up the adrenaline. She began chanting a mantra in her head. *I can handle this, I can handle this, I can handle this.*

"I should be done with the meeting I'm in town for by lunch. I want you to have lunch with me. Catch up on our lives." Bryce patted down his jacket pocket. The tone in his voice betrayed the friendly words. He wasn't interested in catching up on old times. Controlling and manipulating, yes. Honey knew Bryce's interests had nothing to do with her current life but were because of what she had been. "I might even have a surprise for you."

"No, thank you, I have a boyfriend, and I don't think he would like that." Honey calmly explained. She knew Morgan would not only hate it, he would hurt Bryce if he knew he was here talking to Honey.

"Letting a man make decisions for you? I thought you claimed that wasn't your style anymore." Bryce reached into his inner jacket pocket again.

"It's not him making decisions. It's me being honest. He wouldn't like it, and I respect him enough to not do something that would upset him. I don't want to have lunch with you either. However, you are more likely to respect my refusal if you know I have a boyfriend, since you aren't even following the café owner's orders to stay out of here."

"You're not going to serve me?"

"No, I'm not. You need to leave."

He continued conversationally, "So you're dating again? Some little artsy type? A painter? Or are you going to tell me you're still dating models and photographers?"

"It's none of your business who I date, but since you asked, I'm dating a construction worker. We're all caught up. You need to go." Honey leaned to look at the next patron over Bryce's shoulder. She smiled brightly at the woman behind him. "Hi, have you decided what I can get started for you?"

Honey glared at Bryce, then quickly tilted her head to the side, indicating it was time for him to move.

It wasn't until a few customers had come and gone before Honey sighed in relief. She had survived a Bryce interaction, and she didn't feel the urge to hide or throw up.

Lana walked into the shop an hour later with a smirk across her face. "So, Honey, how was your weekend?" Lana asked with a waggle of her eyebrows. Honey could tell she was looking for a juicy story. Lana would be thrilled with the fairytale version of the getaway Honey could remember and not the reality she was certain her brain was purposefully repressing.

"Interesting. I can't decide if I dreamed the whole thing or not. Parts of it were completely unreal."

Lana leaned against the counter, her elbow propped against the counter, her chin resting in one hand. "Tell me about the house."

"Somehow I think you know more than you're telling

me. Have you known who Morgan is this whole time?" Honey asked.

"Not this whole time. But after it looked like you two might be getting together, I looked him up online. He's quite the catch. I followed a link to a vineyard. The pictures had a glorious mansion in the background. Please tell me that's where he took you."

Honey pointed at Lana's grinning face. "You let me think he was some construction worker, and all the while you knew he was the head of a huge corporation with diversified interests."

Lana slowly stood up. "Well…" She let the word draw out. "Sort of. Look, Honey, you needed to get to know him on your own anyway. I figured at some point he would tell you."

"Lana! Oh, my God. He picked me up in this rusted-out old truck. I practically told him I'm in love with him in an old beat-up truck. Then we pull into this mechanic's yard, and the next thing I know, we're speeding up the highway in a car that felt like it wasn't even moving the ride was so smooth. That's how he told me."

Lana's grin was wide and mischievous. "You're in love."

"I am, but I'm not even fully convinced that what really happened wasn't a dream or my brain trying to compensate for an extremely disappointing weekend."

"Oh no. Don't tell me it was disappointing. I was hoping it was like a fairytale." Lana's grin dropped as soon as she thought Honey might have had a bad time.

"So not disappointing. It was actually very much like a fairytale, complete with Prince Charming."

The shop phone began ringing. Lana pushed off the counter and headed into the office. "I've got it."

Lana emerged from the office. "Hey, Honey, can you run an order up the street for me?"

"Since when do we do deliveries?"

"Since the client promised a nice big tip for whoever would bring him four hot coffees and two hot chocolates."

"Fine." Honey sighed and began filling the order.

"Here ya' go." Lana placed two drink carriers on the counter for Honey.

"So where am I taking these?"

"Morgan asked you to bring them to the site office on Wave."

"Lana!" Irritation laced Honey's tone. "Why didn't you tell me it was for Morgan."

"'Cause I wanted to mess with you. I knew you wouldn't say no anyway."

"What if I had?" Honey teased.

"That's easy. Then I would have said it's for Morgan, and you would have become all fluffy and happy and wagging your metaphorical tail, just like you are now."

Honey stacked the loaded drink carriers and headed the few blocks up the hill to the construction site on Wave. A short trailer sat on the grounds serving as a portable office. The only person she saw was a plaid-shirted man who approached her.

"I know you. You're Jim, Morgan's friend who boarded up my window after my apartment got broken into."

"Hi. How's that window? Did they fix it properly for you?" He took the top of the stacked drink carriers.

"They took care of everything nicely. Big new window, and replaced all the window locks too. Thanks for asking. And thanks for your help boarding things up that night."

Jim nodded. "Which of these are the coffees and which the hot chocolates?"

Honey indicated which drinks were which.

"Thanks," he said, handing her back one of the coffees. "That one is for Mr. Palatine. He'll be right in." Jim guided Honey into the office and closed the door, taking the rest of the drinks with him.

The office was small, claustrophobic. Only two small windows on opposite walls let light in. A small desk, really just a folding table, occupied one corner. Honey assumed it was the desk because of the computer sitting on top. Another folding table, covered in blueprints and yellow legal pads with notes scratched on them took up the center of the space.

The door opened and Bryce stepped in. He looked at Honey then reached for his pocket. "Seriously, if you wanted to talk to me, you could have at the coffee shop. No need to follow me. This is terribly embarrassing for you."

Jim followed Bryce into the space. "Mr. Palatine will be right in. You okay, Honey?"

"I think I need to leave." Bile rose in her throat. She had managed him in the café, but there were others present. This office was too small, too confining, to be in it alone with Bryce.

"Is this your construction worker?" Bryce dragged his sneering gaze down Jim, then back up to Jim's face. "Yes, she needs to leave," Bryce emphasized.

"No." Morgan's voice was low, menacing as he stepped into the office. "Thanks, Jim. I've got this." Morgan's presence made her feel secure, but the entire situation set her nerves on edge.

Jim nodded and stepped out of the office.

"Sit, Maplecourt," Morgan demanded.

"The coffee girl needs to go. She doesn't need to be here." Bryce tried to gain control, talking louder than necessary for the small space. For once Honey agreed with Bryce. She didn't need to be here.

"Honey stays." Morgan dropped a file folder on the table in front of Bryce.

"Open it."

Bryce flipped open the cover. Honey could see photos of Bryce hitting her. Of her cowering before him. Her stomach lurched, and she clenched her teeth together, focusing on breathing through her nose. She felt like all the air had been sucked out of the room.

Morgan's voice broke the silence. "Apologize to the lady."

"Why should I? She deserved that."

"No, I didn't." The sound escaped her before she realized she had spoken out loud.

Morgan stood in front of her, a barrier between her and Bryce.

"Apologize!" Morgan growled.

Honey watched as Morgan's shoulders thickened. She ran her hand up his back, feeling the thicker muscled as he pulled his wolf to the surface. Gaining confidence with Morgan's menacing presence, she moved to his side and then said, "This would be my construction worker, Bryce. And I told you he wouldn't like you talking to me."

Bryce looked from Honey to Morgan. "What is this? What are you two up to? Palatine, I will have a little chat with your client about this." His hand reached into his pocket.

"And what?" Morgan scoffed. "You won't like anything she will have to say to you." He pointed towards the file. "That also contains copies of certain financial forms. Cyan del Fuego also has copies. One set is the records you have been submitting to the Cyan Group; the other are the ones that contained the real data. She wants to have a little chat with you. She should be pulling in any moment."

Honey watched Bryce's face turn red with anger.

"I can tell you right now," Morgan continued, "that she's very unhappy with you. Cyan del Fuego does not take well to people who doctor the books or steal her money."

"I'm not afraid of Del Fuego. She can't touch me. I have more powerful friends out there. You've met them already," Bryce sneered.

Morgan nodded. "Met them, took care of them. You haven't seen them around lately, have you?"

Bryce's eyes widened as his skin paled. "You're trying to scare me."

"You should be scared. You have made a very powerful enemy, and I'm going to hand you over all wrapped up with a bow on top," Morgan snarled.

Bryce stood and attempted to move past Morgan. "I'm out of here. I won't let you use scare tactics on me."

"These aren't scare tactics, Maplecourt. This—this is a scare tactic." Morgan's face flashed quickly. Honey cause a glimpse of his brow thickening, his eyes glowing, his cheek-bones protruding. It was as truly frightening as the first time she witnessed his transformation, more so because of the added growling.

Bryce made a noise, a gasp with a hint of terrified squeal. His eyes went wide with fear.

"Now, apologize to Honey." Honey placed her hand on Morgan's arm, not sure if she needed to touch him for her own personal fortitude or if she thought it would calm him. She knew she should be afraid of the entire situation. Bryce, who was abusive, in close quarters with a man who could turn into a wolf. One man who wanted to control her regardless of any pain he might inflict. The other who could tear her to shreds, but would never hurt her.

Bryce stepped back, away from Morgan. His glance shifted from Morgan to Honey and back again. "I...I'm sorry."

"That's not good enough. Say it like you mean it. Like your life depends on me believing you."

"I am truly sorry." Bryce paused.

"Be specific."

"I am repentant that you were hurt." His hand patted the jacket pocket again.

Honey watched as Morgan clenched and unclenched his fist and his nails lengthened and fur grew on the backs of his hands. "I don't like your choice of words," Morgan growled. "Apologize for your actions."

Bryce looked nervously at Honey. "I am truly repentant that I hit you, that I ever caused you pain. Will you forgive me?"

Honey opened her mouth, unsure of what she would say. Her initial reaction was to say it was okay, even though she knew it was not.

Morgan replied for her. "No, she does not forgive you. She never will, and neither will I. If I ever see you again, if I ever find out you came within fifty miles of her, I will hunt you down and I will end you."

"You can't threaten me." Bryce squeaked, his hand touched the pocket again.

"I just did," Morgan growled.

Honey snapped. "What the hell is it with you and that damned pocket?" She reached up and snaked her hand into Bryce's jacket. Her fingers closed on something flat and metal. She pulled her hand out of the jacket and opened her palm.

A small gold oval glinted in the light. *Forza.* She flipped it over and saw, Michelangelo's pattern for the Piazza del Campidoglio.

Honey lashed out and began beating Bryce with closed fists. "You broke into my home. You broke my television." Her words faded into shrieks and grunts of frustration as she continued to hit him.

Bryce tried to cover himself with his arms as he shrank away from the onslaught.

Morgan eased Honey away from Bryce. Her breathing was heavy, and her skin flushed. She struggled to get at him. "I could kill you." She spit in his face.

"Touch me again, and I'll..." Bryce started.

"You'll do nothing." Morgan's voice was a snarl. His face returned to the mask of half wolf, half man.

Bryce started for the door. Morgan growled deep in his chest one last time before stepping out of the way to let Bryce run out the door. A very satisfied evil grin spread across Morgan's face. He sniffed the air. "I think he pissed his pants."

"You let him go?" Honey panted.

"He's not going far. Come." Morgan led Honey from the office. They watched as a long black limousine stopped in front of Bryce. Bryce started to back away. He turned then stopped when he saw Morgan. The limo door opened. Honey watched as a tall woman with intense green eyes and black hair cut in a severe bob stepped out. A burly man grabbed Bryce and forced him into the back of the car.

"That's Cyan del Fuego." Morgan whispered to Honey.

"Thank you for the package delivery," Cyan said to Morgan. "I look forward to working with your family more in the future."

Morgan nodded in acknowledgment. He stopped her

just as she began to climb back into the car. "Whatever you do with him, don't let his bones find their way into my foundation. You paid good money for my work. Don't let that scum undermine it."

Cyan laughed. Honey thought it was a wicked sound. "I doubt there will be that much left of him."

The car door closed behind her.

"That. Was. Terrifying, and brilliant." Honey said, turning to Morgan and wrapping her arms around his waist. "Did you really find something on him? How?"

"I had Dante start an investigation on him when I first found out he abused you. The rest seemed like Maplecourt just handed over the incriminating evidence. Cyan del Fuego does not put up with people trying to double cross her or embezzle her money."

"He's not going to jail, is he?" Honey whispered, her throat dry with the realization of Bryce's future.

"No, he's not. You going to be okay with that?"

Honey bit her lip. She slowly nodded. "He'll never hurt me or another person again."

Morgan nodded.

"That woman—she's scary."

Morgan pulled Honey into his arms. "Yes, and she's a friend."

"You have scary friends."

"Is she really going to—?" Honey swallowed, "You know —" She dropped her voice again. "—kill him?"

"Do you really want to know?"

"Not really. As long as I never see him again, that will be enough." Honey sighed and leaned into Morgan. "I don't want to go back to work."

"Don't. Come with me." Morgan took her hand and led her to his motorcycle.

They rode a few short blocks then parked along the coastal trail. Wordlessly, he helped her off the bike and led her out onto the rocks next to the crashing waves.

Morgan sank to one knee and removed something small from his front pocket. Honey bit into her lip.

Holding up a delicate solitaire diamond ring that sparkled like a thousand stars, Morgan asked, "Honey Rachael Gould, will you accept my ring and agree to be my wife?"

Honey nodded vigorously, her voice caught in her throat.

"Knowing all the shit you know about me, you still want to marry my fat ass?" She wiped tears from her face.

"I want to spend the rest of my life convincing you that your ass is perfect." Morgan began slipping the ring on her finger. "Yes, Honey, I want to marry you. Knowing all that shit about you makes me want you more. I could ask the same of you. Knowing what you know about me and my family, do you want to join me as my wife in the madness that is our lives?"

"Yes." Her squeak was barely audible. Finding her voice she continued, "Yes, Morgan I want to marry you."

Morgan stood, wrapping Honey in his embrace and claiming her lips for his own.

# EPILOGUE 1

Morgan held his hands over Honey's eyes. "Careful," he said as he guided her forward. "There is a big step and another one." He slowly led her up the small set of stairs into the Air Stream.

"Can I see it now?" Honey asked.

"Patience, Miss Gould, patience." Morgan chuckled as he positioned her a few steps further inside.

Honey gasped in delight when he removed his hand. The interior renovations were complete. She slowly rotated, admiring Morgan's decorating and building skills. The interior of the space when she had first seen it had been completely gutted. Folding chairs and a beat-up old couch occupied spaces that now contained a beautifully constructed, built-in dining booth and a luxurious, yet small, living room. The cabinetry that formed the rear wall hiding the bathroom with the jacuzzi tub was complete. No more shower curtain dividing the bathroom from the living space. All grey-blues and blond wood, the interior of the remodeled Air Stream was minimalist with an idealized air of 1960s post-modern design, yet it felt completely contemporary.

"It's perfect, Morgan." Honey gushed. The remodel had turned out better than she imagined that night of their dreadful first date. Like the date, the state of the camper had not foretold the beauty of their future together.

"Think you can live in here for three months with me? Close quarters and all?" Morgan asked.

"It's plenty big for the two of us, Morgan. Definitely more comfortable than a hotel room and more personal than if we stayed in someone's rental property. And you got the big couch!"

"Yep, its folds out into a king-sized bed. Plenty big. You're okay with this as a honeymoon?" Morgan asked. "You don't want to go to Paris or the Caribbean? You sure you want to help build with Habitat? It's not too late to change your mind. You know I'll be wearing those plaid work shirts."

"I've been to Paris. I've been to the islands. I've never been to some of the places we're going, and I've never been to New Orleans. It's supposed to be a fabulous city, Morgan. I get three honeymoon destinations in various places around the US, and I've never done humanitarian work. You are giving me time with you and time to become a better person. I'll just have to suck it up about the plaid. You can always take me to Paris for our first anniversary. I think this plan is kind of perfect."

Morgan backed into the living room, till his legs hit the couch. He fell backwards and pulled Honey down on top of him. "I really think we should test it out before we take it on the road." Morgan began pulling Honey's shirt over her head.

"Do you think that's such a good idea? I mean won't the family frown upon our premarital sex?"

"No one seemed bothered by it last night. Least of all you." Morgan laughed. "Like I'm going to give up touching you until it's no longer premarital."

"Six days until the wedding Eight days until this place is home for a few months." She laid her head against Morgan's chest. She had never felt so safe and so loved.

"You'll be living in a trailer with a construction worker." Morgan stopped removing her clothes and held her close.

"I know." She sighed wistfully.

"Does that make you happy?"

"That makes me very happy Morgan. Very happy."

# EPILOGUE 2

The paper board made a satisfactory zip as Julia opened the FedEx envelope. She wasn't going to allow herself the luxury of a smile until she saw the actual signature.

Yes. There it was in beautiful blue ink. Morgan's signature. Now she could smile. It was done.

She buzzed her assistant, Kathleen. "Could you please schedule a meeting with Cyan del Fuego? It's time I introduced myself to her."

Her office door opened. Ignoring it, she continued to smile at the documents granting her control of the Palatine family's corporation, Truria.

"Don't you look like the evil genius whose plan is rolling out smoothly without a hitch."

Julia cut her eyes up to glare at the intruder. Tall, blond, and with sparkling blue eyes, Roman Aventine smirked as he strutted up to her desk.

"You look maniacally happy." His voice was audible velvet.

"I am maniacally happy." She closed her eyes and

inwardly sighed. She had let him have information she had not intended on sharing. He didn't need to know she felt like cackling with laughter. Morgan had given her the company; now she could soar. "Why are you here? Or did you just come to ruin my mood?"

Roman cocked his head to the side, a very canine maneuver. Then his face split into a dazzling smile. Light refracted from his teeth and eyes with special-effects sparkles.

Julia blinked hard to clear her vision.

He held out a white envelope to her. "I came to deliver some data you might be interested in."

Julia reached up to take the envelope. Roman snatched his hand back and held it up above and behind his head. "I'll show you mine if you show me yours."

Julia let out a slow breath through her nose. Roman had the flirting nuance of a twelve-year-old.

She held up the document she had been smiling at moments before. "I have Truria."

"Congratulations. That means we can move forward with our little genetics program." He held the envelope out to her. "Perfect timing; I have your DNA report."

Julia firmly took the proffered paperwork before Roman could play games again.

She opened her desk drawer and removed a silver dagger.

Roman paused as he removed something from his inner coat pocket. He held his hands up, another folded document clutched in his right hand. "Don't kill me. I'm just the messenger."

Julia rolled her eyes at him and inserted the blade into the envelope, slitting it open. She returned the letter opener to its place in the drawer before closing it.

"I thought we could compare notes. I have my report here," Roman smirked.

Julia scanned her paperwork. The 0.08 percent Sub-Saharan African caused her to raise her eyebrows before she nodded. Yes, that must be the Portuguese. She huffed an almost laugh at the acknowledged Mongolian. The percent was ridiculously low. *Thank you, Mongol Horde.*

She looked up at Roman. His cocky smirk was gone. His pale skin seemed ashen. He wobbled in place. She was out of her chair and around her desk in a flash. With a light hand on his arm she guided him to sit.

Roman did not take his eyes from the report in his hands. He didn't glance up at her, didn't say anything sarcastic and snarky.

"Are you all right?" she asked.

"I have to go to Boston." He sounded shaken.

Julia nodded. "Is it your mother? Is she okay?" Roman's mother had received treatments at Stanford's Cancer Treatment Center until recently.

Roman lifted his face to look at her. He blinked a few times as if he couldn't process what he was looking at. Closing his eyes, he took a deep breath. When he reopened them, Julia noticed their blue had crystalized, turning almost white with black rims. His wolf wanted out.

"Mother is fine. I need to have a little discussion with my father."

He stood, all previous good humor gone. Roman shoved the papers back into the breast pocket of his suit and smoothed the front down.

"Have a good weekend, Julia. Could you possibly have Kathleen call my assistant to have him make travel arrangements for me? I'm headed to the airport now."

Julia watched as Roman coolly walked from her office.

That man confused her on so many levels. But his reaction did have her mildly concerned. He never showed emotions like that in meetings. What had that been about?

∼

*What secret has Roman Aventine's DNA report revealed?*
*Find out in Driven.*
*Keep reading for a sneak preview.*

# DRIVEN, LEGATUM BOOK 2

Julia Palatine is a rare female alpha—smart, sexy, and with a will to match that of ambitious male alpha Roman Aventine. He wants her for his mate, but Julia has no time for entanglements with males of her kind, no matter how seductive. Her mission is to understand wolf shifter genetics so she can keep their existence a secret from the human scientific community. Julia forges an uneasy alliance with Roman, who plans to lure her away under the pretense of business so he can succeed in his ultimate goal of seducing her. They make a great team, but their attraction could prove a costly distraction, putting their lives and fate of their species in jeopardy. The Legatum series continues with a battle of wills, seduction, and danger in *Driven*.

# DRIVEN, LEGATUM BOOK 2

**Excerpt from DRIVEN**

Julia began gathering her papers.

Roman placed a hand on top of her growing stack. "Stay for a bit. We have acquisition papers to go over."

Julia sat back down and gave Roman a side glare. She wasn't aware of any acquisitions they needed to discuss.

Roman was silent until the door clicked shut behind Cindy.

Julia watched him; as soon as he moved to begin speaking, she cut him off. "Don't."

"Don't what?" Roman asked innocently.

"Don't say something witty and slightly flirtatious. I don't have it in me tonight to cross words." She was exhausted. The conference meetings today had thrown her a steep learning curve, and she felt she was not keeping up as she normally would. Business acquisions, mergers, personnel management were all easy concepts. Genomics. Alleles. Arrays. Epistasis. Heterosis. All new vocabulary, all new concepts. Julia hadn't had to deal with this much science since she was in college.

"Then don't," he said evenly. "Don't fight me all the time."

"I don't, Roman, I..." She wiped her hand across her brow, smoothing her hair back from her face. "I can't."

"You're right. In business you don't fight me; that's true. But you never let your guard down around me." Roman paced away from her. "I take that back. You have only let your guard down once. I would dearly like to see that Julia again."

"Seriously, Roman, it was just a kiss," Julia snapped.

"It was hardly just a kiss. It lasted forty minutes; had your brother not interrupted, I'm sure there would have been more than kissing." His tone was heated.

Indignation flooded Julia with the reminder that it hadn't been a simple kiss but rather an aggressive make-out session. "We're doing it right now, arguing."

"Foreplay," Roman countered.

"I'm tired and I don't want this."

Roman stood over Julia as she slumped deeper into her chair.

"You are a smart and strong woman. I am drawn to you like a moth to a flame. You were drawn to me once, but now you fight that urge inside you, don't you? You fight me." Roman's tone was low, gravelly. "As long as you continue to play, I will happily flirt with you. Tell me to stop and I will. Tell me to leave you be and I will. But I want you, Julia, and I don't want to leave you be."

Julia looked up at Roman. Her body yearned for him; there was no denying it. She fought her body's reactions to him constantly. She stared into his eyes; and caught the beginning of an intense glow. She shook her head, not wanting to know he wanted her as much as she wanted him. She didn't know what to say. She didn't want the complication of dealing with a struggle for dominance. She didn't want the confrontations that would come when Roman decided he needed to subdue her.

"I'm tired of the fight," she confessed. "I'm tired of having to put forth a more concerted effort to be taken seriously. I'm tired of my natural dominance being second-guessed."

"I never question your lead. So why are you fighting?"

"Your father never once acknowledged that I was in the room during the accord meetings, and I was there as Morgan's second. The board questions every other move I make. I'm tired."

"I'm not my father, Julia. And your board of directors, with a few exceptions, are all old men trying to stay relevant. Those are different fights; those are not with me. I promise." His tone was soothing. She wanted to lean toward him. She wanted to believe him.

"I'm tired of empty promises."

"Are you tired of me?"

Words were out of her mouth before her mental editor kicked in. "I like you, Roman; I like the attention." Realizing what she said, she froze, and then sighed. "Can we call a truce this week? You back off with the overaggressive flirting, and I'll back off with the overaggressive bitchiness."

Roman held out his hand. Julia slipped her fingers into his palm, allowing him to help her stand. His hand felt warm, soft, and like a caress wrapped around hers. She stood so close she could feel warmth radiating from his body. Her gaze followed the movement as Roman slowly raised her hand to his lips and lightly brushed her knuckles with a kiss. His glowing blue eyes gazed back at her through lowered lashes.

"As you command."

The tone of his voice combined with the flair of glowing passion from his eyes sent a shiver down Julia's spine.

She stumbled back, noticing the faint shimmering aura surrounding Roman. Her chest tightened, and she struggled for breath. Realization of what she was looking at pierced her chest like a spear. "Oh," she said out loud. Internally she began cursing. *Damn.* Julia finally admitted to herself the meaning behind the glow. *That's what Mother meant when she said I'd know; she forgot to mention I needed to accept it for what it was.*

Sign up for Lulu's newsletter to keep up to date with new releases and happenings. And get a free sexy short story.

https://lulumsylvian.com/newsletter/

# ALSO BY LULU M SYLVIAN

**Check out these other series**

**Legatum**

*Paranormal romantic suspense*

**The World of Wet Waterfalls**

*Paranormal reverse harem romance*

**Rockers**

*Contemporary and paranormal rockstar romance*

**Holiday Strippers**

*Contemporary, paranormal, ridiculous, romance*

# ABOUT THE AUTHOR

 Bio-engineered to be the only redhead in a generation of blonds, Lulu feels that "aliens" may actually be the best answer for a life-time of being asked, "Where did you get that red hair from?"

She did not come into writing from years of scribbling words on paper. Her background is rooted in visual arts and making pictures. Encouraged to make those pictures out of words Lulu began writing just to see what would happen. What happened was two full-length manuscripts in three months.

Lulu cannot ride a horse, a motorcycle, spin a hula hoop, or play roller derby. Yes, she has attempted all of those, even if it has been decades since she's been on a horse or a motor-cycle. She embraces the crazy that comes with that one little genetic mutation, and attempts to live up to the reputation that proceeds her. Lulu would like to apologize for her contribution to the hole on the ozone layer from her use of hairspray in the 1980s.

*For more information, visit:*
www.LuluMSylvian.com